DINOSAURS

DINOSAURS

Steve Brusatte

QUERCUS

Contents

5   Introduction

6-7   The Science of Dinosaurs

10-11   Chapter 1: The Origins of the Dinosaurs

12-13   Archosauria: The Ruling Reptiles

26-27   Chapter 2: Dinosaurs of the Late Triassic

28-29   The Rise of the Dinosaurs

34-35   The Prosauropod Dinosaurs

44-45   Chapter 3: Dinosaurs of the Early – Middle Jurassic

46-47   The Triassic-Jurassic Extinction and Pangaea

52-53   The Tetanuran Theropods

60-61   The Sauropods

68-69   Early Ornithischian Dinosaurs

74-75   Chapter 4: Dinosaurs of the Late Jurassic

76-77   The Morrison Formation

86-87   The Coelurosaurian Theropods

90-91   The Origin and Evolution of Birds

116-117   Chapter 5: Dinosaurs of the Early-Middle Cretaceous

118-119   The Cretaceous World

132-133   The Feathered Dinosaurs of China

162-163   Chapter 6: Dinosaurs of the Late Cretaceous

164-165   The Final Act of the Dinosaurs

170-171   New Research on the Tyrant Lizard King

216-217   Chapter 7: The End of the Dinosaurs

220-221   Glossary

222-223   Index

Introduction

Just say the word 'dinosaur' and you immediately conjure up images of a lost world, a fantastic but scary past when the earth was ruled by reptilian giants. There is something about these ancient beasts that captivates the imaginations of children and scientists alike. Perhaps it is the enormous size of some dinosaurs, or the bizarre horns, crests, armour, spikes, claws and teeth that adorned many species. Or maybe it is simply because dinosaurs are no more, a once-great race that rose and fell like so many of the human civilizations that have followed them.

Dinosaurs are more popular today than ever before. Hardly a week goes by without word of an exciting new discovery in the badlands of countries like Argentina or China. New movies, documentaries and television shows focusing on these 'terrible lizards' attract wide audiences. Some palaeontologists – those scientists that find and study dinosaurs – have even become minor celebrities.

But despite the 'rock star' attention that they receive, dinosaurs are not merely a trumped-up media creation. These animals were some of the most important, diverse and dominating creatures ever to inhabit the earth. The first dinosaurs evolved about 230 million years ago, during the Middle Triassic period of geological history. They began as small carnivores that scurried about on two legs, but quickly expanded into a dizzying array of species that spread worldwide. By the end of the Triassic, 200 million years ago, dinosaurs of all sizes were dominating ecosystems across the globe. The dinosaur empire had begun. It would last an astounding 160 million years, until a sudden and catastrophic extinction at the end of the Cretaceous period.

Humans have been fascinated by dinosaurs for nearly two centuries. The first remains of these ancient beasts surfaced in the early 1800s in England. Initially, scientists were bemused. Were these bones actually real? What kind of enormous animal did they belong to? And when did these animals live? It would not be long, however, before further discoveries like Megalosaurus and Iguanodon proved not only that these fossils were real, but also that they belonged to a totally new race of ancient reptile-like creatures that lived during the Mesozoic Era, hundreds of millions of years ago. Some of these animals were colossal – as long as a bus and as tall as a five-storey building – whereas others were small and sleek. Some ate meat, others plants. Some were adorned with spikes and armour befitting a medieval knight, while others were more modest. In all, they were a diverse collection of species, which together ruled the world long before humans came onto the scene.

Over time, and with more and more fossil discoveries, a clear picture of the dinosaur world emerged. Scientists understood that dinosaurs could be divided into three major groups: the carnivorous theropods (including Tyrannosaurus and kin), the long-necked, herbivorous sauropodomorphs (such as Brachiosaurus and Diplodocus) and the beaked, plant-eating ornithischians (among them Stegosaurus, Triceratops and the hadrosaurids). These groups all arose in the Late Triassic and continued to evolve and change as the Age of Dinosaurs progressed. Indeed, the major theme of the dinosaur world was change – continents drifted around, climates shifted and seas expanded and contracted. It is one of the most remarkable evolutionary tales in the history of life.

The rich, unfolding drama of the Age of Dinosaurs is the theme of this book. Instead of simply arranging species by group, the book begins in the Middle Triassic and follows the 160-million-year evolutionary journey of the dinosaurs. Through every twist and turn, past major extinction events and across the drifting continents, it tracks the dinosaurs as they diversified and spread around the world. This ancient story is brought to life by some of the most dramatic and vivid images of dinosaurs ever created. They were produced by the same CGI (computer-generated imagery) technology used in filmmaking, and are based on the most up-to-date and cutting-edge scientific knowledge. The large size of the book allows these images to seen in stunning detail. Some are even life size – which has never been done before. These vibrant images give an exciting overview of one of the greatest stories ever told: the origin, evolution and demise of the dinosaurs.

Steve Brusatte

The Science of Dinosaurs

Dinosaurs are extinct and lived millions of years ago. So how do scientists know so much about them? People have been discovering and studying dinosaurs for nearly 200 years, beginning in England in the early 1800s. Techniques have improved remarkably over the years, and today's dinosaur palaeontologists use many sophisticated scientific tools. But 21st-century research scientists are still driven by the same mission as 19th-century naturalists: to find dinosaur fossils and piece together how these lumps of rock and petrified bone functioned as living animals that ate, slept and ultimately died in a world very different from our own.

Most scientific research begins with a specific question. For instance, a scientist may be interested in the evolution of theropod dinosaurs in the Middle Jurassic period. But how would he or she know where to look for Middle Jurassic fossils? There are five basic steps in the discovery and study of dinosaur fossils. Luckily for palaeontologists, geologists have long been paid to make detailed maps of the world's rock strata, so that businesses can identify rocks containing valuable resources such as coal, oil and diamonds. So the first step for our intrepid palaeontologist is to study geological maps to identify a place where rocks were deposited on land during the Middle Jurassic. China would make a good place to start searching.

Step two sounds simple, but can be very frustrating. Once suitable rock is identified, the scientist must travel to that area and begin the search. Popular movies often portray palaeontology as a technologically sophisticated science. But, although ground-penetrating radar and complicated cameras may sound savvy, they are expensive and nowhere near as dependable as a set of human eyes. So scientists searching for fossils simply stroll around, looking for eroded bone fragments that may indicate a more complete specimen buried nearby. Often the search can be dull, arduous and maddening. Some

scientists walk around an area for months and find nothing. But there is no other way to do it.

Once a dinosaur fossil is found, in this case a Jurassic theropod, it is onwards to step three. The fossil must be removed from the ground, stabilized and transported back to the lab for cleaning and study. This is also a very unsophisticated process. Fossils are usually encased in rock, so excess rock, called matrix, must be hacked away. Field crews will sometimes carefully remove matrix for several weeks before they can encase the fossil in a protective plaster shell. The plaster is the same material used in casts for broken bones, and it shields the

Palaeontology students excavating Late Jurassic dinosaur fossils in Wyoming in the United States. The student in the foreground has discovered a dinosaur bone and is carefully removing it from the surrounding rock.

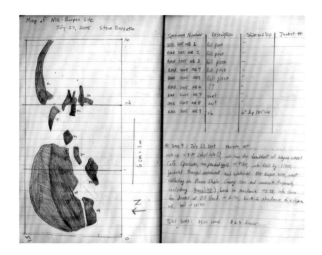

Two pages from the author's (Steve Brusatte) field notebook, detailing a July 2005 excavation of Triceratops fossils in Montana in the United States. Scientists keep a field notebook to record where they have found fossils and to map how the fossils were arranged when discovered.

fossil as it travels back to the lab. This journey can often take months and sometimes involves thousands of miles of transport over land, across the sea or through the air. Unfortunately for palaeontologists, fossils are usually found in dry, sparsely populated badlands, a very long way from the research centres of universities and museums.

Step four begins when the fossil arrives at the lab. There it can be more carefully cleaned, breaks can be prepared, and bones can be put together to create a skeleton. Then it is time for study. First, palaeontologists must figure out what their fossil is: what group it belongs to, how it differs from other members of the group and where it fits into the family tree. This involves careful attention to the anatomy of the fossil. Minute details of the bones must be described and then compared to other fossils. Put together, this information can be used to generate a family tree, which is necessary for studying the bigger picture of the group's evolution. This process is often painstaking, and can take months or even years. When finished, the scientist will write and publish a scientific paper announcing the find to the palaeontological community and using standardized terminology to describe it. This is our palaeontologist's chance to explain what their fossil reveals about theropod evolution in the Middle Jurassic.

The final step of dinosaur research may be to announce the find to the general public. Not all fossil discoveries or research results are groundbreaking. Indeed, much of what scientists do is interesting only to other scientists. But sometimes a discovery is so bizarre or important that it needs to be celebrated, or so revolutionary that it must be communicated to the public at large. The most obvious way to do this is a museum exhibit. Sometimes original fossils are displayed, but often they are too fragile to expose to crowds. In these cases, exact copies of the bones must be made, pieced together into a complete skeleton,

and then mounted using a safe, sturdy framework. This complicated process requires a unique combination of science, art and engineering. The display must be scientifically accurate, but also easy to move, as inexpensive as possible and, most important, visually pleasing. If successful, this mount will be able to teach the general public just how important the new discovery is for understanding theropod evolution in the Middle Jurassic.

Taken together, these five steps can help scientists understand the evolution of the dinosaurs over time. This evolutionary story is the main theme of this book, and is graphically depicted throughout the text by several diagrams, called cladograms. The cladograms show which groups of dinosaurs are closely related to each other, and give a picture of how the entire menagerie of dinosaurs fit together into a single evolutionary story. The Dinosauria cladogram, overleaf, gives an overview of all the dinosaur species and their evolutionary lineages. It reveals that they can be grouped into three major clusters – theropods (meat-eating dinosaurs, including coelophysoids, ceratosaurs, tetanurans, coelurosaurs and birds), sauropodomorphs (the prosauropods and long-necked sauropods) and ornithischians ('bird-hipped dinosaurs' including many plant-eating dinosaurs such as the stegosaurs, ankylosaurs, ceratopsians, pachycephalosaurs and ornithopods). The cladogram also clearly shows that birds evolved from dinosaurs.

Constructing cladograms is one of the primary goals of palaeontology and follows on from detailed laboratory analysis of the fossil. Scientists create cladograms by examining a large number of dinosaur species, measuring and observing all of the bones of the skeleton, and then combining this information into an enormous list of characteristics. For example, one characteristic may be a large spike on the tail, and each dinosaur species is listed as either possessing or lacking this tail spike. Several such characters are added together, creating a large spreadsheet, or data matrix. A computer is then used to analyse the matrix, and produces a family tree that groups dinosaurs depending on what characteristics they share. Creating cladograms is a painstaking process, but is essential in understanding the story of dinosaur evolution.

This cladogram shows how all of the various dinosaur groups are related to each other, just as a family tree of our own families illustrates how we are related to our parents, grandparents, and other ancestors. Although this cladogram is very general and depicts the major groups within the dinosaurs, more specific cladograms that show subdivisions within the major groups are presented throughout the book.

Each dinosaur profile in the book includes a classification of that species. Although many books classify dinosaurs into a dizzying array of groups such as –'orders', 'superorders', 'infraorders', 'families' and 'subfamilies', these ranks are not used in this book as most modern scientists recognize such names as confusing and meaningless. Instead, each species is classified within an indented list of names, which correspond to groups on the cladogram.

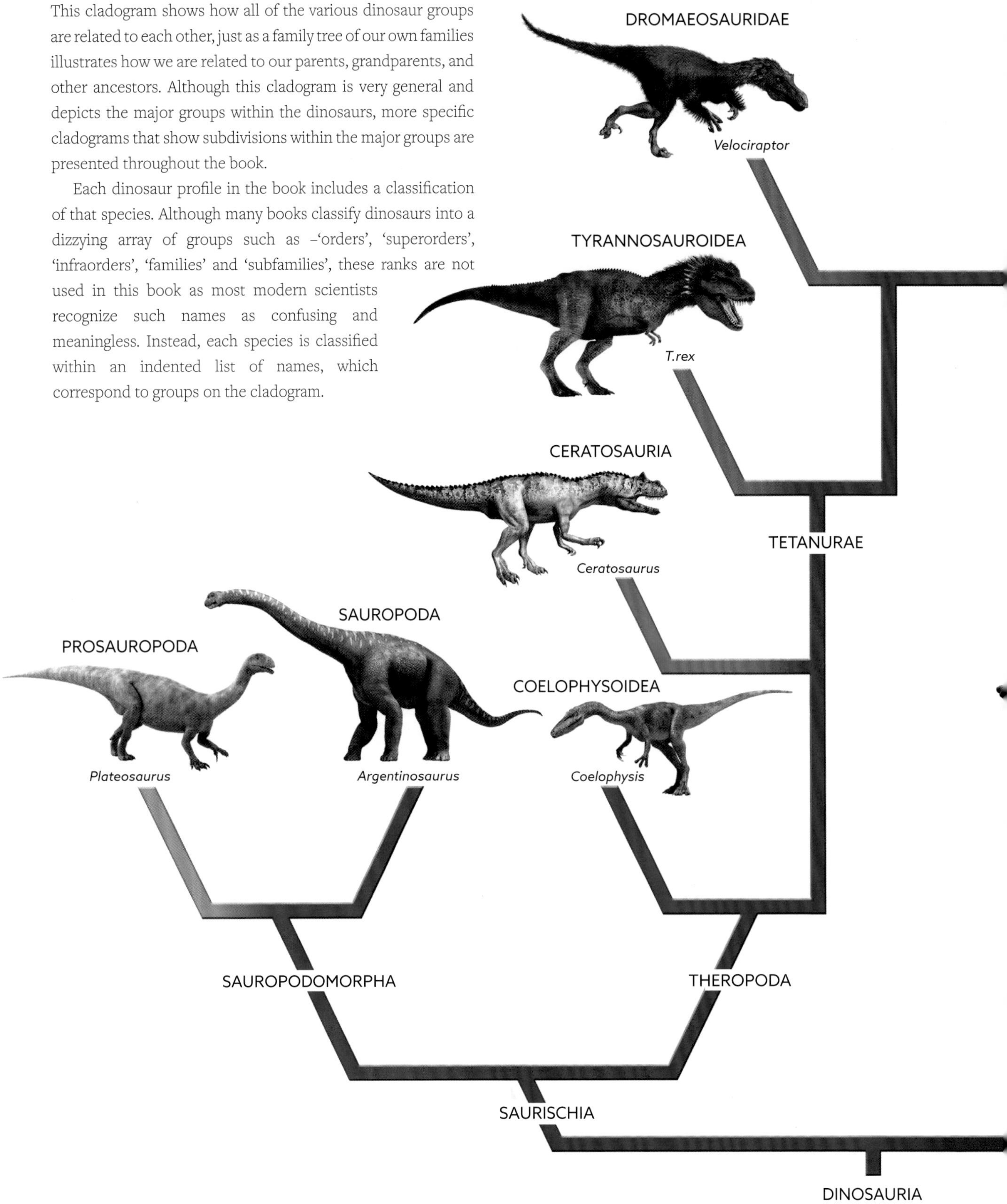

DROMAEOSAURIDAE

Velociraptor

TYRANNOSAUROIDEA

T.rex

CERATOSAURIA

Ceratosaurus

TETANURAE

SAUROPODA

PROSAUROPODA

COELOPHYSOIDEA

Plateosaurus

Argentinosaurus

Coelophysis

SAUROPODOMORPHA

THEROPODA

SAURISCHIA

DINOSAURIA

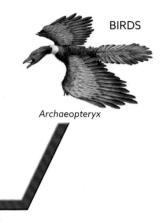

BIRDS

Archaeopteryx

For example, Tyrannosaurus is classified as:

Dinosauria
    Theropoda
        Tetanurae
            Coelurosauria
                Tyrannosauridae

These names comprise a 'nested' set of ever-smaller groups to which *Tyrannosaurus* belongs. Just think of them this way: *Tyrannosaurus* is a tyrannosaurid, all tyrannosaurids belong to Coelurosauria, all coelurosaurs belong to the larger group Tetanurae, all tetanurans are theropods, and theropods are a group of dinosaurs. Visually this can be followed by reference to the cladograms throughout the book.

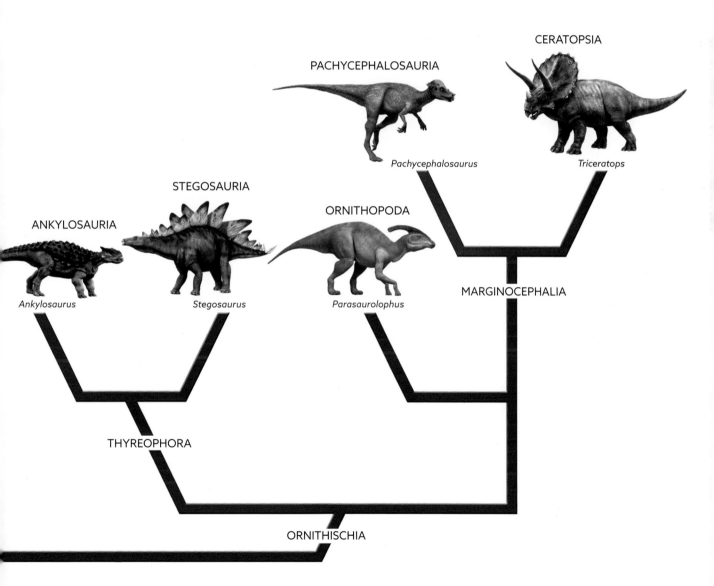

CERATOPSIA

PACHYCEPHALOSAURIA

Pachycephalosaurus

Triceratops

STEGOSAURIA

ORNITHOPODA

ANKYLOSAURIA

Ankylosaurus

Stegosaurus

Parasaurolophus

MARGINOCEPHALIA

THYREOPHORA

ORNITHISCHIA

First bacteria and algae	First animals with hard parts		First land plants	Bony fishes		First mammal-like reptiles
	Trilobites and sponges	First vertebrates	Marine invertebrates		Amphibians	
Worms and jellyfish	Segmented worms	Jawless fish	Cartilaginous fish	First vertebrate land animals	First reptiles	

PRE-CAMBRIAN	CAMBRIAN	ORDOVICIAN	SILURIAN	DEVONIAN	CARBONIFEROUS	PERMIAN
4000.0 – 542.0 MYA	542.0 – 488.3 MYA	488.3 – 443.7 MYA	443.7 – 416.0 MYA	416.0 – 359.2 MYA	359.2 – 299.0 MYA	299.0 – 251.0

The Origins of the Dinosaurs

First dinosaurs

Turtles
and tortoises

Snakes, lizards   Dinosaurs
and crocodiles   dominate

                                          Decline   Mammals   Emergence of
First mammals   First birds   of dinosaurs   dominate   modern humans

TRIASSIC   JURASSIC   CRETACEOUS   PALEOGENE   NEOGENE   QUATERNARY

Archosauria: The Ruling Reptiles

On the surface birds and crocodiles could hardly be more dissimilar. Birds are feathered, crocodiles scaly. Birds are mostly small and hyperactive, whereas crocodiles are mostly large-bodied and sluggish. And, of course, birds fly while crocodiles lurk around the water. But appearances can be misleading. In fact, crocodiles are more closely related to birds than to any other living vertebrates, including lizards and snakes that superficially appear more like them.

This is because birds and crocodiles are the only living members of an ancient group of vertebrates called the Archosauria, the 'ruling reptiles'. Dinosaurs, the evolutionary ancestors of the birds, were archosaurs. So, too, were a host of bizarre animals that lived only in the Triassic period. In today's world, mammals may rule most ecosystems, but during the Mesozoic the archosaurs were kings.

Archosaurs share a number of skeletal features. The most important is an extra opening in front of the eye socket called the antorbital fenestra. This opening most probably housed an extensive system of sinuses, which may have helped archosaurs breathe more efficiently or cool down more quickly. Other hallmarks of this group include an opening near the back of the lower jaw, which probably anchored strong muscles that increased bite force, and dagger-like teeth with serrated margins.

The first known archosaurs date from the Early Triassic, only a few million years after the devastating Permo–Triassic extinction that nearly wiped out all life on earth. Scientists generally divide archosaurs into two groups: a lineage that includes birds and a large group that includes crocodiles. Dinosaurs and pterosaurs, the flying reptiles of the Mesozoic, belong to the bird line. The crocodile line, on the other hand, includes an assortment of peculiar creatures, such as the long-snouted and semiaquatic phytosaurs, the armoured and herbivorous aetosaurs and the fearsome carnivorous rauisuchians. Most of these crocodile cousins lived only during the Middle–Late Triassic, and by the dawn of the Jurassic were completely extinct. Some of these animals were very dinosaur-like, and filled the large carnivore niche in those ecosystems that lacked dinosaurs. However, by the beginning of the Late Triassic true dinosaurs began to spread worldwide, ushering i a 160-million-year period of dominance.

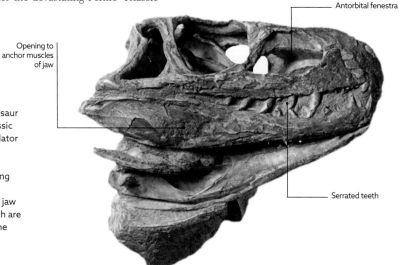

Antorbital fenestra

Opening to anchor muscles of jaw

Serrated teeth

The skull of the primitive archosaur *Euparkeria*, from the Early Triassic of South Africa. This small predator is one of the oldest archosaurs known, and an important early cousin of dinosaurs. The opening in front of the eye (antorbital fenestra), opening in the lower jaw (for muscles) and serrated teeth are important characters that define archosaurs.

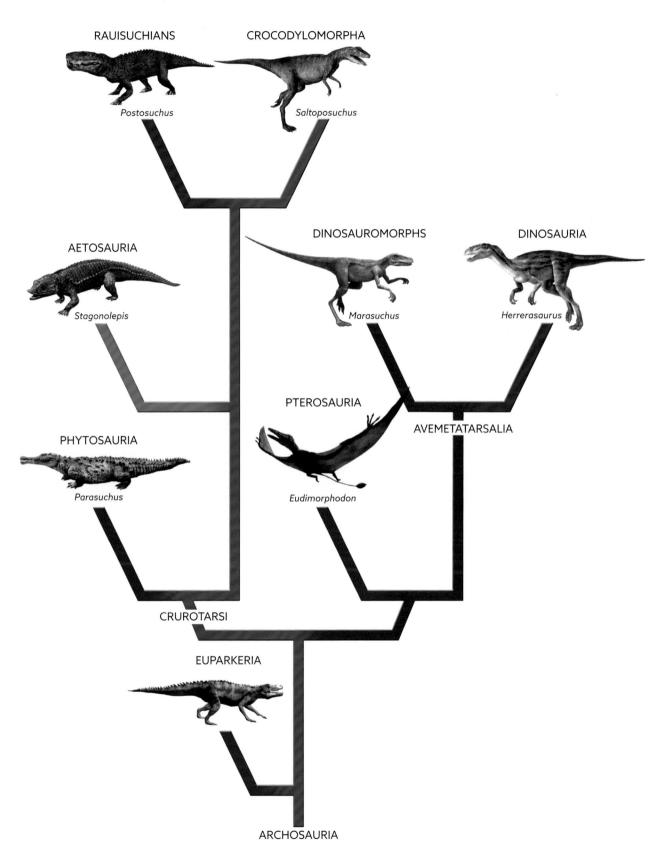

RAUISUCHIANS

CROCODYLOMORPHA

Postosuchus

Saltoposuchus

AETOSAURIA

DINOSAUROMORPHS

DINOSAURIA

Stagonolepis

Marasuchus

Herrerasaurus

PTEROSAURIA

AVEMETATARSALIA

PHYTOSAURIA

Parasuchus

Eudimorphodon

CRUROTARSI

EUPARKERIA

ARCHOSAURIA

EUPARKERIA

Meaning: named in honour of W.K. Parker', is a genus of primitive archosaur
Pronunciation: you-park-air-e-uh

Euparkeria was a moderate-sized animal that played only a minor role in its ecosystem. At first glance, with its sharp, pointed teeth, scaly skin and sprawled stance, it may look just like the many other reptiles that lived in the Triassic. However, look a bit closer and it becomes apparent just how unique and important this small predator was.

Euparkeria has a number of remarkable adaptations that would later be developed in many dinosaur groups. The most important feature linking *Euparkeria* to other archosaurs is the large, oval-shaped opening in front of the eye socket. Also, like many other archosaurs, its back was shielded with numerous bony plates, called osteoderms. Despite its slightly sprawling posture, *Euparkeria* may have stood more upright than other reptiles. Because its forelimbs are significantly shorter than the hindlimbs, many scientists think that *Euparkeria* may have been able to walk on two legs, at least part of the time. So although it barely resembles a dinosaur, crocodile or bird, *Euparkeria* is, in fact, one of the oldest known archosaurs. This means that it is a major evolutionary step on the line leading towards the dinosaurs.

Euparkeria is known from several fossils, all discovered within a small region of South Africa. Rocks in this area date from the very early Triassic period, and record a group of animals that had evolved in the aftermath of the devastating Permo–Triassic extinction event. Therapsids, also known as 'mammal-like reptiles', are commonly found alongside *Euparkeria*. These large, ferocious predators probably preyed on the small archosaur. However, *Euparkeria* was also a predator, and probably fed on smaller vertebrates.

STATISTICS

Habitat:	Africa (South Africa)
Period:	Early Triassic
Length:	28 in (70 cm)
Height*:	8 in (20 cm)
Weight:	15–31 lb (7–14 kg)
Predators:	Therapsids
Food:	Small vertebrates

* All height measurements for dinosaurs are
  taken from the foot to the top of the hip

CLASSIFICATION

Animalia
  Chordata
    Sauropsida
      Archosauria

SIZE COMPARISON

PARASUCHUS

Meaning: 'similar to crocodiles' **Pronunciation:** pah-rah-SOOK-uss

Modern crocodiles are instantly recognizable. No other animal looks remotely like them. Crocodilians possess a unique body plan, which has been fine-tuned by millions of years of evolution to fit their semiaquatic, predatory lifestyle. But, long before modern crocodiles evolved, there were other animals with a similar lifestyle. And one such group, the phytosaurs, looked remarkably similar to crocodiles.

One of the best-known phytosaurs is *Parasuchus*. Its name marks the astonishing similarity between these Late Triassic archosaurs and crocodiles. *Parasuchus* was originally discovered in India and subsequently found in Late Triassic rocks across the world. It is small for a phytosaur, measuring approximately 6 ft (2 m) in length. In contrast, some phytosaurs may have grown to a length of 43 ft (13 m), rivalling *Tyrannosaurus rex* in size.

Like all phytosaurs, *Parasuchus* possesses a long and narrow skull. At the front of the skull is a slender, elongated snout, which houses numerous conical teeth, similar to those of crocodiles and seals. The eyes and nostrils of *Parasuchus* are located close to the top of the skull. In modern animals these features make it easier to see and breathe while partially submerged in water. *Parasuchus* would probably have hidden itself in the water and ambushed its prey, much like the modern crocodiles that it so closely resembles. This is a prime example of convergent evolution: when different groups of animals evolve a similar appearance because they share a similar lifestyle or habitat.

SIZE COMPARISON

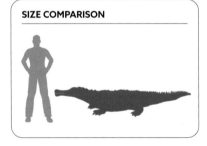

FOSSIL LOCATIONS

STATISTICS

Habitat:	India and worldwide
Period:	Late Triassic
Length:	6 ft (2 m)
Height:	14 in (35 cm)
Weight:	110–220 lb (50–100 kg)
Predators:	Rauisuchian archosaurs, theropod dinosaurs
Food:	Small vertebrates, fish

CLASSIFICATION

Animalia
  Chordata
    Sauropsida
      Archosauria
        Phytosauria

STAGONOLEPIS

Meaning: named for the drop-shaped pits on its scales **Pronunciation:** stag-o-NO-le-pis

Far in the northeastern reaches of Scotland, on the coast of the North Sea, is the small city of Elgin. A cold, wet and windswept place, it was here, in 1844, that quarrymen discovered a series of unusual scales embedded in Triassic sandstone. Drawings of these puzzling fossils were sent to eminent Swiss scientist Louis Agassiz, best known as the man who first realized the earth had undergone an Ice Age. Agassiz had never seen anything quite like these large, plate-like scales, which were ornamented by numerous pits that resembled raindrops in mud. Not knowing what to make of them, Agassiz concluded that they belonged to an enormous fish and named them *Stagonolepis*.

Several years later the equally eminent Thomas Henry Huxley, who later gained fame as one of the strongest supporters of Darwin's theory of evolution, reinterpreted the fossils as being the armour-like plates of a reptile. This new identification set off a long and complicated argument over not only the proper interpretation of the fossil, but also the age of the rocks in Elgin. The argument finally concluded with Huxley victoriously proving the rocks to be Triassic in age and proclaiming that *Stagonolepis* was a key ancestor of modern crocodiles.

Today, nearly 150 years after the clash of these scientific titans, modern scientists no longer regard *Stagonolepis* as an ancestor of crocodiles, but as a close yet distinctive cousin. *Stagonolepis*, along with animals such as *Desmatosuchus* and *Typothorax*, belongs to a group of archosaurs called the aetosaurs. These animals, which lived only during the Late Triassic, were covered with a full body coat of armour, and many also possessed robust spikes around the neck. All aetosaurs were herbivorous; many had a shovel-shaped snout that would have been perfect for uprooting vegetation. Although not closely related, aetosaurs resembled ankylosaurian dinosaurs in general body form.

SIZE COMPARISON

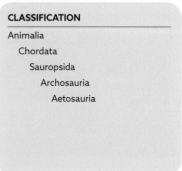

FOSSIL LOCATIONS

STATISTICS

Habitat:	Europe (Scotland) and North America (USA)
Period:	Late Triassic
Length:	10 ft (3 m)
Height:	24 in (60 cm)
Weight:	330–550 lb (150–250 kg)
Predators:	Rauisuchian archosaurs, ornithosuchid archosaurs, theropod dinosaurs
Food:	Plants

CLASSIFICATION

Animalia
  Chordata
    Sauropsida
      Archosauria
        Aetosauria

POSTOSUCHUS

Meaning: named for its discovery near Post, Texas **Pronunciation:** post-o-SOOK-uss

Postosuchus was a large carnivore from the Late Triassic period. It is one of several Triassic archosaurs discovered by Sankar Chatterjee and his colleagues on the empty, dusty plains of west Texas. During the Late Triassic this region was warm and lush, and *Postosuchus* was the top predator in a very diverse ecosystem.

Postosuchus is one of the best-known members of a puzzling group called the rauisuchians, which have been found in Middle–Late Triassic rocks across the world.

In many ways, *Postosuchus* resembles the large theropod dinosaurs of the Jurassic and Cretaceous. In fact, the large, deep skull and blade-like teeth of *Postosuchus* originally confused scientists into believing that it was ancestral to *Tyrannosaurus rex*. However, the ankles of *Postosuchus* and other members of the rauisuchian group share numerous features with crocodiles, conclusively linking the two groups.

Scientists mostly agree about which animals belong to Archosauria, and there is no doubt that phytosaurs, aetosaurs, crocodilians and dinosaurs are members of this group. However, there is considerable disagreement over the family tree of archosaurs, particularly about which groups are most closely related to crocodilians. Currently, most scientists regard phytosaurs and aetosaurs as distant cousins of the crocodiles, and consider the rauisuchians to be more closely related.

Although *Postosuchus* is known from nearly the entire skeleton, most other rauisuchians are represented by much scrappier fossils. This makes it difficult to study the group, and scientists frequently argue over the anatomy, lifestyle and evolutionary relationships of these animals. The recent discovery of more complete rauisuchians, including *Arizonasaurus* and *Effigia* from the southwestern USA and *Batrachotomus* from Germany, should help resolve these debates in the near future.

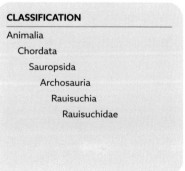

SIZE COMPARISON

FOSSIL LOCATIONS

STATISTICS

Habitat:	North America (USA)
Period:	Late Triassic
Length:	10–13 ft (3–4 m)
Height:	3 ft (1 m)
Weight:	440–660 lb (200–300 kg)
Predators:	None
Food:	Phytosaurs, aetosaurs, other vertebrates

CLASSIFICATION

Animalia
  Chordata
    Sauropsida
      Archosauria
        Rauisuchia
          Rauisuchidae

SALTOPOSUCHUS

Meaning: 'leaping crocodile' **Pronunciation:** salt-o-po-SOOK-uss

FOSSIL LOCATIONS

STATISTICS

Habitat:	Europe (Germany)
Period:	Late Triassic
Length:	3–6 ft (1–2 m)
Height:	10–20 in (25–50 cm)
Weight:	44 lb (20 kg)
Predators:	Rauisuchian archosaurs, theropod dinosaurs
Food:	Small vertebrates

CLASSIFICATION

Animalia
  Chordata
    Sauropsida
      Archosauria
        Crocodylomorpha
          Sphenosuchia

SIZE COMPARISON

Saltoposuchus was a sphenosuchian crocodylomorph, a distant cousin of the crocodile family. While all modern crocodilians appear very similar – crocodiles, alligators, or even long-snouted gharials, are all relatively slow-moving sprawlers, more at home near the water's edge than on dry land – this hasn't always been the case. During the Jurassic and Cretaceous one group of early crocodiles, the metriorhynchids, evolved into monstrous sea-dwelling predators. After the extinction of the dinosaurs a small group called the pristichampsines evolved hooves and lived on land. And even earlier, during the Late Triassic, a very primitive group of crocodiles called the sphenosuchians were important members of terrestrial ecosystems that included the early dinosaurs.

Saltoposuchus was a small animal, probably weighing no more than 44 lb (20 kg) and measuring only 3–6 ft (1–2 m) in length. Numerous fossils of this genus have been discovered in Late Triassic rocks in southwestern Germany, near the city of Stuttgart. A very close but smaller relative, *Terrestrisuchus*, is commonly found in Triassic cave fill deposits in south Wales. Other sphenosuchians are known from across the world, including South Africa, China, Brazil, Argentina and the United States.

The sphenosuchian crocodylomorphs can easily be mistaken for small theropod dinosaurs. Like the early theropods, sphenosuchians were sleek, slender carnivores perfectly suited for running on land. However, unlike theropods, these primitive creatures had not elongated here enough to walk on four legss, and walked on four legs most of the time. Scientists are able to tell that sphenosuchians are related to modern crocodiles because the skeletons of both groups share several important features, such as bony osteoderms running along the back and elongated bones in the wrist.

EUDIMORPHODON

Meaning: named for its multicusped and differentiated teeth
Pronunciation: you-die-MORPH-o-don

Three different vertebrate groups have evolved flight: birds, bats and pterosaurs. Birds and bats are still alive today, and are two of the largest and most diverse groups of vertebrates. Pterosaurs are long extinct, but were an important evolutionary success. These strange archosaurs were the first vertebrates to take to the air, and dominated the skies long before birds and bats existed. The first pterosaur fossils are known from the Late Triassic, some 30 million years before the oldest bird fossils (*Archaeopteryx*). Even after the evolution of the

birds, pterosaurs remained diverse and dominant until their extinction alongside the dinosaurs 65 million years ago.

The skeleton of pterosaurs is finely adapted for flight. Its most surprising feature is the elongated fourth finger of the hand. In some species the finger is nearly as long as the entire body! This stretched finger, along with a unique bone in the wrist called the pteroid, helped to support an extensive wing. Unlike the wing of birds, which is comprised of individual feathers, the aerofoil of pterosaurs was more of a broad sheet

stretching from the fourth finger and connected to the body. Other specializations for flight include a shoulder socket that faced outwards, which helped the wing swing through a broad flight stroke, and extremely hollowed bones, which lightened the animal.

Eudimorphodon is one of the oldest-known pterosaurs. Several fossils have been discovered near Bergamo, a mid-sized city close to Milan in northern Italy. The fossil of a very young individual has also been reported from Greenland. *Eudimorphodon* is distinguished from other pterosaurs by its complex teeth, which have several small points called cusps, and its long, thin tail. It is a relatively small animal, especcialy when compared with Cretaceous pterosaurs such as *Quetzalcoatlus*, whose wingspan of up to 39 ft (12 m) was larger than that of many small planes!

FOSSIL LOCATIONS

STATISTICS

Habitat:	Europe (Italy) and Greenland
Period:	Late Triassic
Length:	3 ft (1 m)
Height:	10 in (25 cm)
Weight:	22 lb (10 kg)
Predators:	Rauisuchian archosaurs, theropod dinosaurs
Food:	Small vertebrates, insects

SIZE COMPARISON

CLASSIFICATION

Animalia
  Chordata
    Sauropsida
      Archosauria
        Pterosauria

MARASUCHUS

Meaning: named for a resemblance to the Patagonian cavy (mara)
Pronunciation: mara-SOOK-uss

The diminutive *Marasuchus* doesn't look very impressive. Barely larger than a rat or a squirrel, this slender little archosaur seems little more than an easy meal for the fearsome rauisuchian predators that lived alongside it. But the small stature of *Marasuchus* belies its critically important role in the evolution of dinosaurs. Although it could easily have been squashed by a *Tyrannosaurus* or a *Diplodocus*, *Marasuchus* is one of the dinosaurs' closest cousins.

Marasuchus lived during the Middle-Triassic, right around the time that the first true dinosaurs originated. Legendary palaeontologist Alfred Romer first discovered fossils of the species in Argentina in the 1960s. He named the fossils *Lagosuchus*, but an error in the original description later led scientists to rename them *Marasuchus*.

Marasuchus, along with several other close dinosaur cousins known from the Middle-Triassic of Argentina, are called dinosauromorphs. They include *Lagerpeton*, *Lewisuchus* and *Pseudolagosuchus*. The dinosauromorphs share several unique skeletal features with dinosaurs. While many archosaurs walked on four legs and had a slightly splayed stance, dinosaurs and their close cousins walked upright and on two legs. The forelimbs of dinosaurs and their cousins, therefore, are very short compared to the hindlimbs, and the socket joint in the pelvis is open to receive the ball-like head of the femur.

Despite these common features the dinosauromorphs were a diverse group. *Marasuchus* had an incredibly elongated tail, while *Lagerpeton* may have hopped around like a kangaroo or rabbit. Both generally resemble small carnivorous dinosaurs, but the newly discovered *Silesaurus* from Poland is an herbivorous quadruped. It would seem that dinosaur cousins have an interesting story to tell.

STATISTICS	
Habitat:	South America (Argentina)
Period:	Middle-Triassic
Length:	12–16 in (30–40 cm)
Height:	4 in (10 cm)
Weight:	4–11 lb (2–5 kg)
Predators:	Rauisuchian archosaurs
Food:	Small vertebrates, insects

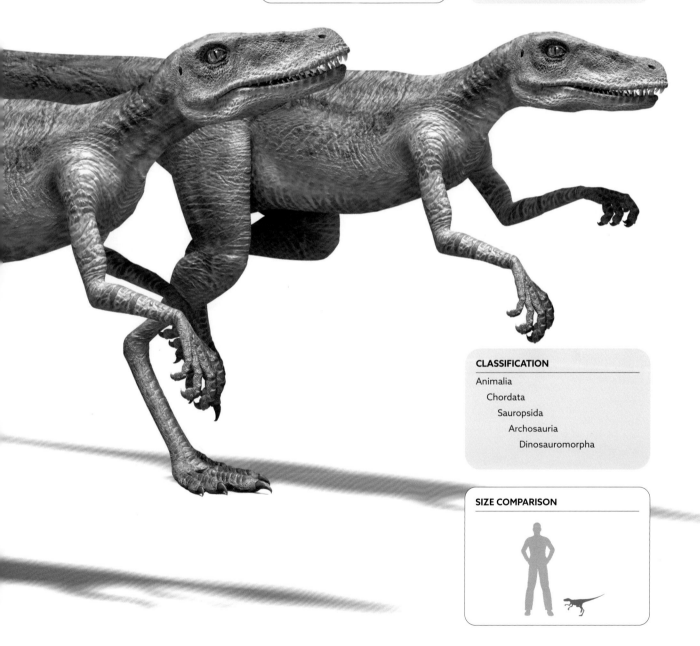

CLASSIFICATION

Animalia
  Chordata
    Sauropsida
      Archosauria
        Dinosauromorpha

SIZE COMPARISON

EORAPTOR

Meaning: 'dawn plunderer' **Pronunciation:** e-o-RAP-tor

FOSSIL LOCATIONS

STATISTICS

Habitat:	South America (Argentina)
Period:	Late Triassic
Length:	3 ft (1 m)
Height:	12 in (30 cm)
Weight:	33–66 lb (15–30 kg)
Predators:	Rauisuchian archosaurs
Food:	Small vertebrates, insects

CLASSIFICATION

Animalia
  Chordata
    Sauropsida
      Archosauria
        Dinosauria
          Theropoda

SIZE COMPARISON

During their 160-million-year reign throughout the Mesozoic the dinosaurs developed an exceptionally diverse array of body types – knife-toothed theropods, long-necked sauropods, plated stegosaurs and heavily armoured ankylosaurs. So what did the common ancestor from which all dinosaurs arose look like? It is virtually impossible to know for sure, since the odds of any single species being preserved as a fossil are mind-numbingly low. However, scientists agree that one early dinosaur in particular, *Eoraptor*, is a good approximation for the size and general body form of the ancestral dinosaur.

Eoraptor is fairly small for a dinosaur, measuring only about 3 ft (1 m) in length. However, compared to the minuscule *Marasuchus* and other close dinosaur cousins *Eoraptor* is quite large. Although the skull generally resembles that of a carnivorous dinosaur, *Eoraptor* has a strange combination of knife-like teeth, useful for cutting meat, and leaf-shaped teeth. commonly seen in plant eaters. However, the elongated hand capped with sharp, robust claws indicates a predatory lifestyle.

Eminent American palaeontologist Paul Sereno discovered the first fossils of *Eoraptor* in Argentina in the late 1980s. Sereno and his colleagues noted several features that *Eoraptor* shared with other dinosaurs, such as an enormous muscle attachment on the humerus (upper bone of the forearm) and additional vertebrae in the hip region, which would have provided extra support and balance. *Eoraptor* also has a few characteristics that are otherwise unique to theropod dinosaurs, such as an elongated hand with the outer two fingers reduced. This has led some scientists to believe that *Eoraptor* is not just a primitive dinosaur, but actually a member of the theropod lineage.

HERRERASAURUS

Meaning: named in honour of its discoverer, Victorino Herrera
Pronunciation: her-RARE-a-sore-uss

Valle de la Luna (Valley of the Moon) sounds as if it is right out of a dream or a fantasy novel. And, at first, the endless stretch of red and grey badlands does give the impression of another world. But a few minutes in the treacherous heat and wind are enough to convince anyone that this is not another planet, but the vast, empty expanses of northwestern Argentina. Here, near the border with Chile, the rolling pampas of eastern Argentina transitions into inhospitable desert. And in this desert, millions of years of slow erosion have exposed a bounty of Late Triassic fossils, including some of the oldest-known dinosaurs and a wealth of early crocodile and mammal relatives.

In the late 1950s, a local artisan named Victorino Herrera came across a puzzling fossil that resembled carnivorous dinosaurs. This was named *Herrerasaurus* in his honour, but remained poorly understood for several decades. Then, in the early summer of 1988, Paul Sereno, just out of graduate school and on his first job, launched an expedition to the Valley in the hope of finding early dinosaurs. Just a few weeks into his trip Sereno struck the jackpot. He noticed a series of eroded vertebrae emerging from a cliff, and further digging revealed a nearly complete skeleton of *Herrerasaurus*. Sereno's discovery showed that this large animal shared many features with dinosaurs, as well as with true theropods. However, other features of the skeleton are strikingly primitive, indicating that *Herrerasaurus* is one of the most archaic dinosaurs known to science.

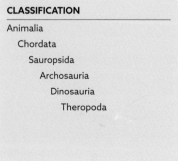

SIZE COMPARISON

FOSSIL LOCATIONS

STATISTICS

Habitat:	South America (Argentina)
Period:	Late Triassic
Length:	10–20 ft (3–6 m)
Height:	3–6 ft (1–2 m)
Weight:	276–660 lb (125–300 kg)
Predators:	Rauisuchian archosaurs
Food:	Large and small vertebrates

CLASSIFICATION

Animalia
  Chordata
    Sauropsida
      Archosauria
        Dinosauria
          Theropoda

		Carnian 228.7 – 216.5 MYA	Hettangian 199.6 – 196.5 MYA	Aalenian 175.6 – 171.6 MYA	
			Sinemurian 196.5 – 189.6 MYA	Bajocian 171.6 – 167.7 MYA	Oxfordian 161.2 – 155.6 MYA
Induan 251.0 – 249.5 MYA	Anisian 245.9 – 237.0 MYA	Norian 216.5 – 203.6 MYA	Pliensbachian 189.6 – 183.0 MYA	Bathonian 167.7 – 164.7 MYA	Kimmeridgian 155.6 – 150.8 MYA
Olenekian 249.5 – 245.9 MYA	Ladinian 237.0 – 228.7 MYA	Rhaetian 203.6 – 199.6 MYA	Toarcian 183.0 – 175.6 MYA	Callovian 164.7 – 161.2 MYA	Tithonian 150.8 – 145.5 MYA
EARLY TRIASSIC 251.0 – 245.9 MYA	MIDDLE TRIASSIC 245.9 – 228.7 MYA	LATE TRIASSIC 228.7 – 199.6 MYA	EARLY JURASSIC 199.6 – 175.6 MYA	MIDDLE JURASSIC 175.6 – 161.2 MYA	LATE JURASSIC 161.2 – 145.5 MYA

TRIASSIC 251.0 – 199.6 MYA   **JURASSIC 199.6 – 145.5 MYA**

Dinosaurs of the Late Triassic

Berriasian 145.5 – 140.2 MYA

Valanginian 140.2 – 133.9 MYA

Hauterivian 133.9 – 130.0 MYA

Barremian 130.0 – 125.0 MYA

Aptian 125.0 – 112.0 MYA

Albian 112.0 – 99.6 MYA

Cenomanian 99.6 – 93.6 MYA

Turonian 93.6 – 88.6 MYA

Coniacian 88.6 – 85.8 MYA

Santonian 85.8 – 83.5 MYA

Campanian 83.5 – 70.6 MYA

Maastrichtian 70.6 – 65.5 MYA

EARLY-MIDDLE CRETACEOUS
145.5 – 99.6 MYA

LATE CRETACEOUS
99.6 – 65.5 MYA

CRETACEOUS 145.5 – 65.5 MYA

The Rise of the Dinosaurs

The Triassic was a critical period in earth history. The preceding period, the Permian, ended with the most destructive mass extinction in the history of the planet. Some estimates suggest that up to 95 per cent of all species went extinct, and at no other time was life so close to complete annihilation. With the dawn of the Triassic came the opportunity for rebirth and recovery on a grand scale. Many ecosystems were empty, waiting for new groups of organisms to evolve, expand and dominate.

It was in this barren world that the archosaurs evolved. Small, generalized animals like *Euparkeria* were the first sign of the archosaur-dominated world to come. Close crocodile relatives, such as rauisuchians, were abundant in the Middle Triassic, and evolved into a range of body forms – large four-legged predators such as *Postosuchus*, swift two-legged runners like *Poposaurus* and strange sail-backed forms such as *Arizonasaurus*. The reign of the rauisuchians, however, would be short lived.

The first dinosaurs must have evolved in the Mid-Triassic, since their closest cousins (*Marasuchus* and *Lagerpeton*) lived at this time. The first definite dinosaur fossils are animals such as *Eoraptor* and *Herrerasaurus*, which are approximately 228 million years old. But these dinosaurs were very rare, and were vastly outnumbered by other reptiles. In the early Late Triassic of Argentina, for instance, dinosaurs comprised only 5 per cent of the individuals in the ecosystem.

However, around 216 million years ago, most rauisuchians and several herbivorous groups went extinct. After this dinosaurs became incredibly common, comprising 50–90 per cent of many ecosystems. The three major groups of dinosaurs – theropods, sauropodomorphs and ornithischians – had evolved prior to the extinction, but the first two groups now began to spread worldwide. Global migration was made possible by a quirk of geological history. At this time, all of the world's continents were joined together in the supercontinent of Pangaea. With no oceans or other barriers to prevent movement, some species were able to spread like wildfire across the globe.

By the close of the Triassic, about 200 million years ago, dinosaurs had taken full advantage of the Pangaean super-highway. A primitive group of theropods (the coelophysoids) and early cousins of the sauropods (prosauropods) dominated ecosystems across the globe. The dinosaur revolution had begun, and the course of earth history had changed forever.

The earth during the Late Triassic, when the dinosaurs first evolved. During this time all of the world's continents were joined together into the giant supercontinent of Pangaea, which allowed animals to easily migrate all around the world. The climate of much of Pangaea was warm and dry during this period.

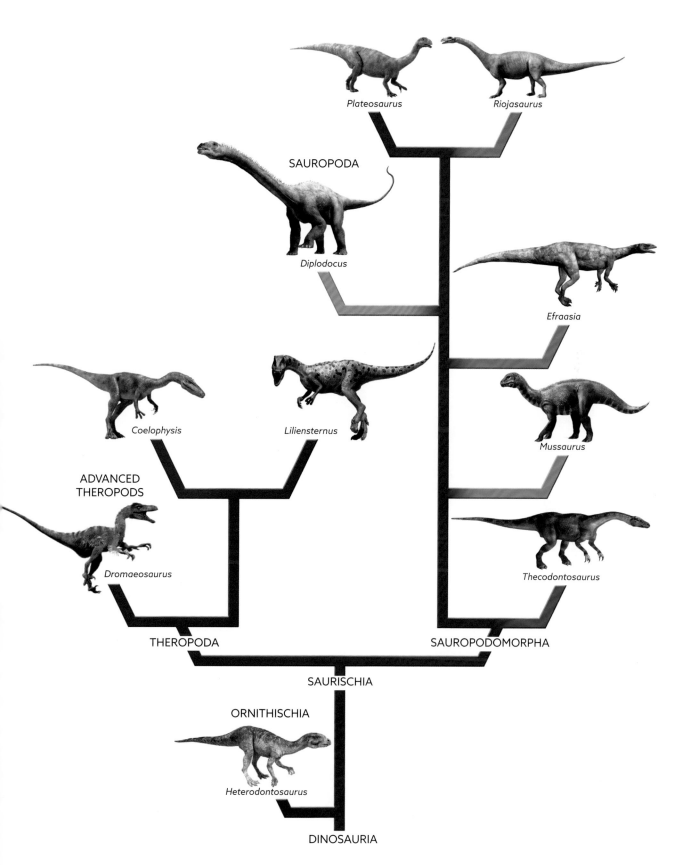

Plateosaurus

Riojasaurus

SAUROPODA

Diplodocus

Efraasia

Coelophysis

Liliensternus

Mussaurus

ADVANCED
THEROPODS

Dromaeosaurus

Thecodontosaurus

THEROPODA

SAUROPODOMORPHA

SAURISCHIA

ORNITHISCHIA

Heterodontosaurus

DINOSAURIA

COELOPHYSIS

Meaning: 'hollow form' **Pronunciation:** see-low-FYS-iss

The history of palaeontology is peppered with colourful characters, but few were as unusual as David Baldwin. A true individual at a time when the American frontier spirit was strong, Baldwin would often excavate fossils in the dead of winter, accompanied only by his mule. But although Baldwin was peculiar he was an outrageously successful fossil collector, who had the distinction of working for both O.C. Marsh and E.D. Cope, the two bitter rivals of the infamous 'Bone Wars'. It was while working for Cope in New Mexico, during the winter of 1881, that Baldwin made one of his more important discoveries.

Although Baldwin had come across only a few small bones, they were enough for Cope to name a new genus of theropod:

Coelophysis. Hailing from the Late Triassic, this slender, lightly built theropod was clearly a sleek and swift predator. However, it would be more than 60 years before more complete remains were discovered. In 1947 an expedition led by the American Museum of Natural History near Ghost Ranch, New Mexico, uncovered dozens of complete skeletons, probably killed by a flash flood.

Over the past few decades, further specimens of *Coelophysis* have been discovered in South Africa and China. Some of these fossils were once referred to as *Syntarsus* and *Megapnosaurus*, but many scientists believe that they all belong to *Coelophysis*. *Coelophysis* is thought to be one of the most primitive theropods, which makes it an important step in the evolution of dinosaurs.

SIZE COMPARISON

FOSSIL LOCATIONS

STATISTICS

Habitat:	North America (USA), Africa (South Africa), Asia (China)
Period:	Late Triassic
Length:	6–9 ft (2–3 m)
Height:	20–36 in (0.5–1 m)
Weight:	55–165 lb (25–75 kg)
Predators:	Crocodylomorph archosaurs
Food:	Small vertebrates, juvenile crocodylomorphs

CLASSIFICATION

Animalia
  Chordata
    Sauropsida
      Archosauria
        Dinosauria
          Theropoda
            Coelophysoidea

LILIENSTERNUS

Meaning: named in honour of German scientist Hugo Rühle von Lilienstern
Pronunciation: lily-IN-stern-uss

The discovery of complete skeletons of *Coelophysis* helped scientists to identify a number of similar Triassic theropods from across the world. These closely related animals are grouped together in the Coelophysoidea, a superfamily of theropods that represents the first major evolutionary radiation of carnivorous dinosaurs.

The giant of the coelophysoids, *Liliensternus*, is nearly 20 ft (6 m) long, much larger than *Coelophysis* at 6–9 ft (2–3 m). The species is represented by two skeletons from the Late Triassic of central Germany. Although the specimens are missing most of the skull, features of the vertebrae, pelvis and hindlimb identify them as coelophysoids.

Most other coelophysoids are represented only by fragmentary fossils. They include *Segisaurus* and *Gojirasaurus* from the southwestern United States and *Procompsognathus* from Germany. The crested *Dilophosaurus* and bizarre South American *Zupaysaurus* are sometimes regarded as coelophysoids, but have recently been reinterpreted as more derived, or evolutionarily advanced, theropods.

SIZE COMPARISON

FOSSIL LOCATIONS

STATISTICS

Habitat:	Europe (Germany)
Period:	Late Triassic
Length:	16–20 ft (5–6 m)
Height:	5–6 ft (1.5–2 m)
Weight:	440–880 lb (200–400 kg)
Predators:	None
Food:	Large and small vertebrates

CLASSIFICATION

Animalia
 Chordata
  Sauropsida
   Archosauria
    Dinosauria
     Theropoda
      Coelophysoidea

The Prosauropod Dinosaurs

Dinosaurs evolved from minuscule, two-legged carnivores such as *Marasuchus* in the Middle Triassic, someW230 million years ago. Very quickly dinosaurs diversified into three major groups: theropods, sauropodomorphs and ornithischians. The first theropod dinosaurs may have been similar to *Eoraptor* and *Herrerasaurus*, the most ancient dinosaurs, but in the Late Triassic coelophysoids evolved. Like the close dinosaur cousin *Marasuchus*, the coelophysoids were slender, agile, fast-running carnivores that walked on two legs. They soon soon became abundant and widespread.

The sauropodomorphs and ornithischians diverged from the primitive dinosaur body plan, evolving into herbivores that often walked on four legs. Ornithischians are rare in Triassic rocks, but seem to have become abundant in the Early Jurassic. Sauropodomorphs, on the other hand, rapidly diversified in the Late Triassic and quickly established themselves across the globe. These Triassic species, which were early cousins and possibly ancestors of the massive sauropods, were the first dinosaurs to spread worldwide and the first to successfully exploit plant eating as a way of life.

Traditionally, these Late Triassic and Early Jurassic sauropodomorphs are referred to as 'prosauropods'. The prosauropod *Thecodontosaurus*, from the Bristol Channel region of England and Wales, was named in 1836, making it only the fourth dinosaur to be named and described. Similar fossils began turning up in Late Triassic rocks across the globe, including South America, Africa and China. Some of these prosauropods, such as *Plateosaurus* from Germany, *Riojasaurus* from Argentina and *Massospondylus* from South Africa, are known from numerous skeletons. Vaguely sloth-like in appearance, these prosauropods ranged in size from 3 to 36 feet (1–11 m), could probably switch between walking on two or four legs, and ate plants, insects and possibly meat.

For much of the 20th century, scientists neglected prosauropods, often dismissing the group as boring and an evolutionary dead end. But in the last decade prosauropod research has taken off. In fact, questions about prosauropod evolution and biology are currently some of the most exciting areas of dinosaur research. One of the most important questions concerns the sauropodomorph family tree. Were the Late Triassic–Early Jurassic prosauropods a transitional series on the evolutionary line to the Early Jurassic–Late Cretaceous sauropods, or did they form their own distinct group, which was closely related to the sauropods? Scientists have also been looking closely at the growth, diet and locomotion of prosauropods. Clearly, prosauropods are anything but boring, and there is still much to learn about this important early group of dinosaurs.

The skeleton of the prosauropod *Plateosaurus* next to a man. *Plateosaurus* is the best-known and best-studied prosauropod dinosaur, and is known from thousands of fossils from Late Triassic rocks in Germany. It was a large plant eater with a massive gut, short neck, and a small head equipped with leaf-shaped teeth for cropping vegetation.

THECODONTOSAURUS

Meaning: 'socket-toothed lizard' **Pronunciation:** the-ko-DON-to-sore-uss

Three hundred million years ago, long before the first dinosaurs evolved, tropical seas covered much of modern England and Wales. This sea deposited a thick layer of limestone, which formed the land surface when primitive dinosaurs and mammals were scurrying around Great Britain in the Late Triassic. Limestone is easily dissolved by groundwater, resulting in caves. And caves are perfect traps for unsuspecting animals.

Today the remains of Late Triassic caves can be found all along the Bristol Channel region of Great Britain. These strange geological formations were first identified near the city of Bristol in the 1830s, and scientists were shocked to find the jumbled and fragmented fossils of many Triassic animals inside. One of the most important of these animals is *Thecodontosaurus*.

Thecodontosaurus was a meek prosauropod, measuring only a few metres in length, a far cry from the huge *Plateosaurus*. Unlike its massive sauropod cousins that walked on four legs, *Thecodontosaurus* probably walked on two legs, like other primitive dinosaurs such as coelophysoids. Many other features of the skeleton are also primitive, leading scientists to consider *Thecodontosaurus* one of the most ancient and unspecialized members of the sauropodomorph lineage.

FOSSIL LOCATIONS

STATISTICS

Habitat:	Europe (England and Wales)
Period:	Late Triassic
Length:	3–10 ft (1–3 m)
Height:	8 in (20 cm)
Weight:	18–44 lb (8–20 kg)
Predators:	Theropod dinosaurs
Food:	Plants, small vertebrates, insects

CLASSIFICATION

Animalia
  Chordata
    Sauropsida
      Archosauria
        Dinosauria
          Sauropodomorpha
            Prosauropoda

SIZE COMPARISON

PLATEOSAURUS

Meaning: 'flat lizard' **Pronunciation:** PLAT-eo-sore-uss

Most dinosaur species are known only from a single fossil, sometimes even a single bone. Palaeontologists seek complete skeletons because they can give a much better understanding of anatomy, lifestyle and evolutionary relationships, but these are scarce indeed.

The prosauropod *Plateosaurus* is a rare exception. More than 50 skeletons of this Late Triassic dinosaur have been discovered by scientists, mostly in the clay pits of Saxony and Bavaria in Germany. Other specimens have turned up in Switzerland, the icy expanses of Greenland and even embedded in Triassic rock more than one mile below the surface of the North Sea.

All of these fossils have given researchers unprecedented insight into the biology of *Plateosaurus*. This species was relatively large for prosauropods, reaching a length of 33 ft (10 m) and a weight of 1540 lb (700 kg). Its deep skull was studded with several leaf-shaped teeth, which were perfect for chewing vegetation and possibly even small prey. Scientists long thought that *Plateosaurus* could walk on either two or four legs, depending on what it was doing. However, recent research shows that the structure of the bones of the forelimb was completely unsuited to locomotion. Other recent research has studied the growth patterns of *Plateosaurus* from embryo to adult. These studies show that its rate of growth depended on the season, which is also true of many living reptiles.

SIZE COMPARISON

FOSSIL LOCATIONS

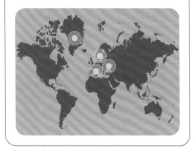

STATISTICS

Habitat:	Europe (France, Germany, Norway, Switzerland) and Greenland
Period:	Late Triassic
Length:	20–33 ft (6–10 m)
Height:	5 ft (1.5 m)
Weight:	1100–1540 lb (500–700 kg)
Predators:	Theropod dinosaurs
Food:	Plants and small vertebrates

CLASSIFICATION

Animalia
  Chordata
    Sauropsida
      Archosauria
        Dinosauria
          Sauropodomorpha
            Prosauropoda

MUSSAURUS

Meaning: 'mouse lizard' **Pronunciation:** muh-SORE-uss

Most animals change quite dramatically as they grow from juveniles into adults. The changes are obvious in humans. Babies are chubby, have large heads in proportion to the body and crawl around on all fours. These helpless infants grow into slimmer, stronger adults that walk on two legs.

But is this the same for dinosaurs? This is a very difficult question to answer, since very few dinosaurs are known from both infant and adult skeletons. But in a few remarkable cases scientists have discovered such remains, known as a 'growth series'. One of the best examples is *Mussaurus* from the Late Triassic of Argentina.

Mussaurus literally means 'mouse lizard', so named because several tiny, fragile juvenile skeletons have been discovered. The smallest skeletons measure only about 8 in (20 cm) in length, making them some of the tiniest dinosaur skeletons ever found. Adults, however, were giants that approached 16 ft (5 m) in length and 265 lb (120 kg) in weight. Scientists have carefully compared the juveniles and adults, and found that infant *Mussaurus* had a large head, big eyes and a round snout. Adults, on the other hand, had a much smaller head and eyes and a more elongated, pointed snout.

FOSSIL LOCATIONS

STATISTICS

Habitat:	South America (Argentina)
Period:	Late Triassic
Length:	10–15 ft (3–5 m) as adults
Height:	30–48 in (0.75–1.25 m)
Weight:	176–265 lb (80–120 kg)
Predators:	Theropod dinosaurs
Food:	Plants and small vertebrates

CLASSIFICATION

Animalia
  Chordata
    Sauropsida
      Archosauria
        Dinosauria
          Sauropodomorpha
            Prosauropoda

SIZE COMPARISON

EFRAASIA

Meaning: named after German scientist Eberhard Fraas **Pronunciation:** e-FRASS-e-uh

Prosauropods have been found across the world, but it is Germany that boasts the largest number of fossil specimens. Late Triassic rocks are particularly common in Germany; they blanket much of the western and central portions of the country. In fact, the Triassic period was originally named for the distinctive series of three rock types – red mudstones, white chalk and black shales – so characteristic of the German countryside. Found within these rocks is an abundance of prosauropod fossils.

Perhaps the most characteristic and best-known prosauropod, *Plateosaurus*, was discovered in the rolling Bavarian hills in 1837. It has the distinction of being the first non-English dinosaur ever named, and only the fifth dinosaur named overall. But these specimens, fragmentary vertebrae and limb bones, were only the first trickle of what would become a flood of German prosauropods.

Within the next 150 years some 11 different prosauropod genera were named from Germany. Many turned out to be invalid, mostly because they were based on scrappy specimens. But one genus that has stood the test of time is the relatively large prosauropod *Efraasia*. For a long while this dinosaur was also known as *Sellosaurus*, but today *Efraasia* is regarded as the correct name. Several specimens of this dinosaur have been discovered in western Germany, near the border with France.

SIZE COMPARISON

FOSSIL LOCATIONS

STATISTICS

Habitat:	Europe (Germany)
Period:	Late Triassic
Length:	16–23 ft (5–7 m)
Height:	4–6 ft (1.25–1.75 m)
Weight:	660–1100 lb (300–500kg)
Predators:	Theropod dinosaurs
Food:	Plants and small vertebrates

CLASSIFICATION

Animalia
  Chordata
    Sauropsida
      Archosauria
        Dinosauria
          Sauropodomorpha
            Prosauropoda

RIOJASAURUS

Meaning: named after La Rioja Province, Argentina **Pronunciation:** re-o-jah-SORE-uss

For many years scientists and museums from North America and Europe dominated dinosaur palaeontology, and little was known about the dinosaurs of other continents. Today, however, Argentina is one of the hot spots of dinosaur research. Few countries can boast as many dinosaurs, and every few months a new species is described.

One man is largely responsible for the growth of palaeontology in Argentina. Jose Bonaparte has discovered over 20 dinosaur species and yet he has no formal training or education in palaeontology. The son of an Italian sailor, Bonaparte grew up in Buenos Aires and began collecting fossils at a young age. He was so successful at finding dinosaurs that he was later given an honorary PhD degree and a prominent position at a museum in his home-town.

One of Bonaparte's most important discoveries is *Riojasaurus*, an enormous prosauropod that is known from more than 20 skeletons. At a length approaching 36 ft (11 m) it is one of the largest prosauropods ever discovered. Many features of the skeleton suggest a close evolutionary relationship with *Plateosaurus*, which is interesting since the two species are from different continents (Europe and South America). However, during the Triassic, all the continents were joined together in one supercontinent, Pangaea, making it easier for animals to disperse across the globe.

SIZE COMPARISON

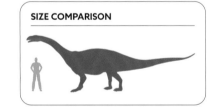

FOSSIL LOCATIONS

STATISTICS

Habitat:	South America (Argentina)
Period:	Late Triassic
Length:	30–36 ft (9–11 m)
Height:	7–9 ft (2.25–2.75 m)
Weight:	1100–1760 lb (500–800 kg)
Predators:	Theropod dinosaurs
Food:	Plants and small vertebrates

CLASSIFICATION

Animalia
  Chordata
    Sauropsida
      Archosauria
        Dinosauria
          Sauropodomorpha
            Prosauropoda

			Hettangian 199.6 – 196.5 MYA	Aalenian 175.6 – 171.6 MYA	
		Carnian 228.7 – 216.5 MYA	Sinemurian 196.5 – 189.6 MYA	Bajocian 171.6 – 167.7 MYA	Oxfordian 161.2 – 155.6 MYA
Induan 251.0 – 249.5 MYA	Anisian 245.9 – 237.0 MYA	Norian 216.5 – 203.6 MYA	Pliensbachian 189.6 – 183.0 MYA	Bathonian 167.7 – 164.7 MYA	Kimmeridgian 155.6 – 150.8 MYA
Olenekian 249.5 – 245.9 MYA	Ladinian 237.0 – 228.7 MYA	Rhaetian 203.6 – 199.6 MYA	Toarcian 183.0 – 175.6 MYA	Callovian 164.7 – 161.2 MYA	Tithonian 150.8 – 145.5 MYA
EARLY TRIASSIC 251.0 – 245.9 MYA	MIDDLE TRIASSIC 245.9 – 228.7 MYA	LATE TRIASSIC 228.7 – 199.6 MYA	EARLY JURASSIC 199.6 – 175.6 MYA	MIDDLE JURASSIC 175.6 – 161.2 MYA	LATE JURASSIC 161.2 – 145.5 MYA

Dinosaurs of the Early-Middle Jurassic

Berriasian 145.5 – 140.2 MYA

Valanginian 140.2 – 133.9 MYA

Hauterivian 133.9 – 130.0 MYA

Barremian 130.0 – 125.0 MYA

Aptian 125.0 – 112.0 MYA

Albian 112.0 – 99.6 MYA

Cenomanian 99.6 – 93.6 MYA

Turonian 93.6 – 88.6 MYA

Coniacian 88.6 – 85.8 MYA

Santonian 85.8 – 83.5 MYA

Campanian 83.5 – 70.6 MYA

Maastrichtian 70.6 – 65.5 MYA

EARLY-MIDDLE CRETACEOUS
145.5 – 99.6 MYA

LATE CRETACEOUS
99.6 – 65.5 MYA

CRETACEOUS 145.5 – 65.5 MYA

The Triassic-Jurassic Extinction and Pangaea

By the close of the Triassic, the three major lineages of dinosaurs had originated, and the theropods and sauropodomorphs had spread across the globe. Dinosaurs were rapidly diversifying, and by this time were the major carnivores and herbivores in terrestrial ecosystems around the world. But the dinosaur revolution was not over, and another extinction event would help the dinosaurs become even more dominant.

Pangaea was an enormous C-shaped landmass that spread across the equator. The body of water that was enclosed within the resulting crescent has been named the Tethys Sea. Owing to Pangaea's massive size, the inland regions appear to have been very hot and dry, however, this vast supercontinent would have allowed terrestrial animals to migrate freely.

The boundary between the Triassic and Jurassic periods, dated at approximately 200 million years ago, is marked by an extinction. Although not as deadly as the end-Permian extinction that helped usher in the age of archosaurs, or the end Cretaceous event that suddenly ended the dinosaurs' long reign, this extinction led to the disappearance of many

vertebrate groups, including the aetosaurs, phytosaurs and rauisuchians. Some experts believe that global warming, triggered by an increase in carbon dioxide in the atmosphere, was to blame.

Regardless of the cause, this extinction removed many groups that were competing with the dinosaurs for food, habitat and other resources. While some dinosaur groups were hard hit by the extinction, dinosaurs as a whole managed to survive. Afterwards they continued diversifying, and in the Jurassic evolved into a range of new body forms. The herbivorous ornithischians, which first evolved in the Late Triassic but remained rare, flourished and spread across the globe. Similarly, the very uniform prosauropods gave rise to true sauropods, the familiar long-necked giants that would become the top herbivores for the next 100 million years. And theropods changed as well, evolving into larger and more fearsome predators.

Meanwhile, the earth was going through some very important changes of its own. For most of the Triassic all of the world's continents were joined together as the supercontinent of Pangaea. This enabled many Triassic dinosaur groups to spread around the world, since there were no oceans or other major barriers to prevent movement. However, during the Early Jurassic Pangaea began to split into the northern region of Laurasia and the southern continent of Gondwana. An ocean formed between these two landmasses, which suddenly cut off an easy migration route. The fragmentation of Pangaea was a major influence on dinosaur evolution. No longer could dinosaurs freely migrate, and the days of a select few species dominating ecosystems across the globe were over. Instead, the world was breaking into many smaller landmasses, each of which would be home to its own unique group of dinosaurs.

The earth during the Early Jurassic, when dinosaurs of all kinds were spreading around the world after the extinction of other archosaur groups. The supercontinent of Pangaea, which linked all of the world's continents during the Triassic, was beginning to break up at this time. It first separated into northern and southern landmasses, called Laurasia and Gondwana. As these landmasses continued to split, unique groups of dinosaurs would inhabit their own continents.

DILOPHOSAURUS

Meaning: 'double-crested lizard'   **Pronunciation:** di-loh-fo-SORE-uss

Most Late Triassic theropods were small to mid-sized animals, typified by the 6–9-ft (2–3-m) *Coelophysis*. Larger theropods began to diversify in the Early Jurassic. They include one of the strangest meat-eating dinosaurs ever discovered: *Dilophosaurus*.

The name *Dilophosaurus* refers to the unique pair of thin, sheet-like crests on the top of the skull. However, there is no evidence that this species had a fleshy neck frill or could spit venom as is often portrayed. Crests, horns, bumps and other bizarre structures are frequently seen on the skulls of dinosaurs. The function of these structures is debatable, but they seem poorly suited for defence from predators and more useful for attracting mates or differentiating males from females.

Dilophosaurus is known only from a few specimens, many of which were found on a Navajo Indian Reservation in northern Arizona. A very similar skeleton was discovered in China and described as a second species, and supposed *Dilophosaurus* footprints have been found everywhere from the northeastern United States to northern Italy. For a long while scientists regarded *Dilophosaurus* as a coelophysoid, a member of the theropod group that contains *Coelophysis* and *Liliensternus*. However, recent studies indicate that *Dilophosaurus* was a member of its own unique group of theropods called the Dilophosauridae, which also includes the crested Antarctic species *Cryolophosaurus*.

SIZE COMPARISON

FOSSIL LOCATIONS

STATISTICS

Habitat:	North America (USA), Asia (China)
Period:	Early Jurassic
Length:	16–20 ft (5–6 m)
Height:	5–6 ft (1.5–2 m)
Weight:	880–1100 lb (400–500 kg)
Predators:	None
Food:	Ornithischian dinosaurs, crocodylomorphs

CLASSIFICATION

Animalia
  Chordata
    Sauropsida
      Archosauria
        Dinosauria
          Theropoda
            Dilophosauridae

CRYOLOPHOSAURUS

Meaning: 'cold crested lizard' **Pronunciation:** cry-oh-lo-fo-SORE-uss

Think of dinosaur digs and you think of deserts and other dry, dusty places where years of wind and heat have exposed the rocky tombs of dinosaur fossils. But dinosaurs are not only found in the Sahara or the Gobi. The first dinosaurs were discovered in the cool, foggy midlands of England, some fossils have been pried from beneath the sea and several dinosaur species are known from one of the coldest and loneliest places on earth, Antarctica.

The first Antarctic dinosaur ever named was *Cryolophosaurus*, a large and primitive theropod from the Early Jurassic. This carnivore was discovered in 1991 deep in the Transantarctic Mountains, a frigid set of hills near the coast of the Ross Sea. Here, at an elevation of over 13,000 ft (4000 m) above sea level, American palaeontologist William Hammer and his team discovered several bone fragments. Additional digging with jackhammers revealed several vertebrae and a partial skull, whose front half had unfortunately been ripped off by a glacier.

Cryolophosaurus is one of only a few theropod dinosaurs known from the Early Jurassic. Its skeleton has a strange mixture of very primitive theropod features seen in coelophysoids and more derived, or advanced, characteristics seen in Middle–Late Jurassic theropods. Recent studies indicate a close relationship with *Dilophosaurus*, *Dracovenator* from South Africa and possibly *Zupaysaurus* from South America. Together, these theropods comprise the Dilophosauridae, the first group of large-bodied theropods to evolve.

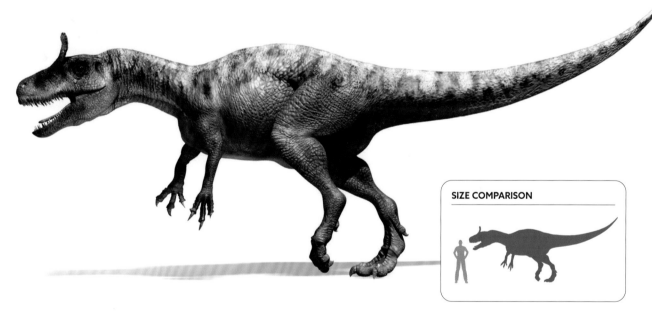

SIZE COMPARISON

FOSSIL LOCATIONS

STATISTICS

Habitat:	Antarctica
Period:	Early Jurassic
Length:	20–26 ft (6–8 m)
Height:	6–8 ft (2–2.4 m)
Weight:	880–1320 lb (400–600 kg)
Predators:	None
Food:	Prosauropod dinosaurs, primitive mammals

CLASSIFICATION

Animalia
  Chordata
    Sauropsida
      Archosauria
        Dinosauria
          Theropoda
            Dilophosauridae

The Tetanuran Theropods

Although they were abundant and dominant worldwide, the theropods of the Late Triassic and Early Jurassic were primitive animals. Most were small in size and lacked the specialized anatomy of many later theropod groups. While species like *Dilophosaurus* and *Cryolophosaurus* sported bizarre cranial crests, the rest of the skeleton retained many primitive features of early dinosaurs and close dinosaur cousins.

A new group of more advanced theropods evolved in the Middle Jurassic. These are the tetanuran theropods, so named because of their stiffened tails. Scientists originally named the group Tetanurae to differentiate many Jurassic and Cretaceous theropods from the more primitive coelophysoids, dilophosaurids and ceratosaurs. These more advanced carnivores include spinosauroids, allosauroids and the coelurosaurs. As will be seen later, the coelurosaurs include a diverse range of bird-like theropods such as dromaeosaurs, ornithomimosaurs, troodontids and birds themselves.

At first glance the splendid array of tetanuran theropods may seem very strange. Many of these animals appear very dissimilar, such as the monstrous, sail-backed spinosaurids and the diminutive, agile dromaeosaurids. However, all of these theropods share a number of derived, or more advanced, features not seen in older, more primitive Late Triassic – Early Jurassic species. The most important of these characteristics are an additional opening in front of the antorbital fenestra (an opening in the skull in front of the eye sockets), a shortened tooth row that ends in front of the eye socket and a hand that is reduced to only three fingers.

The tetanurans must have first evolved in the Early or Middle Jurassic. The oldest fossils of this group are extremely fragmentary, and come from 175-million-year-old rocks in England. The best known of these is Magnosaurus from Dorset, which is known from scrappy remains of the skull, vertebral column and hindlimb. More complete specimens are known from slightly later in China. The best of these is Monolophosaurus, whose crested cranium is one of the most complete dinosaur skulls ever found. By the Late Jurassic the tetanuran theropods had spread worldwide, and these advanced carnivores would dominate much of the world for the next 100 million years.

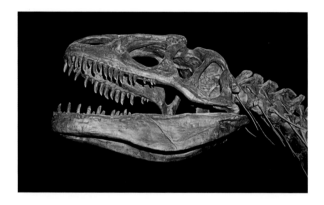

The skull of the tetanuran theropod *Allosaurus*. Allosaurus is one of the best-known and best-studied tetanurans, and is known from thousands of fossils from Late Jurassic rocks in North America and Europe. Allosaurus exhibits two important tetanuran hallmarks: teeth that end in front of the eye and an additional small opening in front of the antorbital fenestra, which cannot be seen in this photo.

The hand of the tetanuran theropod Allosaurus. The hand of tetanurans is reduced to three fingers, which differs from the hands of more primitive theropods like *Herrerasaurus* and Coelophysis that had four or five fingers. The fingers of *Allosaurus* were capped with powerful claws, which would have been used to dismember prey.

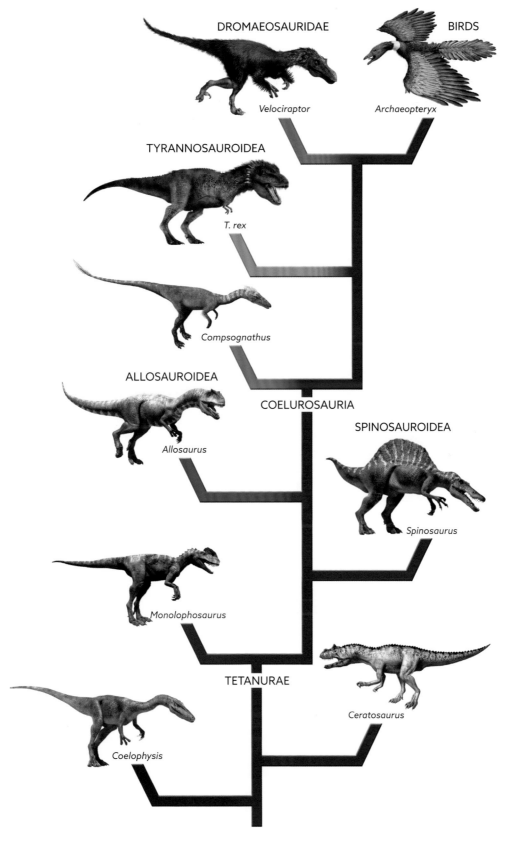

DROMAEOSAURIDAE

Velociraptor

BIRDS

Archaeopteryx

TYRANNOSAUROIDEA

T. rex

Compsognathus

ALLOSAUROIDEA

COELUROSAURIA

Allosaurus

SPINOSAUROIDEA

Spinosaurus

Monolophosaurus

TETANURAE

Ceratosaurus

Coelophysis

MONOLOPHOSAURUS

Meaning: 'single crested lizard' **Pronunciation:** mon-o-loh-fo-SORE-uss

The evolution of Tetanurae marked an important step in theropod evolution. The generalized, primitive theropods of the Late Triassic and Early Jurassic were now being replaced by more advanced species. But tetanurans did not evolve overnight; they developed slowly along an evolutionary lineage.

The Chinese tetanuran *Monolophosaurus* can help scientists understand this long, slow evolutionary transition. *Monolophosaurus* is clearly a tetanuran, since it possesses a number of skeletal features seen only in this group. However, in many ways this Middle-Jurassic species looks like a coelophysoid or a dilophosaurid: it has an elongated skull ornamented by an enlarged, sheet-like crest. This is a sign of evolution in action. Tetanurans evolved from a coelophysoid-

like ancestor, and it makes sense that one of the oldest tetanurans retains many primitive features seen in the ancestor. Later on, as tetanurans continued to evolve, these features were lost by more advanced groups such as allosauroids and coelurosaurs.

Monolophosaurus was discovered in 1981 in the Junggar Basin of Xinjiang Province, a large region that, unlike the rest of China, has a long Muslim heritage. Leading the expedition was respected Chinese palaeontologist Zhao Xijin. Zhao began exploring for dinosaurs in the 1950s, and his numerous discoveries have helped China to earn its reputation as a prime centre for dinosaur research.

SIZE COMPARISON

FOSSIL LOCATIONS

STATISTICS

Habitat:	Asia (China)
Period:	Middle Jurassic
Length:	16–18 ft (5–6 m)
Height:	5–6 ft (1.5–2 m)
Weight:	880–1320 lb (400–600 kg)
Predators:	None
Food:	Sauropod dinosaurs, large vertebrates

CLASSIFICATION

Animalia
  Chordata
    Sauropsida
      Archosauria
        Dinosauria
          Theropoda
            Tetanurae

MEGALOSAURUS

Meaning: 'great lizard' **Pronunciation:** meg-uh-low-SORE-uss

Over 300 years ago, back in 1676, labourers working a limestone quarry near Oxford, England, came across a puzzling object. It sort of resembled a bone, but was certainly too large to be real. The specimen found its way to Oxford professor Robert Plot. After several years of agonized thought, he identified it as the end of a femur (thigh bone). But since it was too big to belong to an animal, he thought it must have come from a mythical giant said to have terrorized England in ancient times.

It took nearly 150 years for the true identity of this specimen to come to light. As is often the case in palaeontology, new information came from the discovery of new specimens. Again they came from a quarry, this time a slate mine in the small town of Stonesfield, on the edge of England's Cotswolds region. Quarrymen uncovered several objects that were clearly large bones, including pieces of a skull, vertebral column and pelvis. These were sent to Oxford professor William Buckland, who in 1824 described them as *Megalosaurus* – not a human giant but a giant reptile.

Soon afterwards, similar fossils began turning up across England. Some clearly belonged to different species of giant reptile, and were given names such as *Iguanodon* and *Hylaeosaurus*. In 1842 Richard Owen grouped these three enormous, extinct species together under the name Dinosauria, the 'fearfully great reptiles'. Thus, Buckland's *Megalosaurus* goes down in history as the first named dinosaur. However, perhaps ironically, this first dinosaur remains one of the most poorly known theropods because only scrappy fossils have been found. These suggest that it was a very primitive member of the tetanuran group.

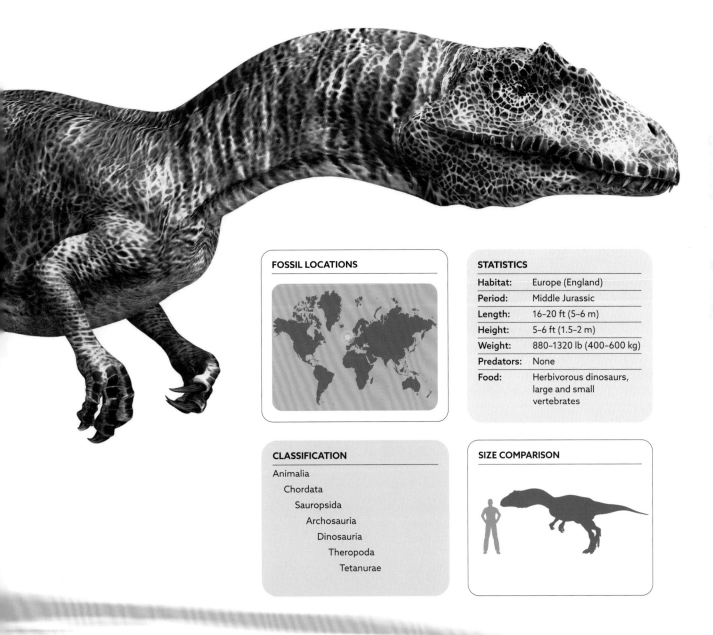

FOSSIL LOCATIONS

STATISTICS

Habitat:	Europe (England)
Period:	Middle Jurassic
Length:	16–20 ft (5–6 m)
Height:	5–6 ft (1.5–2 m)
Weight:	880–1320 lb (400–600 kg)
Predators:	None
Food:	Herbivorous dinosaurs, large and small vertebrates

CLASSIFICATION

Animalia
  Chordata
    Sauropsida
      Archosauria
        Dinosauria
          Theropoda
            Tetanurae

SIZE COMPARISON

EUSTREPTOSPONDYLUS

Meaning: 'well-curved vertebra' **Pronunciation:** you-strept-o-SPOND-o-luss

Although the original fossils were very scrappy, Buckland's *Megalosaurus* quickly became a dinosaur celebrity. Long before *Tyrannosaurus* was discovered, *Megalosaurus* was the quintessential theropod dinosaur. It was often regarded as a model for carnivorous dinosaurs in general, and gained fame in several popular books and museum exhibits in Victorian England. Most famously, a prominent statue of *Megalosaurus* was showcased at the Crystal Palace in London.

But all of this fame had a downside. Because *Megalosaurus* was so popular, scientists would often assign any new theropod fossil to this genus. As a result, over 20 different species of *Megalosaurus* were named from across the world, dating from the Late Triassic to the end of the Cretaceous. Clearly this was outrageous. No genus could be so widespread and long-lived.

More recent scientists have begun to clean up this mess, and have realized that many of these so-called *Megalosaurus* fossils actually belong to entirely new and exciting groups of

theropods. One of these fossils, a nearly complete skeleton from near Oxford, is now known as *Eustreptospondylus*.

This theropod is undoubtedly a tetanuran, and shares many features with the unusual sail-backed spinosaurids. However, *Eustreptospondylus* hails from the Mid-Jurassic, some 40 million years before the first spinosaurids turn up in the fossil record. In addition, it lacks many specializations of the spinosaurids, such as the sail along the back and the highly elongated snout with conical teeth, which spinosaurids probably used to eat fish. This long-misunderstood British theropod is, therefore, an important evolutionary link between early tetanurans and one of the oddest tetanuran subgroups.

SIZE COMPARISON

FOSSIL LOCATIONS

STATISTICS

Habitat:	Europe (England)
Period:	Middle Jurassic
Length:	16–23 ft (5–7 m)
Height:	5–7 ft (1.5–2.1 m)
Weight:	880–1320 lb (400–600 kg)
Predators:	None
Food:	Herbivorous dinosaurs, large and small vertebrates

CLASSIFICATION

Animalia
  Chordata
    Sauropsida
      Archosauria
        Dinosauria
          Theropoda
            Tetanurae
              Spinosuaroidea

GASOSAURUS

Meaning: 'gas lizard' **Pronunciation:** gas-o-SORE-uss

The theropod *Gasosaurus* has a very strange name. Most dinosaurs are named after Latin or Greek words that in some way describe the species. For example, the gigantic *Tyrannosaurus* means 'tyrant lizard', and the horned-and-frilled *Triceratops* means 'three-horned face'. *Gasosaurus* derives from English, and means 'gas lizard'.

The only known fossils of this theropod were discovered during the construction of a gas factory in the western Chinese province of Sichuan. These fragmentary fossils, which include parts of the vertebral column and limbs, were described in 1985 by legendary Chinese palaeontologist Dong Zhiming. Unfortunately, no skull bones were discovered. Since features of the skull are very useful for classifying

dinosaurs, the evolutionary relationships of *Gasosaurus* remain poorly known.

It is most likely that *Gasosaurus* was a primitive member of the tetanuran group, much like *Monolophosaurus*. Both of these dinosaurs come from the Middle-Jurassic of China. Several other fragmentary early tetanurans have also been found in China. In fact, this country is one of the few places where Middle-Jurassic theropods are commonly discovered. During this time China was beginning to break away from the northern continent of Laurasia. Once this separation was complete, China became home to a unique group of dinosaurs that evolved in isolation from the rest of the world.

SIZE COMPARISON

FOSSIL LOCATIONS

STATISTICS

Habitat:	Asia (China)
Period:	Middle Jurassic
Length:	10–13 ft (3–4 m)
Height:	3–4 ft (1–1.2 m)
Weight:	220–880 lb (100–400 kg)
Predators:	None
Food:	Sauropod dinosaurs, large and small vertebrates

CLASSIFICATION

Animalia
  Chordata
    Sauropsida
      Archosauria
        Dinosauria
          Theropoda
            Tetanurae

The Sauropod Dinosaurs

The thundering, long-necked sauropods are among the most familiar of dinosaurs. More than any other group they represent the qualities of colossal size and brute strength that have long captivated the imagination of dinosaur enthusiasts. No other land-living animal has ever approached the size of sauropod giants such as *Argentinosaurus* and *Seismosaurus*, which may have reached lengths of 115 ft (35 m) and weights of over 70 tons. And no other herbivores have so dominated terrestrial ecosystems. The barrel-chested sauropods ate vegetation by the ton, decimating the landscape as they rumbled by. These dinosaurs were a force to be reckoned with – a truly unique group that is simply incomparable to anything in today's world.

Sauropods had their heyday in the Late Jurassic, when familiar species such as *Apatosaurus*, *Brachiosaurus*, *Camarasaurus* and *Diplodocus* were thundering across the floodplains of western North America. Although sauropods started to decline in the Cretaceous, a specialized group called the titanosaurs remained common in the southern hemisphere. The titanosaurs were the last major group of sauropods to evolve. They held on until the end Cretaceous extinction 65 million years ago.

But how did these dinosaur giants evolve? This question has long puzzled scientists, but new research is revealing exciting new answers.

Some of the oldest sauropods ever discovered come from the beginning of the Jurassic, directly after the Triassic–Jurassic extinction boundary. These early sauropods, animals such as *Vulcanodon* from South Africa and *Kotasaurus* from India, look very much like later species that dominated the Late Jurassic and Cretaceous world. They had a long neck, small skull and enormous gut and walked on four legs. But these species do not possess a clear set of primitive features linking them to an ancestral group. So, although scientists had long suspected that the prosauropods were ancestral to the sauropods, there were no transitional fossils between the two groups.

However, several recent discoveries have filled this gap, and there is now clear evidence that the prosauropods gave rise to the sauropods. In fact, several very early sauropod species have recently been discovered in the Late Triassic and Early Jurassic, including *Antetonitrus* from South Africa, *Chinshakiangosaurus* from China and *Lessemsaurus* from Argentina. These animals do not look much like the giant sauropods; their general body form is closer to that of prosauropods. However, they share numerous features with sauropods, proving that they are early members of the group. Because of them, scientists now have a better understanding of sauropod evolution.

The prosauropods were herbivorous but probably also ate insects and some meat. The skulls of these animals were long, with a narrow lower jaw and numerous teeth – features well suited for their omnivorous diet. A few prosauropods may have walked on all fours, but most were two-legged. Their forelimbs were shorter than the hindlimbs and the thumb claw was robust and strongly twisted, allowing the prosauropods to use their hands both for locomotion and grasping plants.

The sauropods had a very different diet and lifestyle. They were enormous animals that ate huge quantities of vegetation and walked on all fours to support their large size. The skull became shortened, some teeth were lost and the lower jaw became wider, all of which helped the sauropods efficiently process their food. The forelimbs grew longer and stronger, and the hand became a wide, circular structure used only to support the animal. These changes did not happen all at once, but evolved gradually in small steps as sauropods diversified. Remarkably, the once poorly understood early evolution of sauropods is now one of the best examples of an evolutionary transition in the fossil record.

TITANOSAURIA

Diplodocus

Apatosaurus

Brachiosaurus

Saltasaurus

Amargasaurus

Camarasaurus

DIPLODOCOIDEA

MACRONARIA

NEOSAUROPODA

Shunosaurus

Barapasaurus

Vulcanodon

SAUROPODA

VULCANODON

Meaning: 'volcano tooth' **Pronunciation:** vul-CAN-o-don

Many new primitive sauropod species have been discovered recently. These have given scientists astonishing insight into the evolution of this unique group. For a long while, however, only one primitive sauropod was known: *Vulcanodon*. As a result, this animal has become a very important species for understanding the transition between small, two-legged, omnivorous prosauropods and the massive, four-footed, plant-guzzling sauropods.

Vulcanodon was small by sauropod standards, measuring only 20 ft (6 m) in length and weighing about 7 tons. This primitive sauropod looks tiny when compared to its later relatives, such as the 70-ton *Argentinosaurus*, but was about the same size as most prosauropods. Thus, *Vulcanodon* is prime evidence that sauropods did not begin as enormous giants, but evolved an extremely large body size later in their history.

Only one definite fossil of *Vulcanodon* is known, a partial skeleton from Zimbabwe that was discovered in the early 1970s. This fossil comes from the earliest part of the Early Jurassic, directly after the extinction event at the end of the Triassic. In fact, *Vulcanodon* may have lived only a few thousand years after the extinction. The presence of a true sauropod in such old rocks was unexpected, so much so that scientists originally dismissed *Vulcanodon* as a strange-looking prosauropod. However, the number of features it shared with true sauropods is overwhelming, such as a four-legged posture and robust, columnar limbs. Today, scientists recognize this ancient beast as one of the most primitive sauropods known.

FOSSIL LOCATIONS

STATISTICS

Habitat:	Africa (Zimbabwe)
Period:	Early Jurassic
Length:	18–23 ft (6–7 m)
Height:	20 ft (6m)
Weight:	5–7 tons
Predators:	Theropod dinosaurs
Food:	Plants (conifers)

CLASSIFICATION

Animalia
  Chordata
    Sauropsida
      Archosauria
        Dinosauria
          Sauropodomorpha
            Sauropoda

SIZE COMPARISON

BARAPASAURUS

Meaning: 'big-legged lizard' **Pronunciation:** bah-RAP-a-sore-uss

FOSSIL LOCATIONS

STATISTICS

Habitat:	India
Period:	Early Jurassic
Length:	50–60 ft (15–18 m)
Height:	17–20 ft (5–6 m)
Weight:	50–55 tons
Predators:	Theropod dinosaurs
Food:	Plants (conifers)

CLASSIFICATION

Animalia
  Chordata
    Sauropsida
      Archosauria
        Dinosauria
          Sauropodomorpha
           Sauropoda

SIZE COMPARISON

Barapasaurus translates as 'big-legged lizard', a fitting name for this important sauropod. At a length of 50–60 ft (15–18 m), *Barapasaurus* was one of the largest land animals alive during the Early Jurassic. Although later sauropods would grow to be much larger, *Barapasaurus* is incredibly massive for a primitive member of the sauropod lineage.

Like *Vulcanodon*, *Barapasaurus* is one of the oldest and most primitive sauropods ever discovered. It is slightly more advanced than *Vulcanodon*, and possesses a number of sauropod hallmarks such as columnar limbs and broad, circular feet used for

body support. Importantly, *Barapasaurus* is the first member of the sauropod lineage to exhibit large body size.

Therefore, while most early sauropods, as well as their prosauropod ancestors, were mid-sized animals, some very primitive species were experimenting with gigantism.

Barapasaurus is also a critical species because it is the most complete primitive sauropod known to science. *Vulcanodon* and other ancient sauropods are mostly known from very scrappy fossils, but *Barapasaurus* is represented by numerous vertebrae and parts of limbs from six different individuals. Unfortunately, only isolated teeth are known from the skull, which prevents a better understanding of the diet and lifestyle of *Barapasaurus*.

Scientists believe that *Barapasaurus* is closely related to *Cetiosaurus* from England and *Patagosaurus* from South America. Although widely separated today, these lands were joined together in the supercontinent Pangaea during the Late Triassic–Early Jurassic. Evidently, this assemblage of primitive species spread worldwide, and was the first diverse and widespread group of sauropods to evolve.

SHUNOSAURUS

Meaning: 'Shu lizard' **Pronunciation:** shu-no-SORE-uss

Over three million people live in the sweltering city of Zigong, in southwestern China's Sichuan Province. For over 2000 years this city has been the centre of China's salt trade, and was once a very wealthy region. Go back about 170 million years, however, and Zigong was home to a flourishing array of dinosaurs.

Fossils discovered in Zigong constitute some of the most complete Middle Jurassic dinosaurs found anywhere in the world. These include a diverse assemblage of species, such as the large tetanuran theropod *Gasosaurus*, the primitive ornithischian *Xiaosaurus* and several long-necked sauropods. The best known of these sauropods is an extraordinary animal called *Shunosaurus*, which is one of only a few sauropods anywhere known from numerous skeletons and well-preserved skulls.

Shunosaurus was small for a sauropod, similar in size to *Vulcanodon* and other primitive members of the group. It is

otherwise very similar in overall body form to *Barapasaurus*, and the two may be closely related archaic sauropods. What sets *Shunosaurus* apart from other sauropods, however, is a remarkable adaptation of the tail. While most sauropods have long tails that gradually taper to a point, the tail of *Shunosaurus* ends with a globular club formed from several fused vertebrae. It is very likely that this structure helped protect *Shunosaurus* from *Gasosaurus* and other predators.

Shunosaurus also has another strange feature: a short neck. As sauropods evolved from prosauropods their neck vertebrae gradually increased in number, which probably helped them to adapt to a lifestyle of feeding on taller plants. *Shunosaurus*, however, deviates from this trend, and so may have fed on shorter shrubs and bushes. This may have been an important evolutionary adaptation that helped *Shunosaurus* coexist with several long-necked sauropods.

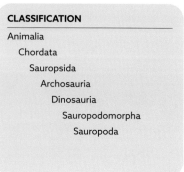

SIZE COMPARISON

FOSSIL LOCATIONS

STATISTICS

Habitat:	Asia (China)
Period:	Middle Jurassic
Length:	30–35 ft (9–11 m)
Height:	13–17 ft (4–5 m)
Weight:	10 tons
Predators:	Theropod dinosaurs
Food:	Plants (conifers)

CLASSIFICATION

Animalia
  Chordata
    Sauropsida
      Archosauria
        Dinosauria
          Sauropodomorpha
            Sauropoda

Early Ornithischian Dinosaurs

Dinosaurs are broadly divided into three major groups: theropods, sauropodomorphs and ornithischians. Each of these groups originated in the Late Triassic, but while coelophysoid theropods and prosauropod sauropodomorphs were dominating Late Triassic ecosystems, the ornithischians remained rare, small in size and restricted to the southern hemisphere.

Much like the Mesozoic mammals that lived in the shadow of the dinosaurs, the ornithischians patiently waited for their chance to evolve and diversify. This opportunity would finally come in the Early–Middle Jurassic, beginning a 100-million-year saga of evolution that ended with the Cretaceous extinction 65 million years ago. Along the way, ornithischians diversified into a range of bizarre forms, including such familiar groups as ankylosaurs, stegosaurs, pachycephalosaurs, ceratopsians and hadrosaurs.

Two ornithischians, the ornithopod *Iguanodon* and the ankylosaur *Hylaeosaurus*, were among the three species that Richard Owen first grouped together as Dinosauria. However, it took nearly 50 more years for scientists to recognize that animals such as stegosaurs, hadrosaurs and ceratopsians were close relatives. The group Ornithischia was first outlined in a landmark 1888 publication by British palaeontologist Harry Govier Seeley, who noticed that these various herbivores all shared a 'bird-like' condition of the pelvis. Like modern birds, the pubis bone at the front of their pelvis projected backwards. In birds this anatomy is possibly related to more efficient breathing, but in ornithischians it helped to accommodate a larger gut that could hold vast quantities of vegetation.

The oldest known ornithischian is *Pisanosaurus*, a fragmentary and puzzling species from the Late Triassic of Argentina. This animal clearly is an ornithischian. In addition to the bird-like pelvis, it shares several other features with the group, including an additional bone at the front of the lower jaw (the predentary), cheeks along the side of the mouth and precise tooth-to-tooth contact. All of these are related to more efficient food processing. Most dinosaurs had unsophisticated eating habits, capable of little more than biting, crunching and

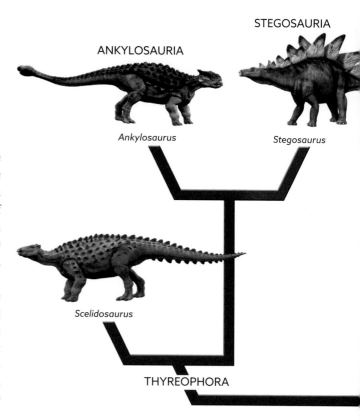

ANKYLOSAURIA

STEGOSAURIA

Ankylosaurus

Stegosaurus

Scelidosaurus

THYREOPHORA

swallowing their food, whereas many ornithischians could chew their food much like humans.

Only a handful of other ornithischians are known from the Late Triassic, including *Eocursor* from South Africa and a group called the heterodontosaurids from South America. All of these animals were small-bodied, and rarely if ever grew to lengths of over 6 ft (2 m). Every Triassic ornithischian fossil discovered comes from the southern hemisphere, and no definitive specimens are known from North America, Europe or Asia.

Ornithischians began to diversify in the Early Jurassic, and by the Mid-Jurassic had evolved into most of the major subgroups. The first thyreophorans (stegosaurs and

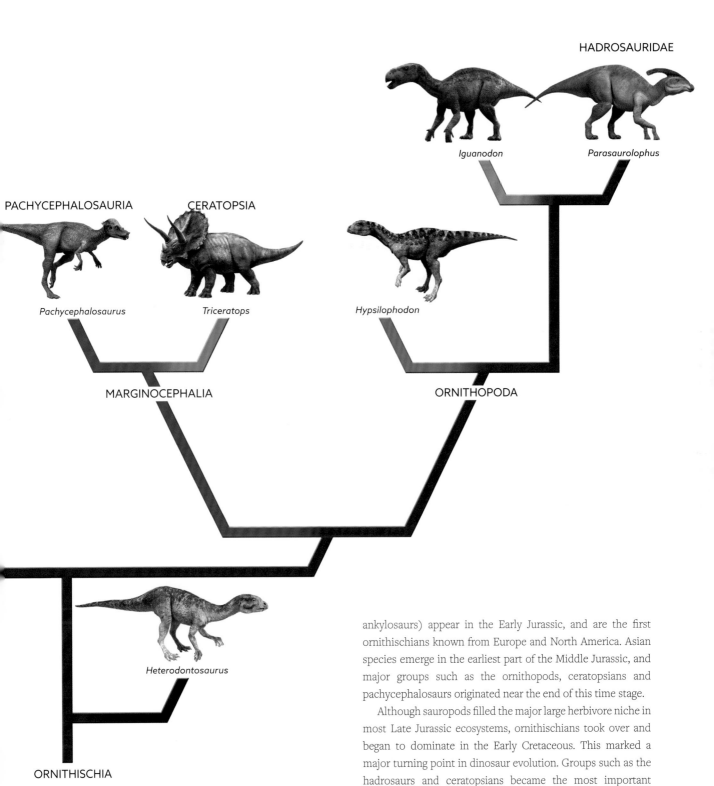

HADROSAURIDAE

Iguanodon

Parasaurolophus

PACHYCEPHALOSAURIA

CERATOPSIA

Pachycephalosaurus

Triceratops

Hypsilophodon

MARGINOCEPHALIA

ORNITHOPODA

Heterodontosaurus

ORNITHISCHIA

ankylosaurs) appear in the Early Jurassic, and are the first ornithischians known from Europe and North America. Asian species emerge in the earliest part of the Middle Jurassic, and major groups such as the ornithopods, ceratopsians and pachycephalosaurs originated near the end of this time stage.

Although sauropods filled the major large herbivore niche in most Late Jurassic ecosystems, ornithischians took over and began to dominate in the Early Cretaceous. This marked a major turning point in dinosaur evolution. Groups such as the hadrosaurs and ceratopsians became the most important herbivores in northern hemisphere ecosystems before their extinction at the end of the Cretaceous.

HETERODONTOSAURUS

Meaning: 'different-toothed lizard' **Pronunciation:** hett-er-o-don-to-SAUR-uss

Although ornithischians were very rare during the Late Triassic and Early Jurassic, one small group lived across much of the world. These were the heterodontosaurids, the first major subgroup of ornithischians to evolve. Heterodontosaurids are known from as far back as the Late Triassic of South America, but the best known species is a diminutive South African animal that gives the group its name: *Heterodontosaurus*.

Unlike many later ornithischian giants, *Heterodontosaurus* was a small animal, measuring no more than 4 ft (1.25 m) in length and weighing about as much as a small child. It would have walked on two legs and was probably a fast runner. Strangely, many bones of the ankle and foot are fused together, which may have provided strength and helped the animal to run faster. The hands of *Heterodontosaurus* are remarkably elongated and capped with powerful claws, suggesting that it may have eaten some meat. However, the teeth indicate that *Heterodontosaurus* was mostly a plant eater.

These teeth are the most distinctive feature of *Hetero-*

dontosaurus, and are the basis for its name. Most dinosaurs have a relatively simple dentition, and all teeth look generally the same. However, *Heterodontosaurus* uniquely possesses three distinct kinds of teeth, as well as a beak that was used to crop vegetation. Directly behind the beak is a set of small, simple, conical teeth. A pair of tusks follows, one on each side of the upper jaw and one on the lower. Finally, behind the tusks are several robust, square-shaped teeth similar to human molars, which would have been used to chew vegetation. The function of the tusks is unknown, but they may have helped to attract mates or been used to root out small bugs to supplement its mostly vegetarian diet.

Other heterodontosaurids include *Abrictosaurus* and *Lycorhinus* from South Africa, as well as unnamed species from South America, North America and Europe. These range from the Late Triassic to the Early Cretaceous, and indicate that heterodontosaurids were a very diverse, widespread and important group of dinosaurs.

SIZE COMPARISON

FOSSIL LOCATIONS

STATISTICS

Habitat:	Africa (South Africa)
Period:	Early Jurassic
Length:	3–4 ft (1–1.25 m)
Height:	2–3 ft (0.5–1 m)
Weight:	44–66 lb (20–30 kg)
Predators:	Theropod dinosaurs
Food:	Plants, small vertebrates, insects

CLASSIFICATION

Animalia
  Chordata
    Sauropsida
      Archosauria
        Dinosauria
          Ornithischia
            Heterodontosauridae

SCELIDOSAURUS

Meaning: 'limb lizard' **Pronunciation:** skeh-lide-o-SORE-uss

The stegosaurs and ankylosaurs are both distinctive groups of dinosaurs. Ankylosaurs are notable for their tank-like appearance, while the plates and tail spikes of stegosaurs are unique to this group. Scientists place these two ornithischian subgroups in the larger group Thyreophora, the 'shielded dinosaurs', because they share several specialized characteristics, most importantly a covering of body armour.

Another animal classified in this group is *Scelidosaurus*, an Early Jurassic herbivore from England. *Scelidosaurus* was first discovered in Dorset in the early 1850s and later named by Richard Owen in 1860. It was the first dinosaur known from a nearly complete and well-preserved skeleton. Today, several skeletons of this small, armoured species are known, some of which rank among the most beautiful and stunning dinosaur fossils ever discovered.

These fossils have helped scientists to learn a great deal about the anatomy and lifestyle of *Scelidosaurus*. *Scelidosaurus* measured approximately 13 ft (4 m) in length, and had small,

leaf-shaped teeth, indicating that it was a herbivore. However, unlike many other ornithischian herbivores *Scelidosaurus* probably did not chew its food. The simple jaws could only move up and down, not sideways as is required for chewing. The most important feature linking *Scelidosaurus* to other thyreophorans is the extensive body armour covering much of the trunk. Parallel rows of scutes covered the back, one row shielded each flank and four rows enclosed the tail. Most of these plates were oval-shaped, but there was also a unique three-pointed plate behind the skull on each side of the body.

Despite the discovery of numerous fossils, scientists are still at odds over the proper classification of *Scelidosaurus*. It is clearly a thyreophoran, but some scientists have regarded it as a stegosaur and others as an ankylosaur. However, *Scelidosaurus* does not possess the specialized characteristics of either group, and is most probably a primitive thyreophoran that evolved prior to stegosaurs and ankylosaurs.

SIZE COMPARISON

FOSSIL LOCATIONS

STATISTICS

Habitat:	Europe (England)
Period:	Early Jurassic
Length:	10–15 ft (3.5–4.5 m)
Height:	2–3 ft (0.5–1 m)
Weight:	550–660 lb (250–300 kg)
Predators:	Theropod dinosaurs
Food:	Plants (low shrubs)

CLASSIFICATION

Animalia
  Chordata
    Sauropsida
      Archosauria
        Dinosauria
          Ornithischia
            Thyreophora

			Hettangian 199.6 – 196.5 MYA	Aalenian 175.6 – 171.6 MYA	
		Carnian 228.7 – 216.5 MYA	Sinemurian 196.5 – 189.6 MYA	Bajocian 171.6 – 167.7 MYA	Oxfordian 161.2 – 155.6 MYA
Induan 251.0 – 249.5 MYA	Anisian 245.9 – 237.0 MYA	Norian 216.5 – 203.6 MYA	Pliensbachian 189.6 – 183.0 MYA	Bathonian 167.7 – 164.7 MYA	Kimmeridgian 155.6 – 150.8 MYA
Olenekian 249.5 – 245.9 MYA	Ladinian 237.0 – 228.7 MYA	Rhaetian 203.6 – 199.6 MYA	Toarcian 183.0 – 175.6 MYA	Callovian 164.7 – 161.2 MYA	Tithonian 150.8 – 145.5 MYA
EARLY TRIASSIC 251.0 – 245.9 MYA	MIDDLE TRIASSIC 245.9 – 228.7 MYA	LATE TRIASSIC 228.7 – 199.6 MYA	EARLY JURASSIC 199.6 – 175.6 MYA	MIDDLE JURASSIC 175.6 – 161.2 MYA	LATE JURASSIC 161.2 – 145.5 MYA

TRIASSIC 251.0 – 199.6 MYA   **JURASSIC 199.6 – 145.5 MYA**

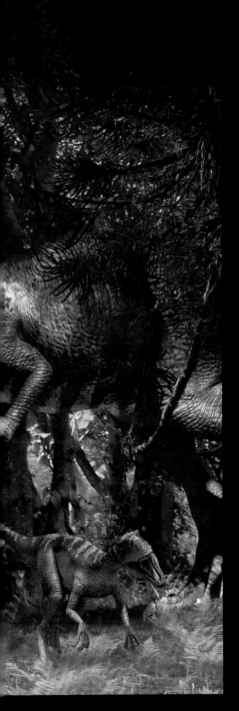

Dinosaurs of the Late Jurassic

Berriasian 145.5 – 140.2 MYA

Valanginian 140.2 – 133.9 MYA

Hauterivian 133.9 – 130.0 MYA

Barremian 130.0 – 125.0 MYA

Aptian 125.0 – 112.0 MYA

Albian 112.0 – 99.6 MYA

Cenomanian 99.6 – 93.6 MYA

Turonian 93.6 – 88.6 MYA

Coniacian 88.6 – 85.8 MYA

Santonian 85.8 – 83.5 MYA

Campanian 83.5 – 70.6 MYA

Maastrichtian 70.6 – 65.5 MYA

EARLY-MIDDLE CRETACEOUS
145.5 – 99.6 MYA

LATE CRETACEOUS
99.6 – 65.5 MYA

CRETACEOUS 145.5 – 65.5 MYA

The Morrison Formation

In the vast empty spaces of the American West are some of the world's most important dinosaur dig sites. Although dry, dusty and sparsely populated today, this area was green and lush during the Late Jurassic, about 150 million years ago. At least 30 different dinosaurs called this area home, including mega predators such as *Allosaurus*, thundering sauropods such as *Apatosaurus* and ornithischians like *Stegosaurus*. Today, their fossils are found throughout a thick unit of rock called the Morrison Formation.

The first Morrison fossils were discovered in 1877, and within a year had become the prize jewel of the 'Bone Wars', a back-and-forth struggle between the great palaeontologists E.D. Cope and O.C. Marsh. Marsh and Cope each desired to be the top fossil researcher in the United States, and over time their rivalry developed into all-out hatred. Theft, sabotage and violence were common ingredients of this feud. Each scientist employed an army of professional collectors with only one job: to find the most spectacular and valuable fossils. These mercenaries were let loose on the Morrison Formation of Colorado and Wyoming, and uncovered a motherload of dinosaur fossils.

Today, many fossils discovered by these minions rank among the best known and most familiar dinosaur species. *Allosaurus*, *Stegosaurus*, *Camarasaurus*, *Apatosaurus* and *Diplodocus* were all discovered as a result of the Cope–Marsh feud. And some 130 years later, scientists are still discovering new dinosaurs in the Morrison Formation. These prolific discoveries have provided a unique window on the Late Jurassic world, a time of global dinosaur dominance but also a critical period in dinosaur evolution.

By the Late Jurassic most of the major groups of dinosaurs had evolved. Primitive groups such as the coelophysoid theropods and prosauropods were long extinct. The more advanced tetanuran theropods and large-bodied sauropods had spread worldwide and were the keystone species in most ecosystems. Ornithischians, although rare for much of the Late Triassic and Early Jurassic, were beginning to diversify and become more important members of dinosaur ecosystems. The supercontinent Pangaea was a distant memory as its fragments continued to drift apart, beginning to resemble the geography of today's world.

The Late Jurassic was the Age of the Sauropods. At no other point in their history were the long-necked, plant-devouring animals so abundant and diverse. As many as 25 different sauropod species have been found in the Morrison Formation alone. Numerous others are known from other classic Late Jurassic fossil sites in Africa, China and Portugal. Most of these

The large theropod Allosaurus, one of the best-known Late Jurassic dinosaurs. Several thousand bones of Allosaurus have been found in the Morrison Formation in the western United States.

species probably fed on conifers, which were incredibly abundant in the warm, dry Late Jurassic landscape. Shorter-necked species such as Diplodocus may have adapted to feed on lower shrubs, bushes and ferns. Differences in diet would have prevented competition and enabled several different sauropods to live together.

However, the reign of the sauropods would soon come to an end. Living alongside the sauropods of the Morrison were mid-sized ornithischian herbivores such as *Camptosaurus* and *Dryosaurus*. These early ornithopods were few in number compared with sauropods, but their later cousins would rise to become the main herbivores in many Cretaceous ecosystems, especially in the northern hemisphere. The ornithopods of the Morrison were the first signs of a critical transition that altered the course of dinosaur evolution for the next 85 million years.

The Morrison Formation of the western United States is one of the most important dinosaur fossil sites in the world. More than 30 species of dinosaur have been found in this rock formation, including familiar animals such as *Allosaurus*, *Stegosaurus*, *Diplodocus* and *Apatosaurus*. Today Morrison Formation rocks are exposed in the dry and dusty badlands of Wyoming, Colorado and other US states. Here several palaeontology students are shown excavating the skeleton of the sauropod *Diplodocus*.

CERATOSAURUS

Meaning: 'horned lizard' **Pronunciation:** sir-AT-o-sore-uss

The advanced tetanuran theropods were kings of the Late Jurassic. Tetanurans such as the large-bodied *Allosaurus* were the keystone predators in most Late Jurassic ecosystems, and smaller, sleeker coelurosaurs were just beginning to diversify. However, some very primitive theropods coexisted with the advanced tetanurans. These were the ceratosaurs, a puzzling group that branched off from the theropod family tree after the very primitive coelophysoids but before the tetanurans.

Ceratosaurs take their name from the genus *Ceratosaurus*, one of the more common theropods in the Morrison Formation of the western United States. Recently fossils of this theropod have also been found in Europe, and some questionable specimens are known from Africa. *Ceratosaurus* was a large theropod, measuring nearly 30 ft (9 m) in length and possibly weighing up to a ton. However, it was smaller

than its contemporaneous Morrison theropods *Allosaurus* and *Torvosaurus*, and may have fed on smaller ornithopods instead of the larger sauropods.

Ceratosaurus was discovered during the infamous 'Bone Wars' and named by O.C. Marsh in 1884. It was named 'horned lizard' for the set of three horns on the skull. A single large, thin horn is present on the snout above the nostril, and thicker circular horns rise over each eye. These may have been useful in attacking predators or fighting over carcasses, but were more likely to be display features used to attract mates. Other unusual features of the skeleton include a row of bony plates along the back, which are more common in ornithischians, and a heavily fused pelvis.

Ceratosaurus was long thought to be a late-surviving coelophysoid, perhaps the last member of this Late Triassic–Early Jurassic lineage. However, recent studies show that *Ceratosaurus* is more derived, or evolutionarily advanced, than the coelophysoids, and thus is a member of its own unique group of theropods. Other ceratosaurs include the slender genera *Elaphrosaurus* and *Spinostropheus* from Africa, as well as a subgroup called the abelisaurids that became very common in the Middle–Late Cretaceous in the southern hemisphere.

SIZE COMPARISON

FOSSIL LOCATIONS

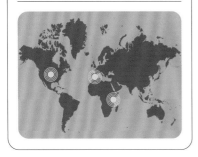

STATISTICS

Habitat:	North America (USA), possibly Europe (Portugal and Africa (Tanzania)
Period:	Late Jurassic
Length:	20–27 ft (6–8 m)
Height:	7–8 ft (2–2.5 m)
Weight:	1100–2200 lb (500–1000 kg)
Predators:	None
Food:	Sauropod and ornithischian dinosaurs

CLASSIFICATION

Animalia
  Chordata
    Sauropsida
      Archosauria
        Dinosauria
          Theropoda
            Ceratosauria

ELAPHROSAURUS

Meaning: 'lightweight lizard' **Pronunciation:** e-LAF-ro-sore-uss

The Tendaguru dinosaur expeditions read like a Hollywood movie script. The sheer size, cost and danger of these early 20th-century expeditions are unmatched in the history of palaeontology. Fieldwork in this small corner of the East African country of Tanzania began with the discovery of bone fragments in 1906. Within a year scientists from Berlin had begun a colossal excavation, which lasted six years and produced some 250 tons of dinosaur fossils.

At its peak the Tendaguru expedition employed 500 men, who excavated, packed and transported every fossil by hand. They were mostly local Africans, drafted at little pay by the German colonial government. In addition to long, hot days working in the blazing sun, workers had to endure drought, monsoons, malaria and even attacks by lions. And, at the end of it all, when it was time to finish up and send the fossils to

Germany, the men formed a human transport line to move hundreds of crates by foot over a hundred miles to the coast. The excruciating journey took nearly a week.

Largely due to their efforts, the Tendaguru fossils are today regarded as the best collection of Late Jurassic dinosaurs outside of the Morrison Formation. Numerous sauropods and theropods have been described from these specimens, including a sleek predator that has long given scientists headaches as they argued about its evolutionary relationships. This is *Elaphrosaurus*, a slender genus that was well adapted for fast running. *Elaphrosaurus* is known from a single skeleton, which lacks the skull but preserves most of the rest of the skeleton. The long hindlimbs and wide cavity for muscles on the pelvis are the hallmarks of a speedy carnivore. Scientists now agree that *Elaphrosaurus* was a ceratosaur, closely related to *Ceratosaurus*.

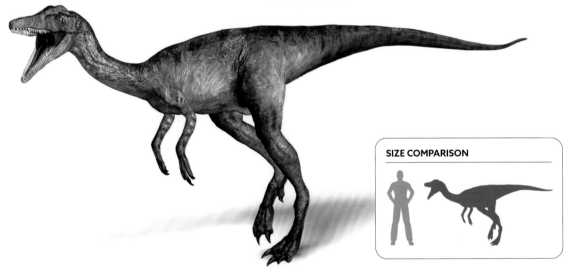

SIZE COMPARISON

FOSSIL LOCATIONS

STATISTICS

Habitat:	Africa (Tanzania)
Period:	Late Jurassic
Length:	15–21 ft (4.5–6.5 m)
Height:	4–5 ft (1.25–1.5 m)
Weight:	440–550 lb (200–250 kg)
Predators:	None
Food:	Sauropod and ornithischian dinosaurs

CLASSIFICATION

Animalia
  Chordata
    Sauropsida
      Archosauria
        Dinosauria
          Theropoda
            Ceratosauria

ALLOSAURUS

Meaning: 'different lizard' **Pronunciation:** al-o-SAUR-uss

Scientists probably know more about *Allosaurus* than any other dinosaur. Hundreds of specimens of this Late Jurassic theropod have been discovered, ranging from juveniles to enormous adults that lived deep into old age, and including several complete skeletons. The bones, muscles and even the brain of *Allosaurus* have been described in painstaking detail by experts. More recently, studies have focused on the growth, feeding strategies and social habits of this typical theropod.

It is surprising, then, that for a long while *Allosaurus* was known only from fragmentary fossil scraps. The first of these was discovered in the Morrison Formation of Colorado in 1869. It would be more than 30 years before the first nearly complete skeleton came to light, but since then new specimens have been discovered at an amazing rate. One fossil site, the Cleveland–Lloyd Quarry of Utah, has produced over 40 *Allosaurus* individuals since work began there in 1960.

Allosaurus was a big theropod, reaching an average length of about 30 ft (9 m). It was smaller than theropod giants such as

Tyrannosaurus, but substantially larger than other Morrison theropods like *Ceratosaurus* and *Torvosaurus*. *Allosaurus* was clearly the keystone predator in the Morrison ecosystem, and probably fed on a range of prey, including an array of large sauropods. Its anatomy was well adapted to a carnivorous diet, particularly the robust, sharp teeth and remarkably strong skull. Computer simulations suggest that the skull was used like a hatchet as the open-mouthed *Allosaurus* violently slashed the flesh of its prey. A set of hornlets over the eyes may have

Habitat:	North America (USA) and Europe (Portugal)
Period:	Late Jurassic
Length:	25–40 ft (7.5–12 m)
Height:	6–7 ft (2 m)
Weight:	2200–3970 lb (1000–1800 kg)
Predators:	None
Food:	Sauropod and ornithischian dinosaurs

CLASSIFICATION

Animalia
  Chordata
    Sauropsida
      Archosauria
        Dinosauria
          Tetanurae
            Allosauroidea

SIZE COMPARISON

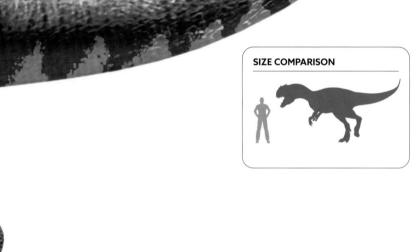

been used to assault prey, but could have been nothing more than display structures.

Allosaurus is one of a handful of primitive tetanuran theropods classified together in the group Allosauroidea. Other members of this group include the Chinese carnivores *Sinraptor* and *Yangchuanosaurus*, as well as the carcharodontosaurids, a subgroup of gigantic predators that were very common in South America and Africa in the middle–Late Cretaceous.

YANGCHUANOSAURUS

Meaning: named after Yangshuan County **Pronunciation:** yang-CHOO-an-o-sore-uss

While *Allosaurus* was prowling the Morrison landscape of North America, a close cousin reigned supreme in China. This was *Yangchuanosaurus*, an allosauroid theropod that was slightly smaller than its more famous relative. However, *Yangchuanosaurus* was anything but meek. At a length of 30 ft (9 m) and weighing about a ton, it was the largest carnivore in an ecosystem bursting with sauropod and stegosaur prey.

Yangchuanosaurus is known from two fossils, each of which has been described as a separate species. These both come from the Shaximiao Formation of Sichuan Province, an area of China that has long been famous for its dinosaur discoveries. Workmen constructing a dam discovered the first skeleton in 1976. It was described three years later and named in honour of the county where it was found. Shortly afterwards another specimen was unearthed, this one with a skull that was over 3 ft (1 m) long.

One of the most unusual features of this dinosaur is its incredibly light skull. Although the skull is long, many of the bones contain hollow chambers, which were probably filled with air. This is especially clear at the front of the snout, where the bone surface is pocketed with numerous openings. As these openings were linked to the sinuses they may have helped the animal smell better or breathe more efficiently. Alternatively, they may have simply lightened the enormous skull.

Another theropod from China, *Sinraptor*, is very similar to *Yangchuanosaurus*. Both of these carnivores are allosauroids and they share the unique, lightened skull. However, *Sinraptor* is several million years older than *Yangchuanosaurus*, and lived during the later part of the Middle-Jurassic. Scientists group the two theropods together in the family Sinraptoridae. Evidently, sinraptorids were the top predators in Asian ecosystems for millions of years.

SIZE COMPARISON

FOSSIL LOCATIONS

STATISTICS

Habitat:	Asia (China)
Period:	Late Jurassic
Length:	25–32 ft (7.5–9.75 m)
Height:	6–7 ft (2 m)
Weight:	1985–2200 lb
	(900–1000 kg)
Predators:	None
Food:	Sauropod and ornithischian dinosaurs

CLASSIFICATION

Animalia
  Chordata
    Sauropsida
      Archosauria
        Dinosauria
          Tetanurae
            Allosauroidea
              Sinraptoridae

The Coelurosaurian Theropods

The history of dinosaurs is a story of evolution and change. Groups originated, became diverse, dominated the landscape and then drifted into extinction as another group rose to take its place. The theropod dinosaurs are typical of this pattern. The first theropods were primitive coelophysoids, which were abundant in the Late Triassic–Early Jurassic. After they faded into extinction the more advanced ceratosaurs and tetanurans came to dominate ecosystems in the Middle–Late Jurassic. But more change was to come, and the new groups would form the cusp of an evolutionary breakthrough.

The Late Jurassic was the breeding ground for the next big step in theropod evolution: the diversification of the bird-like coelurosaurs. The coelurosaurs are a subgroup of tetanurans, more advanced than the allosauroids and other primitive tetanurans that were common in the Middle–Late Jurassic. Classified among the Coelurosauria is a diverse assemblage of theropods. Most were small-bodied, agile carnivores, such as the dromaeosaurids and troodontids. Others resembled large, flightless birds, like the ornithomimosaurs and oviraptorosaurs. And some were truly bizarre, such as the sloth-like therizinosaurids and bug-grubbing alvarezsaurids. The monstrous tyrannosaurids also belong to this group.

Scientists are keenly interested in studying coelurosaurs because modern birds evolved from within this group. Numerous features clearly show that birds evolved from a small, possibly tree-dwelling coelurosaur. Dromaeosaurids and troodontids are universally recognized as the closest relatives to birds, while other coelurosaur groups are more distant cousins. Recently, scientists have identified a number of stunning bird-like characteristics in other coelurosaurs. All coelurosaurs were probably feathered, some could fly, and new evidence shows that certain coelurosaurs grew, reproduced and even slept like birds.

The coelurosaurs were the top predators in many Cretaceous ecosystems. They evolved into an extraordinary range of body forms and their avian descendants still dominate the skies. But for the first 20 or 30 million years of their evolution, coelurosaurs were small, rare and played a minor role in most communities. The oldest well-known coelurosaur is *Proceratosaurus*, a minuscule predator from the Mid-Jurassic of England whose horned skull looks more ferocious than it really was. Other scrappy coelurosaur fossils are known from the Middle-Jurassic, and show that these animals were pint-sized afterthoughts in a world ruled by gigantic allosauroids and ceratosaurs.

But the coelurosaurs continued to evolve, and gradually became larger, more diverse and more important members of dinosaur ecosystems. The most critical period in coelurosaur evolution was the Late Jurassic. During this time all of the main coelurosaur groups evolved, including birds. While most of these groups remained scarce, some coelurosaurs emerged as top predators. The compsognathids, for instance, were common in the Late Jurassic of Europe and later spread worldwide during the Early Cretaceous. Other coelurosaurs, such as *Coelurus* and *Ornitholestes*, were important components of the Morrison community, and probably occupied the mid-sized predator niche in the shadow of *Allosaurus*. The first tyrannosauroids are also known from the Late Jurassic, forerunners of one of the most successful groups of dinosaurs that ever lived.

By the close of the Jurassic the coelurosaur revolution was well under way. Birds had already taken to the air, compsognathids were dispersing across the globe and tyrannosaurids were beginning their path to dominance. Everything was set for these bird-like theropods to take over the Cretaceous world.

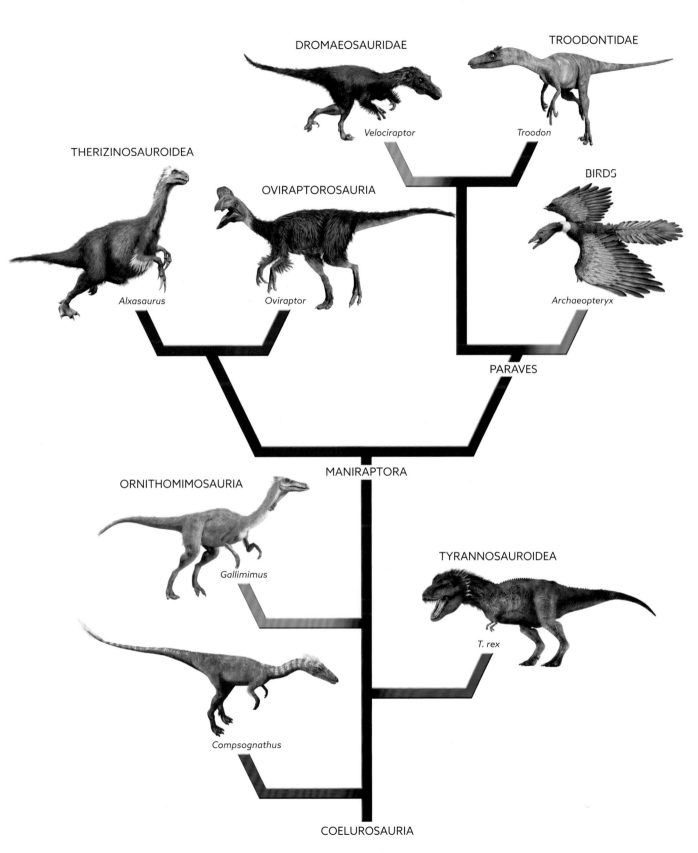

DROMAEOSAURIDAE

Velociraptor

TROODONTIDAE

Troodon

THERIZINOSAUROIDEA

OVIRAPTOROSAURIA

BIRDS

Alxasaurus

Oviraptor

Archaeopteryx

PARAVES

MANIRAPTORA

ORNITHOMIMOSAURIA

TYRANNOSAUROIDEA

Gallimimus

T. rex

Compsognathus

COELUROSAURIA

COMPSOGNATHUS

Meaning: 'elegant form' **Pronunciation:** komp-sog-NAY-thuss

It is very likely that the first coelurosaur to evolve – the common ancestor of the entire group—was sleek, small and fast. This ancestor must have lived in the Mid-Jurassic, several million years before the Late Jurassic *Compsognathus* was hopping around the islands of Europe. However, the Middle-Jurassic fossil record is notoriously poor, leaving *Compsognathus* as the best-known primitive coelurosaur.

Compsognathus was the smallest dinosaur ever found until the recent discovery of minuscule dromaeosaurs in China. It weighed about as much as a small dog, but its light, sturdy build was ideal for hunting small vertebrates. One specimen was found with a lizard skeleton preserved in the gut. *Compsognathus* is known from two specimens, a smaller skeleton from Bavaria and a larger specimen from France.

Both come from the Late Jurassic, a time when much of Europe was flooded and only small islands of land existed.

The Bavarian specimen was discovered in the famous Solnhofen Limestone deposits, the same rocks that yielded the early bird *Archaeopteryx* in the 1850s. *Compsognathus* quickly became a key piece of evidence supporting the dinosaur–bird evolutionary link, since it clearly shared numerous features with birds. In more recent years, scientists have discovered a host of close relatives around the world, some of which were covered with feathers. These theropods, classified together as Compsognathidae, include the famous feathered *Sinosauropteryx* from China and the newly described *Juravenator* from Germany.

SIZE COMPARISON

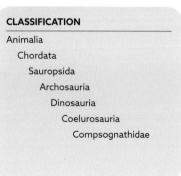

FOSSIL LOCATIONS

STATISTICS

Habitat:	Europe (France, Germany)
Period:	Late Jurassic
Length:	3–5 ft (1–1.5 m)
Height:	1–2 ft (25–60 cm)
Weight:	11–22 lb (5–10 kg)
Predators:	Large theropod dinosaurs
Food:	small mammals, insects

CLASSIFICATION

Animalia
　Chordata
　　Sauropsida
　　　Archosauria
　　　　Dinosauria
　　　　　Coelurosauria
　　　　　　Compsognathidae

ORNITHOLESTES

Meaning: 'bird robber' **Pronunciation:** or-nith-o-LESS-tees

Mega predators such as *Allosaurus*, *Ceratosaurus* and *Torvosaurus* ruled the Morrison Formation. *Allosaurus*, the largest and strongest of the three, probably hunted big game: the thundering sauropods and giant stegosaurs. *Ceratosaurus* and *Torvosaurus*, which were slightly smaller and slimmer, may have gone after more manageable prey, such as ornithopods. But these large predators were not the only theropods in the Morrison community. Although often overlooked, numerous smaller theropods lived alongside *Allosaurus* and the other giants of the Late Jurassic.

Ornitholestes is one of the best-known smaller Morrison theropods. A primitive coelurosaur that was slightly larger than *Compsognathus*, *Ornitholestes* was probably a generalist predator that fed on small vertebrates, juvenile dinosaurs and perhaps even insects.

It was slender of build but very fast, and possessed the characteristic sharp teeth and claws of predatory dinosaurs.

These were useful not only for catching prey, but also to avoid becoming the prey of *Allosaurus* and other larger theropods.

Ornitholestes is known only from one fossil, a nearly complete skeleton discovered in 1900 at Como Bluff, Wyoming. Como Bluff, a low ridge of Morrison Formation rock stretching across the desolate plains of southern Wyoming, is one of the world's most famous dinosaur sites. It was originally worked by O.C. Marsh's fossil hunters during the 'Bone Wars', and later excavated by groups from the American Museum of Natural History. As many as 20 different dinosaur species have been found there, including another primitive coelurosaur, the slender predator *Coelurus*.

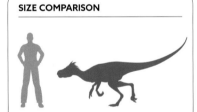

SIZE COMPARISON

FOSSIL LOCATIONS

STATISTICS

Habitat:	North America (USA)
Period:	Late Jurassic
Length:	7 ft (2 m)
Height:	2–3 ft (0.5–1 m)
Weight:	33–44 lb (15–20 kg)
Predators:	Large theropod dinosaurs
Food:	Lizards, small mammals, insects

CLASSIFICATION

Animalia
  Chordata
    Sauropsida
      Archosauria
        Dinosauria
          Theropoda
            Coelurosauria

The Origin and Evolution of Birds

One of the greatest discoveries of modern palaeontology is that birds evolved from small, carnivorous theropod dinosaurs. This idea was first introduced by legendary scientist Thomas Henry Huxley in the 1860s, a few years after the extraordinary discovery of the primitive bird *Archaeopteryx* in Germany. Huxley noted the uncanny resemblance between *Archaeopteryx* and a theropod dinosaur from the same rock unit, *Compsognathus*. The only major difference between the two skeletons was that *Archaeopteryx* was cloaked in a coat of feathers. Huxley's conclusion was simple but revolutionary: birds must have evolved from theropod dinosaurs.

Since then scientists have vigorously debated Huxley's theory. Many researchers dismissed his ideas, mostly because the fossil record of early birds was so poor that it could be interpreted in many different ways. Over the past 40 years, however, palaeontologists have amassed a stunning weight of evidence that points clearly to an unmistakable truth: Huxley was correct and birds evolved from dinosaurs. This means that the descendants of dinosaurs are alive in today's world.

The first exhibit in the modern study of bird origins came from the badlands of the western United States. In 1964 John Ostrom and his team came across a nearly complete skeleton of a small theropod in southern Montana. Later named *Deinonychus*, this dromaeosaurid was incredibly bird-like in its overall anatomy, and possessed several unique features of the wrist and arm only seen in modern birds. Discoveries over the next two decades added supporting evidence, and by the mid-1980s most scientists were convinced that birds had evolved from dinosaurs. Features long considered the hallmarks of birds, such as hollow bones, a wishbone and a wrist that could fold inwards, were appearing in theropod fossils.

Some of the most jaw-dropping evidence in support of the dinosaur–bird link has come to light over the past decade. Most spectacularly, several theropods covered in feathers have been found in China. These include not only very close bird cousins such as dromaeosaurs, but also more primitive coelurosaurs like compsognathids. None of these dinosaurs could fly, which suggests that feathers must have evolved for other purposes long before birds took to the sky. Some of these feathered dinosaurs are tiny and probably lived in trees. They provide a perfect transitional sequence between coelurosaurs, most of

which were large carnivores that ran on the ground, and true birds, which are much smaller and mostly live in trees.

The oldest known bird is still *Archaeopteryx*, which roosted among the European islands of the Late Jurassic some 150 million years ago. No other Jurassic birds are known, but by the Early Cretaceous primitive birds had spread worldwide. Thousands of bird fossils have been found in Early Cretaceous rocks in China alongside the famous feathered dinosaurs. One of these, *Confuciusornis*, is known from hundreds of complete skeletons, and is one of the most common vertebrate fossils ever discovered. Other Chinese species belong to numerous subgroups of primitive birds, showing that avians became incredibly diverse early in their history.

One of the more important subgroups is the Enatiornithes, the so-called 'opposite birds', named because they differ from modern birds in features of the foot and shoulder. The closest cousin to the enatiornithines is a group called Ornithurae, a major division of birds that includes all modern forms. These two diverse groups evolved sometime in the Late Jurassic or Early Cretaceous. The enatiornithines quickly diversified, spread worldwide and dominated the Cretaceous airways before going extinct at the Cretaceous–Tertiary boundary. The ornithurines, on the other hand, were much rarer during the Cretaceous. The first modern birds are found in the Late Cretaceous, but did not diversify explosively until after the opposite birds had gone extinct. Then, very quickly, modern birds evolved into all of the major groups within the first few million years after the dinosaur extinction. Today, there are approximately 10,000 species of birds, ranging from penny-sized hummingbirds to the enormous, flightless ostriches.

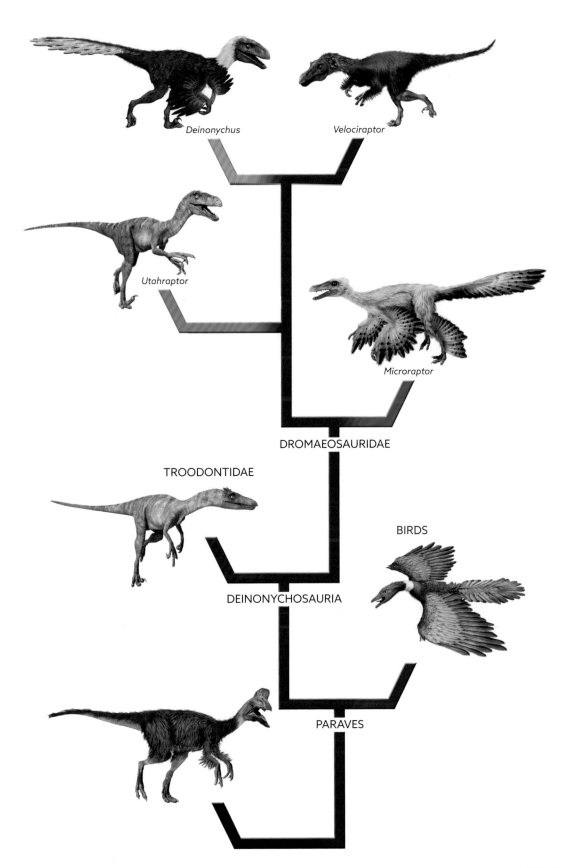

Deinonychus

Velociraptor

Utahraptor

Microraptor

DROMAEOSAURIDAE

TROODONTIDAE

BIRDS

DEINONYCHOSAURIA

PARAVES

ARCHAEOPTERYX

Meaning: 'ancient wing' **Pronunciation:** ark-e-op-ter-IX

Archaeopteryx, the oldest and most primitive bird ever discovered, is a true celebrity of the dinosaur world. No other Mesozoic fossil has been so celebrated, so debated or so carefully studied. *Archaeopteryx* has played a central role in many of the most heated debates in evolutionary biology. Today, it is recognized as a key piece of evidence supporting the dinosaur–bird link, and is treasured by scientists who study the origin and early evolution of birds.

A single feather of *Archaeopteryx* was found in 1860. The first skeleton was unearthed a year later, in the famous Solnhofen Limestone quarries of Bavaria. Frozen in fossilized time, the stretched and squashed body of this animal seemed to be a strange chimera of reptile and bird. The long, bony tail and teeth were similar to those of reptiles, but the stunningly preserved feathers and light, hollow bones were trademark features of birds.

In a strange twist of fate, *Archaeopteryx* was discovered only two years after Charles Darwin first published his theory of evolution. Confused and upset by his ideas, the public demanded clear evidence of evolution in action. The half-bird, half-reptile *Archaeopteryx* was a perfect transitional form between these two groups, an unquestionable evolutionary intermediate. The exquisite feathers and generally reptilian body of this little fossil formed the first real, visual evidence of evolution that could be shown to the public. In large part, *Archaeopteryx* helped to prove that evolution was real.

Since the landmark discovery of *Archaeopteryx* in 1861 nine other fossils of this bird have been found, all within the same quarries in Germany. The large wing and very sophisticated brain show that *Archaeopteryx* could fly, but a lack of strong muscle attachments on the breastbone and upper arm indicate that it could not fly as well as most modern birds. Also, unlike most modern birds, the feet of *Archaeopteryx* were poorly adapted for perching in trees. It may have spent most of its time on the ground, hunting small vertebrates and insects. The hands of *Archaeopteryx* were enormous and capped with sharp claws, like the hands of close coelurosaur cousins but unlike the shortened and fused hands of modern birds. The forearms of *Archaeopteryx* may have been used for both flight and hunting, whereas in modern birds they are almost exclusively used for flying.

The Berlin *Archaeopteryx* was discovered in 1876 or 1877 near Eichstätt, Germany. Seemingly half dinosaur and half bird, it has been called a fossil caught in the act of evolution. It is certainly one of the most famous fossils in the world and is on display at the Museum für Naturkunde in Berlin, Germany.

FOSSIL LOCATIONS

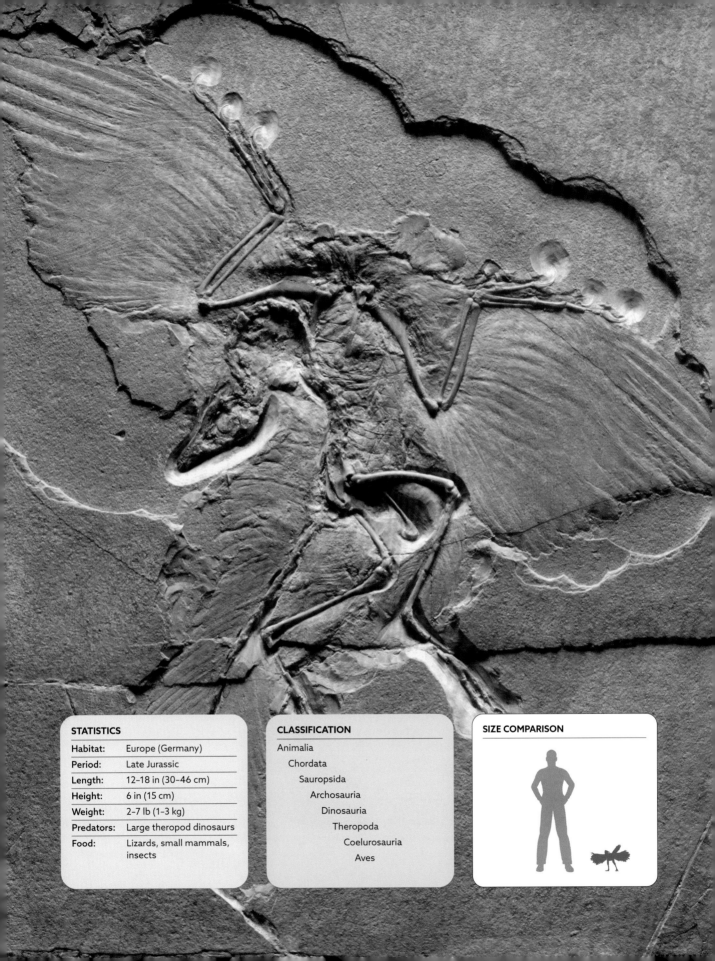

STATISTICS

Habitat:	Europe (Germany)
Period:	Late Jurassic
Length:	12–18 in (30–46 cm)
Height:	6 in (15 cm)
Weight:	2–7 lb (1–3 kg)
Predators:	Large theropod dinosaurs
Food:	Lizards, small mammals, insects

CLASSIFICATION

Animalia
  Chordata
    Sauropsida
      Archosauria
        Dinosauria
          Theropoda
            Coelurosauria
              Aves

SIZE COMPARISON

ARCHAEOPTERYX

MAMENCHISAURUS

Meaning: named after its discovery site in China **Pronunciation:** ma-mench-e-SORE-uss

The Late Jurassic sauropod *Mamenchisaurus* is a record-setter. It has the longest neck of any known dinosaur, a skinny, snake-like organ that stretched nearly 40 ft (12 m) and measured over half of the entire length of the animal! In fact, no land animal in the history of the world has had a neck longer than this monstrous Chinese herbivore.

Mamenchisaurus is one of the largest sauropods ever discovered, and was by far the biggest animal in Asia during the Late Jurassic. Some individuals may have measured up to 80 ft (25 m), only slightly smaller than the grandest sauropods known, such as *Argentinosaurus*. Even for a sauropod *Mamenchisaurus* was a strange-looking animal. The head,

which is never large in a sauropod, looks even smaller compared to the noodle-like neck. And the extreme length of the neck results in a bizarre, front-loaded posture. It almost looks as if *Mamenchisaurus* is about to tip head over heels.

Seven different species of *Mamenchisaurus* have been named, most of which come from the same rock formation in China's Sichuan Province. The first specimen was discovered in 1952 during highway construction and later named by C.C. Young, who is widely recognized as the father of Chinese palaeontology. A trove of additional fossils has turned up recently, including numerous complete skeletons.

Careful study of these fossils indicates that *Mamenchisaurus*

STATISTICS

Habitat:	Asia (China)
Period:	Late Jurassic
Length:	65–82 ft (20–25 m)
Height:	16–20 ft (5–6 m)
Weight:	20–25 tons
Predators:	Theropod dinosaurs
Food:	Plants (conifers)

CLASSIFICATION

Animalia
  Chordata
    Sauropsida
      Archosauria
        Dinosauria
          Sauropodomorpha
            Sauropoda

SIZE COMPARISON

is more advanced than the Early Jurassic sauropods like *Vulcanodon* and the slightly later Middle-Jurassic genera such as *Shunosaurus*. It appears to be a close cousin to the Neosauropoda, a sauropod subgroup that includes more advanced species such as *Diplodocus*, *Apatosaurus*, *Brachiosaurus* and the titanosaurids. At the same time that *Mamenchisaurus* was thundering across Asia, many neosauropods were beginning to dominate ecosystems in North America and Africa.

BRACHIOSAURUS

Meaning: 'arm lizard' **Pronunciation:** BRACK-e-o-sore-uss

Only a few dinosaurs enjoy the widespread popularity of *Brachiosaurus*. For many years this Late Jurassic sauropod was the largest dinosaur known to science. Although it has been eclipsed in recent years by new discoveries such as *Argentinosaurus* and *Seismosaurus*, *Brachiosaurus* is still one of the most massive animals that ever walked the earth.

Brachiosaurus was about as long as *Mamenchisaurus*, as both sauropods measured up to 82 ft (25 m) in length. However, *Brachiosaurus* was much more massive, and may have weighed as much as 50 tons. The skull of *Brachiosaurus* is unique among sauropods, and the top is expanded into a broad dome. This may have housed a resonating chamber to produce sound for communication purposes. The teeth are wide and spatula-shaped, and would have been well suited for feeding on tougher vegetation such as the conifers that were wildly abundant in the Late Jurassic landscape.

Perhaps the most unique feature of *Brachiosaurus* was its forelimbs, which were longer than the hindlimbs. In most other dinosaurs, and most other land animals, the hindlimbs are at least slightly longer. This strange condition would have helped raise the head of *Brachiosaurus*, and perhaps given it easier access to taller vegetation. Such an adaptation may have been critical, since *Brachiosaurus* shared the Late Jurassic terrain with several other sauropods that were very likely to have been competing for the same food.

Brachiosaurus is known from only a few fossils, among them two partial skeletons from the Morrison Formation of the western United States. Several other specimens, including skulls, have been found in the Tendaguru Formation of Africa, alongside the theropod *Elaphrosaurus*, so it seems that North America and Africa had similar dinosaur communities during the Late Jurassic. Recently, close relatives of *Brachiosaurus* have been found in the Early Cretaceous of North America. These animals, which include *Sauroposeidon* and *Cedarosaurus*, show that brachiosaurids continued to survive long after their Late Jurassic heyday.

FOSSIL LOCATIONS

STATISTICS

Habitat:	North America (USA) Africa (Tanzania)
Period:	Late Jurassic
Length:	65–82 ft (20–25 m)
Height:	17–20 ft (5–6 m)
Weight:	30–50 tons
Predators:	Theropod dinosaurs
Food:	Plants (conifers)

CLASSIFICATION

Animalia
  Chordata
    Sauropsida
      Archosauria
        Dinosauria
          Sauropodomorpha
            Sauropoda
              Brachiosauridae

SIZE COMPARISON

DIPLODOCUS

Meaning: 'double beam' **Pronunciation:** dip-lo-do-KUSS

In the late 1890s American business tycoon Andrew Carnegie was in a giving mood. His steel company had risen to become the most profitable business in the entire world, and the self-styled 'captain of industry' turned his attention to grander endeavours. Not satisfied with merely making money, Carnegie wanted to make history. He desired to push the boundaries of human discovery and imagination, just as he had revolutionized big business a generation earlier. So Carnegie sent a handful of his best men into the wilderness of the American West with one simple goal: to find the largest creature that had ever walked the earth.

This is how *Diplodocus*, one of the grandest and most awesome of the dinosaurs, was discovered. True, fragmentary remains of this herbivore had been found at Como Bluff, Wyoming, in the 1870s. But it was the nearly complete skeleton unearthed by Jacob Wortman, on orders from Carnegie, that gave scientists their first glimpse of an entire sauropod skeleton. Carnegie was so proud of his dinosaur that he sent cast copies across the world. These were exhibited in museums as far away as Europe, and introduced scores of ordinary people to the bizarre world of dinosaurs.

Carnegie's ambitious dream was not too far off the mark. At the time it was found, *Diplodocus* was one of the largest dinosaurs ever discovered, and even today it ranks in the upper tier of dinosaur giants. *Diplodocus* lived in the Morrison ecosystem alongside other monsters such as *Brachiosaurus* and *Apatosaurus*. Compared to *Brachiosaurus* it was slightly longer but much less massive. The two sauropods probably also ate different plants. The robust teeth of *Brachiosaurus* enabled it to eat tougher vegetation, while *Diplodocus* possessed smaller, simpler pencil-like teeth that were suitable for softer plants such as ferns.

Diplodocus had a longer neck than most other sauropods, although not nearly as long as *Mamenchisaurus*. Recent studies conclude that these necks could not reach high into the treetops as was often assumed, but rather were used like vacuum cleaners to sweep through ferns, bushes and other low-lying plants.

The tail of *Diplodocus* was exceptionally long. It contained over 80 separate bones, whereas most sauropods had approximately 40 tail vertebrae. The end of the tail was comprised of about 30 very simple, tubular vertebrae, which may have been used as a whip-like device to fend off predators. This would have been very useful in a landscape infested with mega carnivores like *Allosaurus*.

STATISTICS

Habitat:	North America (USA)
Period:	Late Jurassic
Length:	82–95 ft (25–29 m)
Height:	10–13 ft (3–4 m)
Weight:	12–16 tons
Predators:	Theropod dinosaurs
Food:	Plants (low shrubs and ferns)

CLASSIFICATION

Animalia
  Chordata
    Sauropsida
      Archosauria
        Dinosauria
          Sauropodomorpha
          Sauropoda
            Diplodocoidea

SIZE COMPARISON

APATOSAURUS

Meaning: 'deceptive lizard' **Pronunciation:** a-pat-o-SORE-uss

Apatosaurus, another plodding sauropod from the Morrison Formation, was formerly known as *Brontosaurus*. This confusion stems from the 'Bone Wars', when O.C. Marsh and E.D. Cope were naming each and every bone fragment as a new species in an endless bid to one-up the other. Marsh originally named a few scraps as *Apatosaurus* in 1877, and two years later described a much better specimen as *Brontosaurus*. *Brontosaurus*, the quintessential 'thunder lizard', became one of the most popular dinosaurs. However, later study revealed that *Apatosaurus* and *Brontosaurus* were in fact the same animal. The older name had priority, and *Brontosaurus* was relegated to history.

Today *Apatosaurus* is one of the best-known sauropods. At least ten nearly complete skeletons have been discovered in the badlands of the western United States. These have been separated into three different species. The skeleton of *Apatosaurus* is generally very similar to that of *Diplodocus*, although *Apatosaurus* was slightly taller and *Diplodocus* was a little bit longer. Scientists classify *Diplodocus* and *Apatosaurus*,

along with *Barosaurus*, together in the Diplodocidae. This family was one of the most successful and important groups of Late Jurassic sauropods, and close cousins persisted into the Early Cretaceous.

Recently scientists have studied the large collection of *Apatosaurus* fossils to learn more about how the giant sauropods grew. Many early researchers suggested that sauropods grew slowly throughout their life, and therefore must have lived to be several hundred years old. However, the recent studies reveal a very different answer. *Apatosaurus* reached adulthood at about 13 years of age, meaning that it grew astronomically fast during childhood – possibly gaining up to 33 lb (15 kg) in weight each day! The amount of food needed to fuel such growth would have been enormous, and it is very likely that these rapidly growing sauropods were warm-blooded.

SIZE COMPARISON

FOSSIL LOCATIONS

STATISTICS

Habitat:	North America (USA)
Period:	Late Jurassic
Length:	62–82 ft (19–25 m)
Height:	10–16 ft (3–5 m)
Weight:	25–28 tons
Predators:	Theropod dinosaurs
Food:	Plants (conifers)

CLASSIFICATION

Animalia
  Chordata
    Sauropsida
      Archosauria
        Dinosauria
          Sauropodomorpha
            Sauropoda
              Diplodocoidea

CAMARASAURUS

Meaning: 'chambered lizard' **Pronunciation:** kam-ah-ra-SORE-uss

Camarasaurus is certainly the best-known sauropod. Over 20 specimens of this stocky herbivore have been discovered in the Morrison Formation, including a number of nearly complete skeletons, several of which include skulls. In contrast, very few other sauropod skulls are known, probably because the skull was small, lightweight and only loosely connected to the body. Much of what is known about sauropod cranial anatomy comes from careful study of *Camarasaurus*.

The skeleton of *Camarasaurus* is shorter and stockier than most other Late Jurassic sauropods. The neck is particularly short and only measured about 10 ft (3 m). This may indicate that *Camarasaurus* was feeding differently from *Brachiosaurus*, *Diplodocus* and *Apatosaurus*, all of which had longer necks. The neck of *Brachiosaurus* was more than twice the length of the neck of *Camarasaurus*, but the two had similar teeth and skulls. Thus, the two sauropods may have fed on similar kinds of plants, probably conifers, with *Camarasaurus* focusing on low-lying shrubs and *Brachiosaurus* on taller trees.

Although the first *Camarasaurus* fossils were found in 1877 new research is still focused on this sauropod. The brain of *Camarasaurus* was recently described and is startling because of its small size. The brain is only about 5 in (13 cm) long – approximately 200 times smaller than the skeleton! Not only is the entire brain small, but the olfactory tracts are also proportionally tiny. This suggests that *Camarasaurus* probably couldn't think or smell very well. Other recent research has looked at how the skeleton changed during growth. This work, based on comparison of juvenile and adult skeletons, indicates that the neck became proportionally longer and the bones slimmer as *Camarasaurus* grew up. Perhaps juveniles fed on slightly different plants from the adults.

SIZE COMPARISON

FOSSIL LOCATIONS

STATISTICS

Habitat:	North America (USA)
Period:	Late Jurassic
Length:	59–69 ft (18–21 m)
Height:	10–16 ft (3–5 m)
Weight:	15–20 tons
Predators:	Theropod dinosaurs
Food:	Plants (conifers)

CLASSIFICATION

Animalia
  Chordata
    Sauropsida
      Archosauria
        Dinosauria
          Sauropodomorpha
            Sauropoda
              Diplodocoidea

HUAYANGOSAURUS

Meaning: named for Huayang (Sichuan) Province **Pronunciation:** hwa-yang-o-SORE-uss

The Stegosauria are a group of ornithischians, which includes a variety of heavily armoured herbivores that lived from the Middle Jurassic until the Early Cretaceous. A row of plates along the back and a bundle of spikes on the tail make these four-legged species immediately recognizable.

The oldest and most primitive stegosaur is *Huayangosaurus* from the Middle Jurassic of China. Careful study of this genus has helped scientists to understand the early history of the stegosaurs, as well as to place them within the larger family tree of ornithischians. *Huayangosaurus* is known from a complete skeleton, which fortunately includes a complete, well-preserved skull. The skeleton shares many features with other stegosaurs, such as stretched vertebrae that served to expand the gut and a row of plates on the back. However, unlike the broad and thin plates of *Stegosaurus*, the armour of *Huayangosaurus* was sharper and more spike-like.

Later stegosaurs possessed long, thin skulls that were incredibly narrow when looked at from above, whereas many other ornithischians had wider and more box-like skulls. Remarkably, the cranium of *Huayangosaurus* was robust and wide, and very similar to that of ankylosaurs and *Scelidosaurus*. Indeed, scientists now classify all of these animals together into the Thyreophora. The skull shape of *Huayangosaurus* shows that primitive stegosaurs looked much more similar to

their cousins. Additionally, most stegosaurs lost teeth at the front of the jaw, and replaced them with a beak for cropping vegetation. *Huayangosaurus*, on the other hand, retained these teeth, again showing that primitive stegosaurs were much more similar to other ornithischian groups.

This important early stegosaur was first found in 1982, and since then several more skeletons have been reported. It is one of the best-known dinosaurs from the Middle Jurassic of China, and would have lived alongside fearsome predators such as *Gasosaurus*. It has been suggested that a series of huge spikes above the hips were specifically used to deter *Gasosaurus* and other large theropods.

FOSSIL LOCATIONS

STATISTICS

Habitat:	Asia (China)
Period:	Middle-Jurassic
Length:	15 ft (4.5 m)
Height:	5 ft (1.5 m)
Weight:	1985–2200 lb
	(900–1000 kg)
Predators:	Theropod dinosaurs
Food:	Plants (low shrubs, ferns)

CLASSIFICATION

Animalia
  Chordata
    Sauropsida
      Archosauria
        Dinosauria
          Ornithischia
            Thyreophora
              Stegosauria

SIZE COMPARISON

STEGOSAURUS

Meaning: 'roofed lizard'   **Pronunciation:** steg-o-SORE-uss

There is no mistaking *Stegosaurus*. Along with *Tyrannosaurus*, *Triceratops* and *Brachiosaurus*, this plate-backed herbivore is one of the most recognizable dinosaurs. Its remarkably odd body plan is unlike that of any other animal alive or extinct. The tiny head, low-slung shoulders, arched back, prominent saucer-like plates and menacing tail spikes combined to create a mega herbivore that would have stood out in lush Late Jurassic landscape.

Many features of *Stegosaurus* seem strange. The skull is tiny compared with the rest of the animal, and the brain was particularly minuscule. The forelimb is much shorter than the hindlimb, which, along with the arched vertebral column, gave *Stegosaurus* a distinct hump-backed appearance. This posture also

placed the skull very close to the ground, giving *Stegosaurus* easy access to low-lying plants. Some of these plants may have been too low for the giant sauropods to feed on, providing *Stegosaurus* with a unique resource that helped it compete with the many other herbivores of the Late Jurassic.

However, the wackiest features of *Stegosaurus* were certainly its back plates and tail spikes. The thin, triangular plates formed two alternating rows down the back of the animal. The largest plates were located over the hips and measured 2 ft (0.5 m) wide by 2 ft (0.5 m) deep—the size of a small table! The end of the tail was adorned with four intimidating spikes, which were nearly 3 ft (1 m) long. There is no doubt that the tail spikes were used as defence from mega predators such as *Allosaurus*. Many fossilized spikes show injuries caused by impact, and one *Allosaurus* vertebra is even dented with a deep hole that perfectly matches a *Stegosaurus* spike. However, the function of the plates is more controversial. They may have been used for defence, but were more likely to be display structures or used to cool the animal.

Stegosaurus is known from numerous fossils discovered in the Morrison Formation, as well as more fragmentary specimens from Portugal. It is only one of several dinosaurs found in both areas, and indicates that North America and Europe had a very similar dinosaur community in the Late Jurassic.

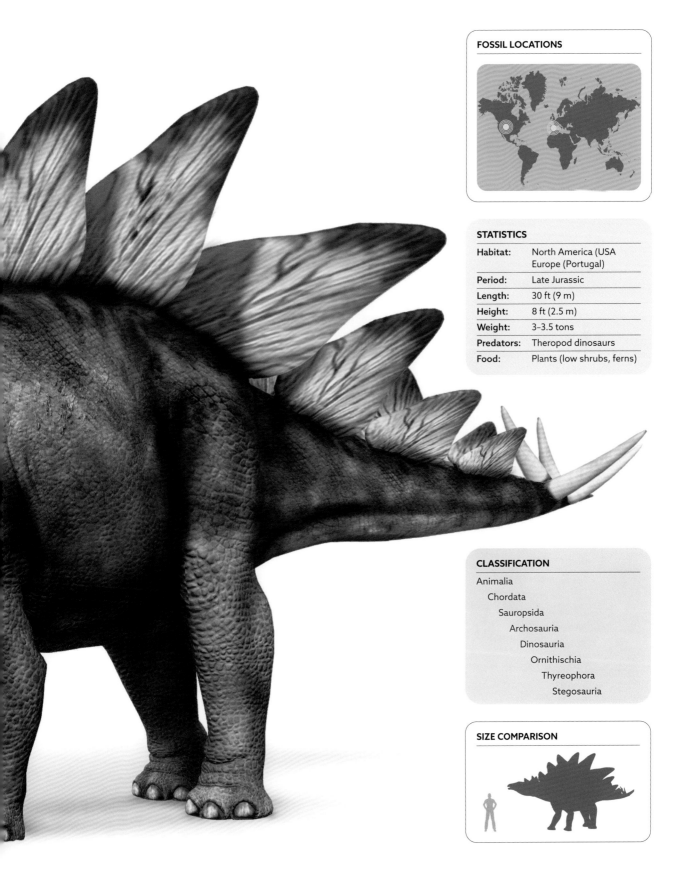

FOSSIL LOCATIONS

STATISTICS

Habitat:	North America (USA Europe (Portugal)
Period:	Late Jurassic
Length:	30 ft (9 m)
Height:	8 ft (2.5 m)
Weight:	3–3.5 tons
Predators:	Theropod dinosaurs
Food:	Plants (low shrubs, ferns)

CLASSIFICATION

Animalia
  Chordata
    Sauropsida
      Archosauria
        Dinosauria
          Ornithischia
            Thyreophora
              Stegosauria

SIZE COMPARISON

DACENTRURUS

Meaning: 'very sharp tail' **Pronunciation:** da-SEN-troo-russ

The first stegosaur ever discovered was *Dacentrurus*, a large herbivore from the Late Jurassic of Europe. The first bones of this species were recovered in the 1870s and named by Richard Owen in 1875. He originally called it *Omosaurus*, the 'forelimb reptile', because of its incredibly short forelimbs. However, this name had already been used for a dinosaur, so this species was rebranded *Dacentrurus*.

The name *Dacentrurus* describes the dangerously sharp tail spikes, which had razor-like edges. These were much sharper than the spikes of other stegosaurs, and were probably a keen defensive weapon against *Megalosaurus* and other large tetanuran predators. *Dacentrurus* is often regarded as a small stegosaur, and most individuals were probably in the 15–23 ft (4.5–7 m) range. However, some fossil discoveries show that

Dacentrurus could reach larger sizes, with some individuals approaching the length of *Stegosaurus*.

Dacentrurus fossils were first found in England, and numerous fragments have been unearthed in the counties of Dorset, Wiltshire and Cambridgeshire. Other excellent fossils have been found in France, Portugal and Spain. Evidently *Dacentrurus* was common across Europe in the Late Jurassic, but no fossils have been found outside the continent. The dominant North American *Stegosaurus*, on the other hand, extended its range into Europe, indicating that some stegosaur species were more widely distributed than others. Whether *Stegosaurus* and *Dacentrurus* coexisted is uncertain, but both were clearly major herbivores in their ecosystems.

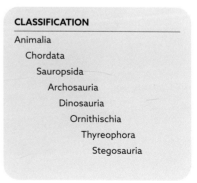

SIZE COMPARISON

FOSSIL LOCATIONS

STATISTICS

Habitat:	Europe (England, France, Portugal, Spain)
Period:	Late Jurassic
Length:	15–33 ft (4.5–10 m)
Height:	6.5 ft (2 m)
Weight:	3090–4410 lb (1400–2000 kg)
Predators:	Theropod dinosaurs
Food:	Plants (low shrubs, ferns)

CLASSIFICATION

Animalia
  Chordata
    Sauropsida
      Archosauria
        Dinosauria
          Ornithischia
            Thyreophora
              Stegosauria

KENTROSAURUS

Meaning: 'pointed lizard' **Pronunciation:** ken-tro-SORE-uss

Not all stegosaurs were as large as the colossal *Stegosaurus*. The genus *Kentrosaurus*, from the Late Jurassic of Africa, was substantially smaller and lighter. In fact, at an average length of 15 ft (4.5 m), *Kentrosaurus* was about half as long as its more famous North American cousin.

Kentrosaurus is known from hundreds of bones discovered during the legendary Tendaguru expeditions in Tanzania. Many of these specimens were displayed in German museums that were bombed during the Second World War. Although the specimens were destroyed, luckily they had been well described.

The armour of *Kentrosaurus* is unique among stegosaurs, and much simpler than that of *Stegosaurus* and other species.

The neck was ornamented with pairs of small, thin plates, which were nowhere near the table-like proportions of *Stegosaurus* These plates transitioned to flattened spines on the back and then pairs of sharper, more robust spikes on the tail. In addition, a set of massive horizontal spines projected sideways along the trunk. These were certainly defensive weapons against *Elaphrosaurus* and other Tendaguru carnivores.

Most stegosaurs had very complex teeth with several pointed projections, called denticles, for cropping vegetation. The teeth of *Kentrosaurus*, however, were much simpler and have only seven denticles. Perhaps *Kentrosaurus* ate softer plants than other stegosaurs.

SIZE COMPARISON

FOSSIL LOCATIONS

STATISTICS

Habitat:	Africa (Tanzania)
Period:	Late Jurassic
Length:	13–16 ft (4–5 m)
Height:	5 ft (1.5 m)
Weight:	1–1.5 tons
Predators:	Theropod dinosaurs
Food:	Plants (low shrubs, ferns)

CLASSIFICATION

Animalia
  Chordata
    Sauropsida
      Archosauria
        Dinosauria
          Ornithischia
            Thyreophora
              Stegosauria

GARGOYLEOSAURUS

Meaning: 'gargoyle lizard' **Pronunciation:** gahr-GOYL-o-sore-uss

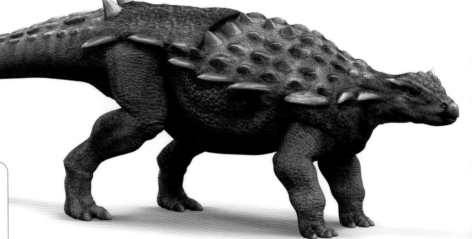

FOSSIL LOCATIONS

STATISTICS

Habitat:	North America (USA)
Period:	Late Jurassic
Length:	10 ft (3 m)
Height:	3.5 ft (1 m)
Weight:	1985–2425 lb
	(900–1100 kg)
Predators:	Theropod dinosaurs
Food:	Plants (low shrubs, ferns)

CLASSIFICATION

Animalia
  Chordata
    Sauropsida
      Archosauria
        Dinosauria
          Ornithischia
            Thyreophora
              Ankylosauria

Ankylosaurs, the heavily armoured and tank-like herbivores so common in museum displays, are another characteristic group of dinosaurs. These plodding, armadillo-like creatures were especially common in the middle–Late Cretaceous, and were dominant herbivores in many North American and Asian ecosystems. Numerous species have been described from every continent apart from Africa. They were finally snuffed out at the Cretaceous–Tertiary extinction.

Like most dinosaur groups, ankylosaurs began as very rare animals and only later became more common and spread worldwide. One of the oldest and most primitive ankylosaurs is a bizarre-looking creature from the Late Jurassic of Wyoming. This dinosaur was so hideous in appearance that it was named *Gargoyleosaurus* after the grotesque stone statues that adorn medieval churches.

Gargoyleosaurus was one of the smallest ankylosaurs. Its skeleton was only about 10 ft (3 m) long, merely a third of the length of Late Cretaceous giants such as *Ankylosaurus*. The box-like skull was also tiny, measuring less than 12 in (30 cm), but it shares important features with other ankylosaur skulls. For instance, it is heavily fused, covered with sculptured armour plates and lacks many cranial openings seen in other dinosaurs. It is likely that these openings, which include the antorbital fenestra (in front of the eye sockets) and the mandibular fenestra of the lower jaw, were closed in order to make the skull of the *Gargoyleosaurus* more compact and rigid. The teeth of *Gargoyleosaurus* were simple and conical like those of other ankylosaurs, and were probably used to tear but not chew soft plants.

Scientists regard *Gargoyleosaurus* as a very primitive ankylosaur, and possibly the most primitive member of the subgroup Ankylosauridae. This subgroup includes giant animals such as *Ankylosaurus* and *Euoplocephalus*, whose tails were capped with a bony club. The skull of *Gargoyleosaurus* is also very similar to that of the stegosaur *Huayangosaurus*, providing more evidence that ankylosaurs and stegosaurs are closely related groups.

CAMPTOSAURUS

Meaning: 'bent lizard' **Pronunciation:** kamp-to-SORE-uss

By the Late Jurassic all of the major groups of ornithischians had evolved. Some ornithischians, such as stegosaurs, were important and abundant herbivores in many areas of the world. Others, such as ankylosaurs, were just beginning to diversify. So too were the ornithopods, the group of ornithischians that includes large-bodied herbivores such as *Iguanodon*, hypsilophodontids and hadrosaurids.

The stocky herbivore *Camptosaurus* is one of the oldest known ornithopods. A handful of smaller, fragmentary ornithopods have been found in slightly older rocks in China, but these look very little like the enormous iguanodontids and hadrosaurids. *Camptosaurus*, on the other hand, was a massive plant-muncher that is obviously a close cousin to these more derived, or evolutionarily advanced, groups that spread like wildfire during the Cretaceous.

Camptosaurus was a mega herbivore. Its skull was fitted with several leaf-shaped teeth, which were perfect for cropping tough vegetation and, like all ornithopods, its upper jaw could rotate outwards while feeding, which helped to give more strength to the bite and allowed *Camptosaurus* to chew its food. These adaptations may have allowed *Camptosaurus* to feed on smaller quantities of more nutrient-rich food, whereas contemporary sauropods and stegosaurs had to ingest huge amounts of nutrient-poor vegetation because they could not chew their food. Initially, these different feeding strategies probably allowed *Camptosaurus* and other ornithopods to coexist alongside other dinosaur herbivores. In the long run, however, their sophisticated chewing ability probably helped ornithopods to eclipse sauropods as the main herbivores of the Cretaceous.

Camptosaurus was a large animal, similar in size to its more advanced hadrosaurid cousins. It probably walked on two legs most of the time, and may have been able to reach high into the trees while feeding. However, the forelimbs were long and stocky and the hand was robust, fused and obviously adapted for weight bearing, enabling *Camptosaurus* to assume a four-footed stance. It is possible that this herbivore rested on all fours, but switched to two legs when feeding or running.

FOSSIL LOCATIONS

STATISTICS

Habitat:	North America (USA), Europe (England)
Period:	Late Jurassic
Length:	16–25 ft (5–7.5 m)
Height:	5–8 ft (1.5–2.5 m)
Weight:	880–1985 lb (400–900 kg)
Predators:	Theropod dinosaurs
Food:	Plants (conifers, shrubs)

CLASSIFICATION

Animalia
  Chordata
    Sauropsida
      Archosauria
        Dinosauria
          Ornithischia
            Ornithopoda

SIZE COMPARISON

DRYOSAURUS

Meaning: 'oak lizard' **Pronunciation:** dry-oh-SORE-uss

Most ornithopods were large, stocky herbivores that plodded along on all fours. Occasionally some species could stand on two legs, but probably only when feeding. These lumbering, slow animals probably avoided predators by sticking together in large herds.

But some of the most primitive members of the group had a much different anatomy and posture. *Dryosaurus*, from the Late Jurassic of North America and Africa, is one of the best-known primitive ornithopods. In overall body form this small herbivore looks more like a theropod than a hadrosaurid. It was slender and light, and certainly a fast runner. The forelimbs were incredibly short, and so *Dryosaurus* could walk only on two legs. Its skull, however, was similar to that of other ornithopods: fronted with a beak and well suited for chewing plant matter.

Dryosaurus lived alongside *Camptosaurus* in the Morrison ecosystem of North America. The two ornithopods probably exploited different lifestyles, as the more massive *Camptosaurus* is twice as long and weighed ten times as much as *Dryosaurus*. Hundreds of isolated *Dryosaurus* bones have also been found in the Tendaguru Formation of Tanzania. However, *Camptosaurus* is unknown from Africa. As the Morrison and Tendaguru were overflowing with mega predators, such as *Allosaurus*, *Ceratosaurus* and *Elaphrosaurus*, it is no wonder that *Dryosaurus* was strongly adapted for running.

SIZE COMPARISON

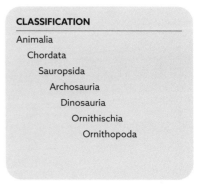

FOSSIL LOCATIONS

STATISTICS

Habitat:	North America (USA), Africa (Tanzania)
Period:	Late Jurassic
Length:	8–14 ft (2.5–4.3 m)
Height:	5 ft (1.5 m)
Weight:	176–198 lb (80–90 kg)
Predators:	Theropod dinosaurs
Food:	Plants (conifers, low shrubs)

CLASSIFICATION

Animalia
  Chordata
    Sauropsida
      Archosauria
        Dinosauria
          Ornithischia
            Ornithopoda

			Hettangian 199.6 – 196.5 MYA	Aalenian 175.6 – 171.6 MYA	
		Carnian 228.7 – 216.5 MYA	Sinemurian 196.5 – 189.6 MYA	Bajocian 171.6 – 167.7 MYA	Oxfordian 161.2 – 155.6 MYA
Induan 251.0 – 249.5 MYA	Anisian 245.9 – 237.0 MYA	Norian 216.5 – 203.6 MYA	Pliensbachian 189.6 – 183.0 MYA	Bathonian 167.7 – 164.7 MYA	Kimmeridgian 155.6 – 150.8 MYA
Olenekian 249.5 – 245.9 MYA	Ladinian 237.0 – 228.7 MYA	Rhaetian 203.6 – 199.6 MYA	Toarcian 183.0 – 175.6 MYA	Callovian 164.7 – 161.2 MYA	Tithonian 150.8 – 145.5 MYA
EARLY TRIASSIC 251.0 – 245.9 MYA	MIDDLE TRIASSIC 245.9 – 228.7 MYA	LATE TRIASSIC 228.7 – 199.6 MYA	EARLY JURASSIC 199.6 – 175.6 MYA	MIDDLE JURASSIC 175.6 – 161.2 MYA	LATE JURASSIC 161.2 – 145.5 MYA

TRIASSIC 251.0 – 199.6 MYA   **JURASSIC 199.6 – 145.5 MYA**

Dinosaurs of the Early-Middle Cretaceous

Berriasian 145.5 – 140.2 MYA

Valanginian 140.2 – 133.9 MYA

Hauterivian 133.9 – 130.0 MYA

Barremian 130.0 – 125.0 MYA

Aptian 125.0 – 112.0 MYA

Albian 112.0 – 99.6 MYA

Cenomanian 99.6 – 93.6 MYA

Turonian 93.6 – 88.6 MYA

Coniacian 88.6 – 85.8 MYA

Santonian 85.8 – 83.5 MYA

Campanian 83.5 – 70.6 MYA

Maastrichtian 70.6 – 65.5 MYA

EARLY-MIDDLE CRETACEOUS
145.5 – 99.6 MYA

LATE CRETACEOUS
99.6 – 65.5 MYA

The Cretaceous World

The Cretaceous was the heyday of the dinosaurs. At no other time in their history were dinosaurs so diverse, so abundant or so dominant. Like humans today, dinosaurs had spread to every corner of the world during the Cretaceous. No spot was left untouched by these behemoths – their fossils are even found in the polar highlands of Alaska and the ice shelves of Antarctica. Early mammals, which had originated in the Late Triassic, were continuing to evolve at low diversity. So too were other reptiles and dinosaur descendants, the birds. But the Cretaceous belonged to the dinosaurs.

Many critical events in earth history also occurred during the Cretaceous. The supercontinent of Pangaea was no more than a distant memory. By the middle of the Cretaceous North America and Europe were separated, and the southern continent of Gondwana was beginning to drift apart.

The major landmasses were now separated by oceans, which prevented the easy dispersal of plants and animals. Each continent developed its own unique communities, which explains why dinosaur ecosystems were so different on different landmasses.

The Cretaceous world was a hothouse; global temperatures were among the warmest ever recorded. Tropical plants flourished in Alaska and Greenland and warm, shallow seas flooded the continents. One such sea nearly divided North America in half. Plesiosaurs, mosasaurs, ichthyosaurs and primitive birds flourished and many dinosaurs made their homes alongside the sea. Certain groups such as the nodosaurid ankylosaurs and some hadrosaurids seemed especially well suited for living at the water's edge. Shallow seas divided landmasses into many smaller regions, which promoted the rise of new and diverse species of dinosaurs.

The most influential event of the Cretaceous, however, was the evolution of flowering plants. The angiosperms, which include everything from oaks and magnolias to grasses and garden flowers, first evolved in the Early–middle Cretaceous. Up to then conifers, cycads and other more primitive plants had flourished, providing a vast food resource for the giant sauropods and stegosaurs. Flowering plants were more

A reconstruction of the Middle-Late Cretaceous environment. The Cretaceous witnessed the evolution of angiosperms, or flowering plants, which drastically reshaped the landscape. Many new kinds of bushes, flowers and even primitive grasses evolved in the Cretaceous, supplanting the evergreen conifers as the primary type of vegetation. This may have enabled new groups of herbivorous dinosaurs such as the ceratopsians and hadrosaurs to exploit this new resource and become very common.

nutritious, and were soon exploited by new groups of dinosaurian herbivores such as the hadrosaurids, ceratopsians and pachycephalosaurs.

Entirely new groups of dinosaurs evolved, such as the ceratopsians. Lineages that had arisen earlier, such as the coelurosaurs, explosively diversified. Even very ancient groups, such as the ceratosaurs, allosauroids and sauropods, enjoyed renewed success, especially in the southern hemisphere. Northern hemisphere communities were dominated by giant tyrannosaurid predators and mega herbivores well suited for guzzling angiosperms, most importantly the hadrosaurids and ceratopsians. The isolated southern hemisphere communities were quite different. Tyrannosaurids were absent, so allosau-roids and ceratosaurs evolved into giants that ruled most ecosystems. There were no ceratopsians and ornithopods were rare, so unique sauropod lineages occupied the main herbivore role. But even this is an oversimplification: each continent had its own quirky dinosaur fauna, and no two places in the world looked the same.

The earth during the Late Cretaceous. The supercontinent of Pangaea was little more than a distant memory, as the globe was beginning to resemble our modern world. The separation of major continents such as Africa, South America, Asia, Europe and North America prevented easy migration across the world, which allowed unique communities of dinosaurs to evolve on each landmass.

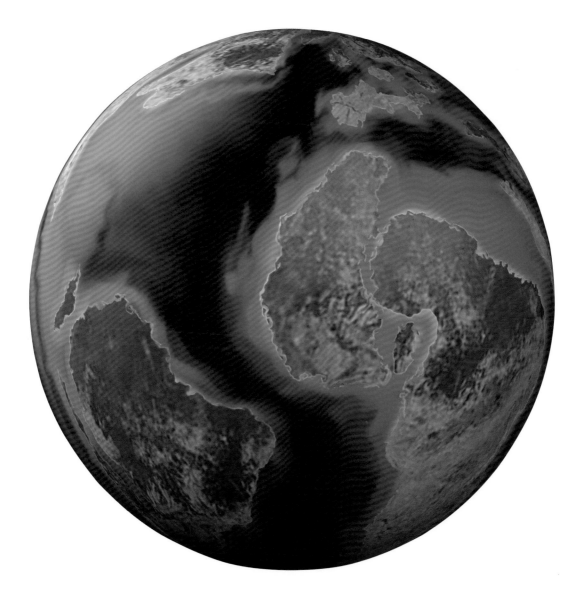

SPINOSAURUS

Meaning: 'spine lizard' **Pronunciation:** spine-o-SORE-uss

STATISTICS

Habitat:	Africa (Egypt, Morocco, Niger)
Period:	Early-middle Cretaceous
Length:	33–60 ft (10–18 m)
Height:	8–10 ft (2.5–3 m)
Weight:	6–9 tons
Predators:	None
Food:	Theropod, ornithischian, and sauropod dinosaurs

CLASSIFICATION

Animalia
  Chordata
    Sauropsida
      Archosauria
        Dinosauria
          Theropoda
            Tetanurae
              Spinosauroidea

SIZE COMPARISON

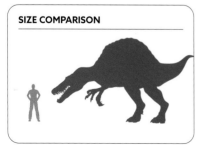

In 1910 a German aristocrat named Ernst Stromer boarded a steamship bound for Egypt. Stromer was born into a noble bloodline—his father was mayor of Nuremberg—but for the next several months he was leaving behind the comforts of Europe and heading into the treacherous desert of North Africa. Very little was known about Africa's fossil record at that time, and Stromer was determined to find dinosaurs.

Stromer's expedition was a remarkable success. He and his assistants uncovered a wide sample of fossils, which included many new dinosaur species. One of these dinosaurs, the gargantuan theropod *Spinosaurus*, was unlike anything that had ever been found before. Fragmentary pieces of the skull suggested a long, low cranium very similar to those of crocodiles. Most remarkably, the back vertebrae extended into tall, thin sheets that looked like they supported a sail. And clearly this animal was a giant. The scrappy remains were all substantially larger than the bones of other predatory dinosaurs.

The intriguing fossils of *Spinosaurus* were made the centrepiece of an exhibit in Munich. However, the museum was located close to Nazi headquarters, and was accidentally destroyed during an Allied bombing raid in 1944. The only known fossils of *Spinosaurus* were turned to dust, leaving scientists with nothing more than Stromer's description and illustrations.

Recently a handful of new *Spinosaurus* fossils have been found, but most are fragmentary, and no one has yet found an even moderately complete skeleton. However, these new fossils confirm the strange appearance of *Spinosaurus* and suggest that it may have been the largest carnivore ever to walk the earth. A newly discovered skull is nearly 6 ft (2 m) long – the largest skull of any theropod. Based on this skull and other fossils, scientists have estimated the length of *Spinosaurus* as anywhere from 33 to 60 ft (10–18 m). The largest *Tyrannosaurus* individuals, in contrast, rarely measure over 40 ft (12 m). Weight estimates of *Spinosaurus* also vary, but this dinosaur could have reached 20 tons, larger than many sauropods. This figure is an extreme, though, and it is more likely that *Spinosaurus* weighed 6–9 tons, which is still enormous for a predatory dinosaur.

BARYONYX

Meaning: 'heavy claw' **Pronunciation:** bah-ree-ON-icks

Amateur fossil hunter William Walker spent a lifetime searching for fossils all around England. In 1983 he made the discovery of his career. While combing a brick company's claypit in Surrey, Walker came across an almost unbelievable fossil: a 10-in (25-cm) long claw of a theropod dinosaur. But that wasn't all. Further digging revealed a nearly complete skeleton of a theropod very similar to *Spinosaurus*.

Baryonyx was a large theropod, about the size of *Allosaurus* and only slightly smaller than giants such as *Tyrannosaurus*. It was substantially smaller than *Spinosaurus*, but shares numerous features with this mysterious African predator. Most importantly, the back vertebrae were expanded to form a great sail. Long, thin spines rose upwards from each vertebra to support the sail. The spines were short in *Baryonyx*, but in some spinosaurids they stretched for nearly 7 ft (2.1 m)! The skull was long and narrow, with a thin snout full of conical

teeth much like those of crocodiles. In most theropods the forelimb is small, but spinosaurids had a long, robust forelimb capped with monstrous sharp claws that made a powerful hunting weapon.

Given their strange anatomy, what were the feeding habits and lifestyle of these animals? It seems likely that they were similar to those of crocodiles. Walker's *Baryonyx* fossil had fish scales in its gut, conclusively proving that spinosaurids ate fish. It is probable that *Baryonyx* lurked by the water's edge, much like a grizzly, waiting for shoals of fish to move downstream. Their long, narrow skulls were perfectly suited for quick darts into the water, and the strong, clawed arms may have been used for spearing fish. However, *Baryonyx* was also found with bones of *Iguanodon* in its gut, indicating that it was probably more of a generalist feeder. Certainly, a 43-ft (13-m) long spinosaurid was the top predator in its ecosystem and could eat whatever it wanted.

SIZE COMPARISON

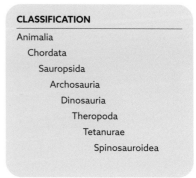

FOSSIL LOCATIONS

STATISTICS

Habitat:	Europe (England)
Period:	Early Cretaceous
Length:	30–43 ft (9–13 m)
Height:	6–8 ft (1.8–2.5 m)
Weight:	5500–11,900 lb (2500–5400 kg)
Predators:	None
Food:	Sauropod and ornithischian dinosaurs

CLASSIFICATION

Animalia
  Chordata
    Sauropsida
      Archosauria
        Dinosauria
          Theropoda
            Tetanurae
              Spinosauroidea

IRRITATOR

Meaning: 'the irritating one' **Pronunciation:** ear-e-tate-OR

The South American spinosaurid *Irritator* has a quirky name. It is derived from English, not Latin or Greek, and literally means 'the irritating one'. The only known fossil, a nearly complete skull, was originally discovered by commercial fossil hunters in Brazil. They touched it up with plaster and added several fake features, all in the hopes that a prettier specimen would bring more money. When scientists finally studied the skull they had a difficult time interpreting which parts were real bone and which were phony additions. This was painstaking and irritating, hence the name.

But the irritation was worth it, because the skull of *Irritator* is the most complete cranium of a spinosaurid ever discovered. *Baryonyx*, and to a lesser extent *Spinosaurus*, helped to outline the major cranial features of spinosaurids, but *Irritator* gave scientists their first glimpse of what an entire skull would look like.

Overall, the skull is crocodile-like and well adapted for eating fish. The snout is very narrow and filled with unserrated, conical teeth. Such teeth are also found in many crocodiles, seals and other creatures that eat fish, and were perfect for biting down on slippery prey. In addition, the front of the snout is expanded into a bulbous rosette, which held numerous teeth for snaring and killing fish. Internally, there is a secondary palate, which separates the mouth from the nostrils. This feature is seen in crocodiles, and allows the animal to feed underwater but still breathe through its nose. It is also thought to make the skull stronger and increase bite force, which would be necessary in mega predators like spinosaurids that ate a range of prey.

Irritator comes from the Santana Formation of Brazil, a world-famous rock unit that has yielded hundreds of beautiful fish and pterosaur fossils. Another spinosaurid, *Angaturama*, was described from this formation based on a single fossil: the front portion of a snout. However, scientists now think that this piece was ripped off the skull of *Irritator*.

Spinosaurid fossils, especially teeth, are common in South America and Africa, but unknown in North America and most of Asia. Spinosaurids were probably a mostly southern group that occasionally spread into northern continents (Europe). Clearly, they were some of the most dominant and important predators in the southern hemisphere during the Cretaceous.

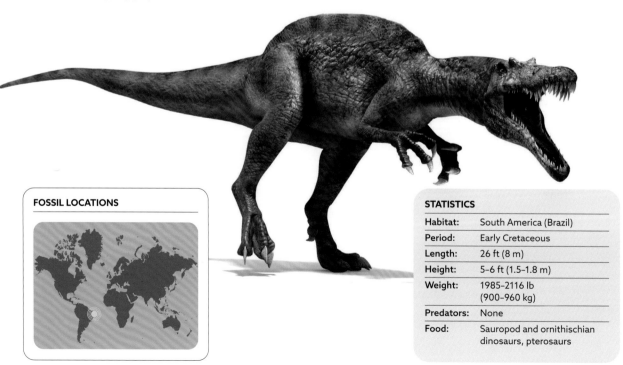

FOSSIL LOCATIONS

STATISTICS

Habitat:	South America (Brazil)
Period:	Early Cretaceous
Length:	26 ft (8 m)
Height:	5–6 ft (1.5–1.8 m)
Weight:	1985–2116 lb (900–960 kg)
Predators:	None
Food:	Sauropod and ornithischian dinosaurs, pterosaurs

SIZE COMPARISON

CLASSIFICATION

Animalia
  Chordata
    Sauropsida
      Archosauria
        Dinosauria
          Theropoda
            Tetanurae
              Spinosauroidea

ACROCANTHOSAURUS

Meaning: 'high-spined lizard' **Pronunciation:** ak-row-can-tho-SORE-uss

The most fearsome predator in North America during the Early Cretaceous was *Acrocanthosaurus*. At 40 ft (12 m) long it was the size of *Tyrannosaurus*, and at 3–4 tons it was one of the largest land predators that has ever existed. Fossils of this humongous beast are known from the American plains, and are found alongside a rich diversity of sauropods and ornithopods. Although these herbivores were large, they were no match for the strong jaws and sharp claws of *Acrocanthosaurus*.

Acrocanthosaurus was an allosauroid theropod, a member of a subgroup called the tetanurans that was very common in the Late Jurassic. In some ways it looks more like a spinosaurid or a tyrannosaurid, and indeed was often classified as a member of these theropod groups. The giant skull, which was over 4 ft (1.25 m) long and studded with dagger-like teeth, looks much like that of a tyrannosaurid. The back vertebrae expanded upwards into plate-like spines, which supported a sail or back hump as in spinosaurids. However, recent studies clearly link *Acrocanthosaurus* with the allosauroids, based on numerous features across the entire skeleton.

Acrocanthosaurus is very similar to another allosauroid subgroup called the carcharodontosaurids, which includes the African *Carcharodontosaurus* and the South American *Giganotosaurus*.These enormous animals were amazingly diverse on the southern continents during the Early–middle Cretaceous and

FOSSIL LOCATIONS

STATISTICS	
Habitat:	North America (USA), Asia
Period:	Early Cretaceous
Length:	40 ft (12 m)
Height:	6–8 ft (1.8–2.5m)
Weight:	3–4 tons
Predators:	None
Food:	Ornithischian dinosaurs, crocodylomorphs

clearly the top predators in their ecosystems. Aside from large size, *Acrocanthosaurus* shares many other characteristics with these giants, such as a large bony swelling over the eye, vertebrae hollowed by air sacs and a pubis bone that ends in a large, boot-like expansion that would have anchored powerful hindlimb muscles. The conclusion is unmistakable: *Acrocanthosaurus* is a bizarre northern representative of this group of southern giants.

Fossils of *Acrocanthosaurus* have been found in the states of Texas and Oklahoma. Four excellent skeletons are known. Scientists have even been able to study details of the brain that are usually impossible to see in most fossils.

In addition, countless large theropod footprints have been found in Early Cretaceous rocks in Texas, most of which were probably made by *Acrocanthosaurus*. One trackway near Glen Rose, Texas, may even show an *Acrocanthosaurus* tracking sauropod prey. This is one of the few instances of predatory behaviour directly preserved in the fossil record.

CLASSIFICATION

Animalia
  Chordata
    Sauropsida
      Archosauria
        Dinosauria
          Theropoda
            Tetanurae
              Allosauroidea
                Carcharodontosauridae

SIZE COMPARISON

CARCHARODONTOSAURUS

Meaning: 'shark-toothed lizard' **Pronunciation:** car-car-o-don-to-SORE-uss

Living alongside the colossal *Spinosaurus* was another theropod that was nearly as large. The allosauroid *Carcharodontosaurus* was slightly smaller and more slender, but just as fearsome. Together, these carnivores would have terrorized the deltas and floodplains of northern Africa during the Early Cretaceous. It was not the ideal time to be a small herbivorous dinosaur!

Like *Spinosaurus*, *Carcharodontosaurus* was originally described by German palaeontologist Ernst Stromer, based mostly on fragmentary scraps. And like the original fossils of the sail-backed giant, these scraps were destroyed during the Second World War. However, recent fossil-hunting expeditions led by Paul Sereno have unearthed several *Carcharodontosaurus* fossils. One of these specimens, a nearly complete skull, is one of the largest theropod skulls ever found. It measures over 5 ft (1.5 m) in length, making it longer than the skull of *Tyrannosaurus* and nearly as long as that of *Spinosaurus*.

But while the skull of *Spinosaurus* was long, narrow and well adapted for catching fish, the head of *Carcharodontosaurus* was deep, robust and perfect for taking down large prey. The teeth of *Carcharodontosaurus* are unique for theropods, and give the predator its name. Like the teeth of sharks, those of *Carcharodontosaurus* are long, thin, blade-like and finely serrated, making them perfect for slicing through the flesh of prey. Uniquely, the skull of *Carcharodontosaurus* has an enlarged, window-like antorbital fenestra (opening in front of the eye sockets). This probably served to reduce weight and make the massive skull easier to carry.

Carcharodontosaurus teeth are found all across northern Africa, indicating that it was a dominant and widespread predator for much of the Early–middle Cretaceous. Recently, a second species of *Carcharodontosaurus* has been described from Niger. This species differs from fossils discovered in Egypt and Morocco and may represent a unique, southern form that evolved in isolation when shallow seas divided much of northern Africa into separate regions during the middle Cretaceous.

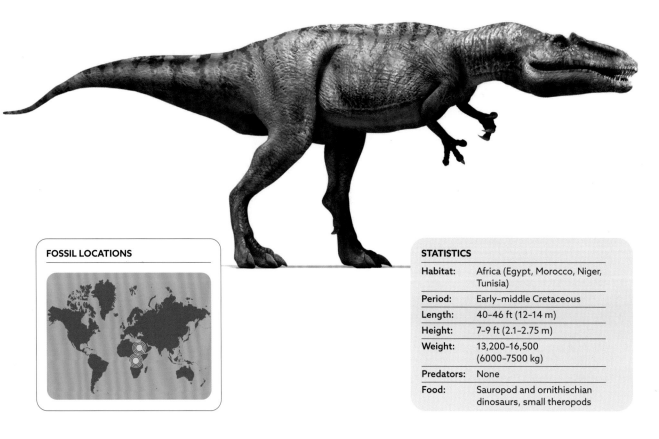

FOSSIL LOCATIONS

STATISTICS

Habitat:	Africa (Egypt, Morocco, Niger, Tunisia)
Period:	Early–middle Cretaceous
Length:	40–46 ft (12–14 m)
Height:	7–9 ft (2.1–2.75 m)
Weight:	13,200–16,500 (6000–7500 kg)
Predators:	None
Food:	Sauropod and ornithischian dinosaurs, small theropods

SIZE COMPARISON

CLASSIFICATION

Animalia
   Chordata
      Sauropsida
         Archosauria
            Dinosauria
               Theropoda
                  Tetanurae
                     Carcharodontosauridae

GIGANOTOSAURUS

Meaning: 'giant southern lizard' **Pronunciation:** ji-gan-ote-o-SORE-uss

While *Carcharodontosaurus* was stalking ornithopods in northern Africa, its close cousin *Giganotosaurus* was sinking its teeth into gigantic sauropods in South America. These two allosauroids were among the most frightening predators of the dinosaur world, and are prime examples of how carcharodontosaurids ruled the Early–middle Cretaceous ecosystems of the supercontinent Gondwana.

The first remains of *Giganotosaurus* were found in 1993 and named in 1995. Their discovery sparked a rush of excitement because the fossil was nearly complete, which is rare for large theropods. However, 'large' does not come close to describing *Giganotosaurus*. Better words would be 'giant', 'massive', 'colossal' or 'enormous'. It is difficult to imagine an animal of this size. The largest individuals may have reached well over 45 ft (14 m). Although *Spinosaurus* may have been larger, there are no nearly complete skeletons to give a clear picture of its size. Next to the skeleton of a *Giganotosaurus*, a man looks more insignificant than a mouse.

Its size enabled *Giganotosaurus* to become the keystone carnivore of its ecosystem, and it probably feasted on giant sauropods and ornithopods. In fact, some of the largest sauropods ever to live are found either alongside *Giganotosaurus* or in slightly

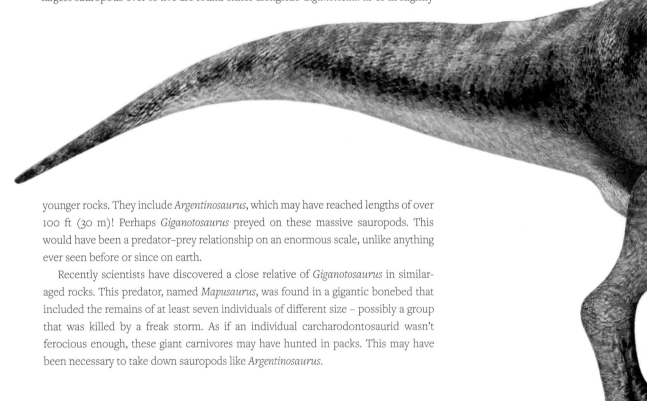

younger rocks. They include *Argentinosaurus*, which may have reached lengths of over 100 ft (30 m)! Perhaps *Giganotosaurus* preyed on these massive sauropods. This would have been a predator–prey relationship on an enormous scale, unlike anything ever seen before or since on earth.

Recently scientists have discovered a close relative of *Giganotosaurus* in similar-aged rocks. This predator, named *Mapusaurus*, was found in a gigantic bonebed that included the remains of at least seven individuals of different size – possibly a group that was killed by a freak storm. As if an individual carcharodontosaurid wasn't ferocious enough, these giant carnivores may have hunted in packs. This may have been necessary to take down sauropods like *Argentinosaurus*.

FOSSIL LOCATIONS

STATISTICS

Habitat:	South America (Argentina)
Period:	Early-middle Cretaceous
Length:	40–46 ft (12–14 m)
Height:	7–9 ft (2.1–2.75 m)
Weight:	13,200–15,400 lb
	(6000–7000 kg)
Predators:	None
Food:	Sauropod and ornithischian dinosaurs, small theropods

CLASSIFICATION

Animalia
  Chordata
    Sauropsida
      Archosauria
        Dinosauria
          Theropoda
            Tetanurae
              Carcharodontosauridae

SIZE COMPARISON

The Feathered Dinosaurs of China

There is no doubt that birds evolved from theropod dinosaurs. The 1861 discovery of *Archaeopteryx* gave palaeontology its first bona fide missing link between the two groups: a small creature that retained a dinosaurian bony tail and sharp teeth, but was feathered and could fly like a bird. A century later, John Ostrom's discovery of the dromaeosaur *Deinonychus* provided yet another important link in the chain: a swift, agile dinosaur with many bird-like features in the skull, wrist and shoulder. These discoveries, along with years of careful research, closed the book on bird origins. But many mysteries remained. When and why did feathers evolve? Did flight evolve in dinosaurs that ran on the ground or perched in the trees? And which exact group of dinosaurs gave rise to birds?

A remarkable fossil site in China has helped palaeontologists answer these questions and many more. Located in far northeastern China, along the border with North Korea, is the province of Liaoning. Today this region is home to rolling farms and sprawling factories, as well as nearly 50 million people. About 125 million years ago, however, the area boasted large lakes and teemed with life, from schools of fish and crustaceans to early birds, small theropod dinosaurs and some of the first flowering plants. Distant volcanoes occasionally erupted with great force, burying plants and animals, which turned into fossils.

-Although such fossils had been known for 50 years or more, it wasn't until the mid-1990s that scientists began to explore Liaoning carefully. Very quickly they made some extraordinary discoveries. The first of these, a squashed creature covered in feathers, was pried from an Early Cretaceous rock unit called the Yixian Formation. This fossil was named *Sinosauropteryx* in 1996 and described as the most primitive bird – an animal potentially more important than *Archaeopteryx*. Scientists noticed something very strange, however. Yes, the specimen was sheathed in a feathery coat, but the skeleton was almost identical to the theropod dinosaur *Compsognathus*. Two years later researchers came to a stunning conclusion: *Sinosauropteryx* was not a bird, but a true theropod dinosaur with feathers.

-This was a groundbreaking discovery. Although there was no doubt that birds evolved from dinosaurs, this fact was based on lots of technical anatomical evidence that was mostly

The remarkable feathered dinosaur *Microraptor*. This tiny dinosaur was a member of the dromaeosaur lineage, and possessed feathered wings on both the arms and legs.

Left: The skull of the feathered dinosaur *Sinosauropteryx*. Discovered in 1996, *Sinosauropteryx* was the first feathered dinosaur fossil found in China's Liaoning Province.

Below: The primitive bird *Confuciusornis*. Thousands of fossils of this early bird have been discovered in Liaoning, China, in the same rocks that have yielded feathered dinosaurs. It is one of the oldest and most primitive birds known.

understandable only to scientists. A feathered theropod was the final proof, the jaw-dropping visual evidence needed to convince everyone that birds are dinosaurs.

-But the story didn't end with *Sinosauropteryx*. These 125-million-year-old rocks continued to produce feathered theropods at a breathtaking pace. First came the downy *Caudipteryx* and *Protarchaeopteryx*, both relatives of the oviraptorids, then the therizinosaurid *Beipiaosaurus*, the dromaeosaurid *Sinornithosaurus* and the tiny glider *Microraptor*. Recently, a primitive cousin of the tyrannosaurids, *Dilong*, has been found with feathers. This avalanche of discovery shows that many theropods were covered with feathers, not just the very bird-like ones. Obviously, animals like tyrannosaurs and compsognathids could not fly, so their feathers must have evolved for some other purpose. Perhaps they were originally used for display or insulation and were later altered into aerofoils for flight.

Careful study of the famous feathered theropods of Liaoning has helped scientists to address many important evolutionary questions. A comparison of different feather types in different species reveals a spectacular evolutionary sequence. The 'protofeathers' of *Sinosauropteryx* were short, simple and dense, and provided a fuzzy body covering like the hair of mammals. Later, dromaeosaurids such as *Sinornithosaurus* developed larger feathers with a more complicated internal structure. Some of these dromaeosaurids had true flight feathers, with a central shaft and broad outline. This shows that feathers gradually evolved from simple strands into more complex structures for flight, and also indicates that the dromaeosaurids are the closest relatives of birds. Some of these dromaeosaurids, such as *Microraptor*, were tiny animals that probably lived in the trees. So, bird flight probably evolved from gliding animals that floated down from the treetops, not from running animals that took off from the ground.

Today, the countryside of Liaoning is crawling with fossil hunters hoping to find the next great, feathered theropod. Almost every year new species are discovered, which continues to help scientists understand one of the most important evolutionary transitions in the history of life: the evolution of birds from dinosaurs.

MICRORAPTOR

MICRORAPTOR

Meaning: 'small thief' **Pronunciation:** my-krow-rap-TOR

The little theropod *Microraptor* is perhaps the most important of China's feathered dinosaurs. Notable for its small size in a world ruled by behemoths, this downy dinosaur was only a few feet long and weighed less than 10 lb (4.5 kg). It was a primitive member of the dromaeosaurid group, the closest dinosaurian relatives of birds. The bizarre anatomy and feather arrangement of *Microraptor* are helping scientists to understand how bird flight evolved.

Microraptor fossils comprised one half of the infamous 'Archaeoraptor', a fake built in 1999 from several different Liaoning fossils, that was thought to be a key missing link on the line to birds. Scientists quickly uncovered the forgery, but then noticed that part of the fake was stunning in its own right. With its long tail and full covering of feathers, *Microraptor* was described as a very close bird cousin by Xu Xing and colleagues in 2000. With a trunk length of only 2 in (5 cm), it was the first known dinosaur smaller than *Archaeopteryx*. This was important, since some critics had argued that theropod dinosaurs were too large to evolve into the much smaller birds.

Additionally, *Microraptor* had curved and slender claws on its feet. These claws, along with other features, were perfectly suited for living in the trees. This was also important, since it was long debated whether birds evolved from ground-running animals or arboreal creatures that lived in trees. Up until *Microraptor* no dinosaur showed such obvious tree-living adaptations. Since this dromaeosaur is so closely related to birds, it is likely that the first birds evolved in the trees.

The feathers of *Microraptor* were also unique. Three years after their initial description, Xu and his team described a second species of *Microraptor* from the same rocks. This animal proved even more bizarre and important than the original species. It was also very bird-like, extremely small and showed tree-living adaptations. But this new animal had fully developed, feather-covered wings not only on its arms, but also on its legs. The presence of four wings was a shock to palaeontologists. All living birds have wings only on their arms, but *Microraptor* suggests that birds may have first evolved as four-winged animals that flew like a biplane. And, like these early aeroplanes, *Microraptor* may have glided with its forewings and hindwings at different levels, a distinctive behaviour unknown in other animals.

SIZE COMPARISON

FOSSIL LOCATIONS

STATISTICS

Habitat:	Asia (China)
Period:	Early Cretaceous
Length:	18–29 in (45–75 cm)
Height:	9–14 in (22–36 cm)
Weight:	4–9 lb (2–4 kg)
Predators:	Theropod dinosaurs
Food:	Small vertebrates, insects

CLASSIFICATION

Animalia
  Chordata
    Sauropsida
      Archosauria
        Dinosauria
          Theropoda
            Tetanurae
              Coelurosauria
                Dromaeosauridae

CAUDIPTERYX

Meaning: 'tail feather' **Pronunciation:** kaw-DIP-ter-icks

The peacock-like *Caudipteryx* was one of the first feathered dinosaurs unearthed in China. Despite the thick coat of feathers that ran down its arms, hands and tail, scientists consider *Caudipteryx* to be a very primitive member of the oviraptorosaur group, a bizarre assemblage of theropods that includes the famous *Oviraptor* from the Gobi Desert.

The oviraptorosaurs were one of the strangest groups of dinosaurs. These advanced, very bird-like coelurosaurs were mostly small animals, characterized by a short, light skull ornamented with a midline crest. Most species completely lacked teeth and probably ate seeds, nuts, shellfish or small vertebrates. However, *Caudipteryx* is more primitive in its overall anatomy than many other oviraptorosaurs. It also retained four teeth at the upper end of its snout and had a much heavier skull, so it may have been more of a predator than other members of the group.

Caudipteryx was certainly fast. Its skeleton was light, the arms were reduced and the legs were long and slender. Compared to most dinosaurs the tail was short, and ended in a stiffened, fused portion very similar to the knob-like pygostyle in birds. This is the 'parson's nose' so familiar from roast turkey or chicken dinners. The end of the tail sported a tuft of slender feathers, which radiated outwards into a broad fan. This was probably a display structure. The arms and hands were sheathed with larger, stronger and more complex feathers that were similar to the flight feathers of modern birds. However, true flight feathers are asymmetrical around the central axis. Those of *Caudipteryx* were symmetrical, indicating that this oviraptorosaur could not fly.

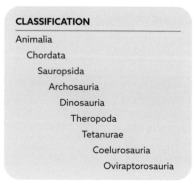

SIZE COMPARISON

FOSSIL LOCATIONS

STATISTICS

Habitat:	Asia (China)
Period:	Early Cretaceous
Length:	3–4 ft (1–1.25 m)
Height:	4–5 ft (1.2–1.5 m)
Weight:	463–476 lb (210–216 kg)
Predators:	Theropod dinosaurs
Food:	Small vertebrates, insects

CLASSIFICATION

Animalia
  Chordata
    Sauropsida
      Archosauria
        Dinosauria
          Theropoda
            Tetanurae
              Coelurosauria
                Oviraptorosauria

INCISIVOSAURUS

Meaning: 'incisor-toothed lizard' **Pronunciation:** in-sice-i-vo-SORE-uss

Incisivosaurus, a very close relative of *Caudipteryx* from Liaoning, is a most unusual theropod. It, too, is a very primitive member of the oviraptorosaur group, and like *Caudipteryx* was a fast, two-legged runner that was probably feathered, although poor preservation has destroyed any signs of these structures. The most puzzling features of *Incisivosaurus* are in its skull, which along with some fragments of the vertebral column is the only part of this animal that has been found.

Most oviraptorosaurs lacked teeth, and instead possessed sharp, bird-like beaks that were perfectly suited for cracking nuts or seeds. Caudipteryx had a few teeth in its upper jaw but was otherwise toothless. Incisivosaurus, however, possessed a full array of teeth in both the upper and lower jaws. Four teeth protrude from the upper jaw at the front of the snout. The first of these is a long, strong, flattened tooth that shows clear signs of wear on its inner surface. Similar wear patterns are seen on the teeth of rodents that gnaw on tough vegetation. This suggests that *Incisivosaurus* was not eating seeds like other oviraptorosaurs, or even meat like most other theropods, but was actually a herbivore!

Teeth further back in the upper jaw, as well as those in the lower jaw, are simpler cone-like structures. They also have wear facets, further telltale signs of plant eating. Other features of the skull are also unique among oviraptorosaurs. The 4-in (10-cm) long cranium was longer and more slender than in other members of the group, which mostly possessed short, box-like skulls. Additionally, although the skull of *Incisivosaurus* was somewhat light it wasn't nearly as hollow and fragile as in other oviraptorosaurs. Perhaps the skull of

Incisivosaurus needed to be stronger to endure the powerful biting forces associated with chewing plants.

SIZE COMPARISON

FOSSIL LOCATIONS

STATISTICS

Habitat:	Asia (China)
Period:	Early Cretaceous
Length:	40 in (1 m)
Height:	4 ft (1.25 m)
Weight:	13–15 lb (6–7 kg)
Predators:	Theropod dinosaurs
Food:	Small vertebrates, insects

CLASSIFICATION

Animalia
  Chordata
    Sauropsida
      Archosauria
        Dinosauria
          Theropoda
            Tetanurae
              Coelurosauria
                Oviraptorosauria

DEINONYCHUS

Meaning: 'terrible claw' **Pronunciation:** die-NON-e-kus

The 1964 discovery of the bird-like theropod *Deinonychus* was a revolutionary moment in palaeontology. Up until this point dinosaurs were dismissed as stupid, sluggish, evolutionary failures whose primitive lifestyles doomed them to extinction. But John Ostrom's description of *Deinonychus* caused a titanic shift in how scientists viewed dinosaurs. This animal was no dim-witted plodder, but an agile, energetic predator that terrorized its ecosystem. It was also remarkably similar to birds, and helped resurrect Huxley's forgotten ideas of a dinosaur-bird evolutionary linkage (see page 90).

Deinonychus is a member of the dromaeosaur lineage, and in many ways is the quintessential 'raptor'. It was a midsized animal, measuring about 10 ft (3 m) in length but weighing a lithe 176–220 lb (80–100 kg). The skeleton was fine-tuned for predation and speed. The streamlined skull was light and strong, and filled with a battery of razor-like teeth. Compared to other dinosaurs *Deinonychus* was intelligent and keen. The brain was massive and the eyes were large, both perfect weapons for outsensing and outsmarting prey.

But the skull was only the first of this raptor's arsenal of weapons. The forelimb was longer than in most other theropods and all three fingers were crowned with menacing claws. An incredibly mobile shoulder joint allowed the arm to swing in a wide arc, an ideal technique for slashing and grasping prey. The tail was long, stiffened and stuck out straight. This would have helped increase balance and agility. The long, slender hindlimbs sported an enormous, sharp claw on the second toe that could not only slash flesh, but also enabled *Deinonychus* to grasp the sides of its prey in a deadly embrace.

Fossils of *Deinonychus* are known from Early Cretaceous rocks in the western United States. Many of these, especially shed teeth, are found alongside the herbivorous ornithischian *Tenontosaurus*. It is possible that *Deinonychus* hunted in packs, which enabled it to take down the much larger *Tenontosaurus*. Many scientists speculate that swarms of *Deinonychus* would attack by leaping through the air, latching onto the flanks of *Tenontosaurus* with their claws and then ripping their prey to death. This was not a nightmare or a movie, but reality on the American plains of 110 million years ago.

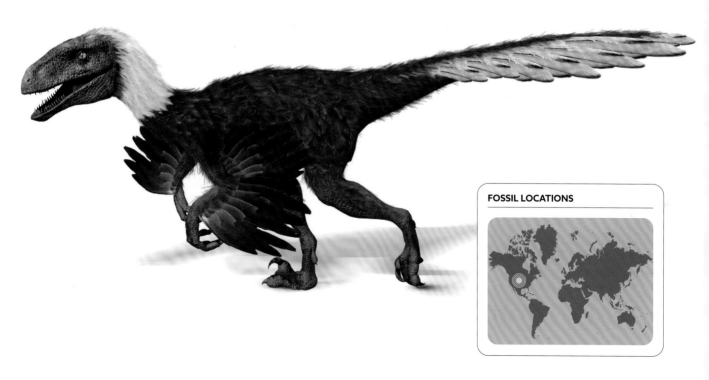

FOSSIL LOCATIONS

STATISTICS

Habitat:	North America (USA)
Period:	Early Cretaceous
Length:	10–11 ft (3–3.5 m)
Height:	36–42 in (1 m)
Weight:	176–220 lb (80–100 kg)
Predators:	None
Food:	Herbivorous dinosaurs

CLASSIFICATION

Animalia
  Chordata
    Sauropsida
      Archosauria
        Dinosauria
          Theropoda
            Tetanurae
              Coelurosauria
                Dromaeosauridae

SIZE COMPARISON

UTAHRAPTOR

Meaning: 'thief from Utah' **Pronunciation:** you-taw-rap-TOR

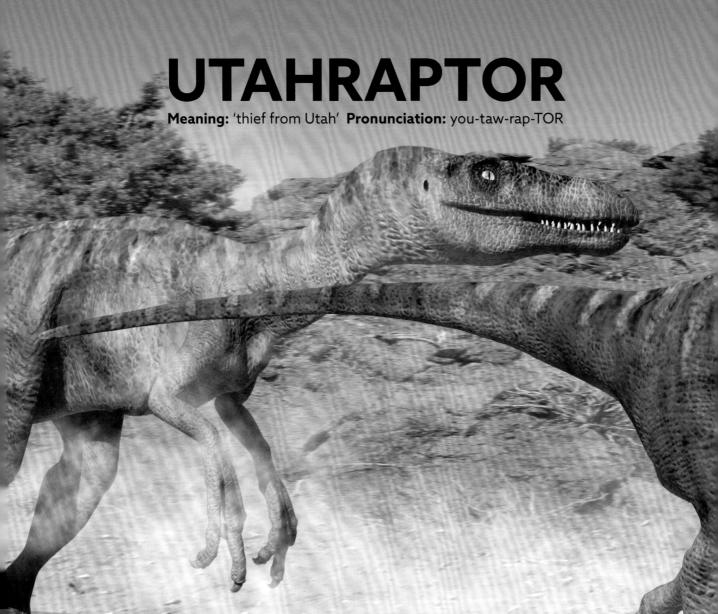

The Early Cretaceous theropod *Utahraptor* was like a monster out of a bad dream. It was a dromaeosaurid, a member of the same group of agile, intelligent, claw-slashing 'raptors' as *Deinonychus*. However, while *Deinonychus* was a modest-sized predator *Utahraptor* was a giant. It was more than double the size of its close cousin, and is the largest member of this bird-like group ever discovered.

Utahraptor has all of the classic dromaeosaurid hunting weapons: a large, sickle claw on the second digit of the foot, a slender hindlimb adapted for speed, a stiffened tail used for balance and razor-like teeth for dismembering prey. This mega predator probably hunted in a similar fashion as *Deinonychus*, only on a much grander scale. A pack of *Allosaurus*-sized raptors is a mind-numbing thought, but would have been everyday reality for the herbivorous dinosaurs that lived alongside *Utahraptor* 125 million years ago. These include brachiosaurid sauropods like *Cedarosaurus*, iguanodontid ornithopods like *Planicoxa* and ankylosaurs like *Gastonia*.

Utahraptor lived several million years before *Deinonychus*, indicating that raptors terrorized the Cretaceous world of North America for tens of millions of years. Dromaeosaurs were also remarkably diverse worldwide, and continued to rule ecosystems everywhere from Asia to South America late into the Cretaceous.

Both the gigantic *Utahraptor* and the minuscule *Microraptor* from China are among the oldest dromaeosaurids. However, they are not particularly closely related: *Microraptor* is regarded as a very primitive form and *Utahraptor* as a much more advanced species. Scientists believe that dromaeosaurs first evolved as very small animals, and only later in their history erupted into giants.

FOSSIL LOCATIONS

STATISTICS

Habitat:	North America (USA)
Period:	Early Cretaceous
Length:	20–23 ft (6–7 m)
Height:	6 ft (1.8 m)
Weight:	1540–1875 lb (700–850 kg)
Predators:	None
Food:	Herbivorous dinosaurs

CLASSIFICATION

Animalia
  Chordata
    Sauropsida
      Archosauria
        Dinosauria
          Theropoda
            Tetanurae
              Coelurosauria
                Dromaeosauridae

SIZE COMPARISON

AMARGASAURUS

Meaning: named after its discovery site in Argentina   **Pronunciation:** ah-mar-ga-SORE-uss

STATISTICS

Habitat:	South America (Argentina)
Period:	Early Cretaceous
Length:	26–30 ft (8–9 m)
Height:	10–12 ft (3–3.7 m)
Weight:	3–4.7 tons
Predators:	Theropod dinosaurs
Food:	Plants

CLASSIFICATION

Animalia
  Chordata
    Sauropsida
      Archosauria
        Dinosauria
          Sauropodomorpha
            Sauropoda
              Diplodocoidea

SIZE COMPARISON

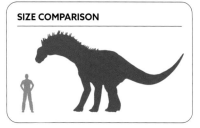

The Argentine *Amargasaurus* did not look like an average sauropod. For starters, it was substantially smaller than most of the long-necked behemoths in the group. While close relatives *Apatosaurus* and *Diplodocus* were growing to nearly 100 ft (30 m) in length, *Amargasaurus* was limited to about 30 ft (9 m). But more noticeably, the neck and back of *Amargasaurus* were shielded with a fantastic array of long, twig-like spines. No other theropod had such prominent ornamentation.

Amargasaurus is known from a single incomplete skeleton, which was discovered by oil geologist Luis Cazau near the town of La Amarga, Argentina. Found in the same 125-million-year-old rock unit were several other long-necked species, but only a single theropod: the tiny, frail *Ligabueino*. At less than 3 ft (1 m) in length *Ligabueino* was no match for even a small sauropod, and it is more likely that *Amargasaurus* was preyed upon by large carcharodontosaurid theropods.

It is possible that the spines of *Amargasaurus* helped to defend it against such predators, but it is more likely that they had a decorative function. Individual spines are too thin and weak to offer any protection, but together they may have supported a broad sail or frill. The spines of the neck are the longest and most complex. Two parallel rows extend across the neck, reaching their greatest height at the midpoint. Each spine curves strongly backwards and is up to three times as tall as the actual vertebra. As the spine row continues backwards, it collapses into a single line of much smaller spines, which means that the sail would have been tallest and most noticeable over the neck, but short over the hips.

Many sauropods had short spikes on top of their vertebrae, but only *Amargasaurus* and very close relatives sported a large sail. The closest relatives of this bizarre sauropod include the Late Jurassic African genus *Dicraeosaurus*, as well as the recently discovered South American *Brachytracelopan*. This new sauropod also comes from the Late Jurassic, suggesting that *Amargasaurus* was a late-surviving relic of an older group of aberrant herbivores.

ARGENTINOSAURUS

Meaning: 'Argentina lizard' **Pronunciation:** ar-jen-TEE-no-sore-uss

FOSSIL LOCATIONS

STATISTICS

Habitat:	South America (Argentina)
Period:	Early–middle Cretaceous
Length:	108–135 ft (33–41 m)
Height:	20–24 ft (6–7.3 m)
Weight:	75–90 tons
Predators:	Theropod dinosaurs
Food:	Plants

Dinosaurs are fascinating for many reasons, but it is their huge size that captures many people's imaginations. The 'terrible lizards' of the Mesozoic were among the largest animals ever to live. And of all of the dinosaurs ever found, the South American sauropod *Argentinosaurus* is probably the largest. This record-holder may have approached lengths of 135 ft (41 m) and weights of 90 tons, making it not only the largest dinosaur, but also the largest-ever land animal.

Argentinosaurus was a hulking, thundering giant that was not only long but also bulky. It was so large that even the contemporary *Giganotosaurus*, one of the biggest theropods ever, had no hope of taking it down. Perhaps large packs of *Giganotosaurus* attacked smaller *Argentinosaurus* individuals, or targeted injured or diseased animals. They must have done, because in a one-on-one fight the mighty *Giganotosaurus* would have been humiliated by this Cretaceous colossus.

Argentinosaurus is known only from a fragmentary set of vertebrae and limb bones. The skull, tail and neck are missing. This makes it very difficult to estimate the size of the animal. However, scientists have been able to compare the fossils of *Argentinosaurus* with close cousins known from entire skeletons. Differences in size between individual bones of *Argentinosaurus* and more complete sauropods can tell scientists approximately how much bigger this Argentine giant was. Some of the largest estimates border on 120–135 ft (37 m) and 80–90 tons, but these are only educated guesses based on very incomplete fossils.

No matter its exact length and weight it is clear that *Argentinosaurus* was a huge animal, as were many of its close cousins. Scientists consider these species to be primitive members of a very important sauropod subgroup, the Titanosauria. This group includes animals like *Saltasaurus* and *Rapetosaurus*, which were very common in the southern continents of Gondwana during the Cretaceous. In fact, they were the primary herbivores in the south at this time. Meanwhile, in the north, sauropods were becoming rare and various ornithischian groups (ornithopods and ceratopsians) would come to dominate ecosystems.

CLASSIFICATION

Animalia
  Chordata
    Sauropsida
      Archosauria
        Dinosauria
          Sauropodomorpha
            Sauropoda
              Titanosauria

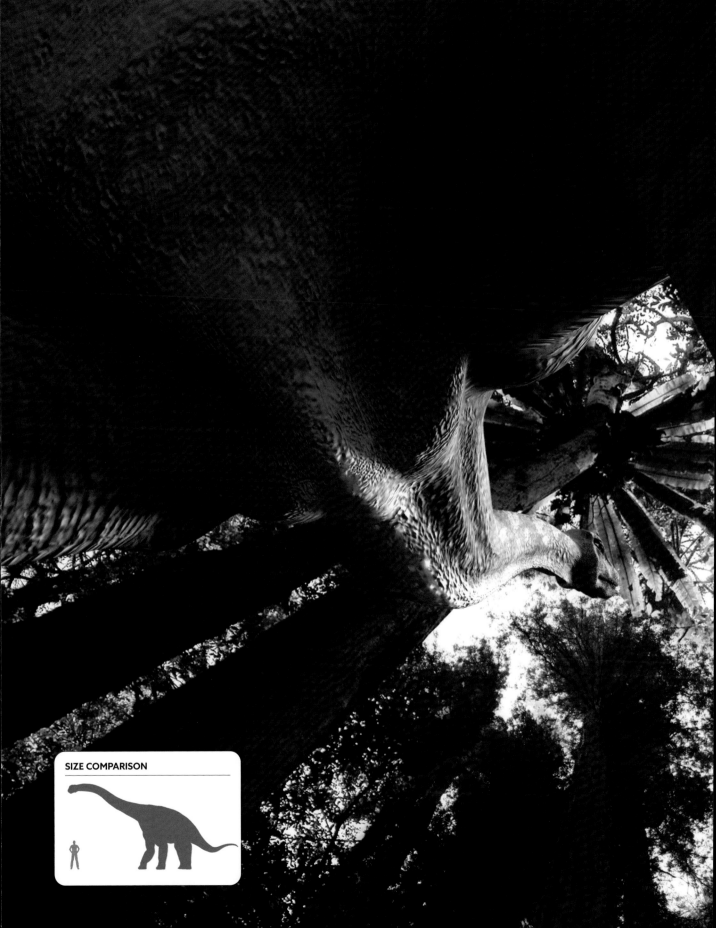

SIZE COMPARISON

GASTONIA

Meaning: named after Rob Gaston **Pronunciation:** gas-TONE-e-uh

The Early Cretaceous landscape of Utah was a dangerous place. The cunning slasher *Utahraptor* needed to eat constantly to fuel its bird-like metabolism and hulking body size. Herbivorous dinosaurs were on the menu, and were relentlessly pursued by packs of raptors. Protection was the only option. These herbivores had to defend themselves, or face the cold reality of nearly a ton of carnivorous power channelled through knife-like claws and razor-blade teeth.

No prey species was as well equipped as *Gastonia*. This herbivore was an early member of the ankylosaurian lineage, a group of heavily armoured, tank-like species that plodded around on four legs. The characteristic body armour of ankylosaurs was a perfect protective device for *Gastonia*. Even the fearsome *Utahraptor* would have had difficulty piercing the thick, bony carapace. But more than likely it would never have had the chance. The neck of *Gastonia* was studded with large, erect spines above the shoulders. These were clearly defensive weapons used to ward off *Utahraptor* and other predators, and thwart attacks long before they turned dangerous.

Gastonia was a mid-sized ankylosaur, averaging about 12 ft (3.7 m) in length. However, like other species it was incredibly bulky, and probably weighed at least two tons. Four or five well-preserved skeletons of this herbivore were discovered side by side, and may indicate that *Gastonia* travelled in small herds.

Scientists disagree about the evolutionary relationships of *Gastonia*. It is definitely an ankylosaurian but more precise relationships are controversial. Some scientists regard it as one of the most primitive members of the subgroup Ankylosauridae, those ankylosaurs with globular tail clubs. Others see similarities with the Late Jurassic *Gargoyleosaurus* and the Early Cretaceous *Polacanthus*, and argue that these species should be classified in their own subgroup, the Polacanthidae. Researchers vigorously debate alternatives. The question may only be solved by finding new fossils.

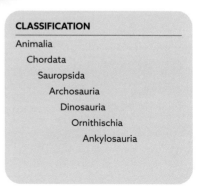

SIZE COMPARISON

FOSSIL LOCATIONS

STATISTICS

Habitat:	North America (USA)
Period:	Early Cretaceous
Length:	8–15 ft (2.5–4.5 m)
Height:	2–4 ft (0.6–1.25 m)
Weight:	1.5–3.7 tons
Predators:	Theropod dinosaurs
Food:	Plants

CLASSIFICATION

Animalia
  Chordata
    Sauropsida
      Archosauria
        Dinosauria
          Ornithischia
            Ankylosauria

SAUROPELTA

Meaning: 'shield lizard' **Pronunciation:** sore-oh-PEL-ta

One of the best-known ankylosaurian dinosaurs is *Sauropelta*, another animal that was well adapted to endure dromaeosaurid attacks. Fossils of *Sauropelta* have been found in Early Cretaceous rocks across the western United States, particularly in Wyoming and Montana. These same rocks are packed with dromaeosaurid fossils, especially the shed teeth of the vicious raptor *Deinonychus*. *Sauropelta* may have been prime prey, but defended itself with a heavy arsenal of spikes, plates and body armour.

Several skeletons of *Sauropelta* have been found, allowing scientists to reconstruct the entire array of body armour. Few other ankylosaurs are understood in such detail. Two rows of domed scutes covered the top of the neck, while the back and tail were sheathed with a random display of keeled plates interspersed with smaller bony ossicles. Over the hips the plates and ossicles fused together into a large, solid shield. This feature gives the animal its name, which means 'shield lizard'.

Along the flanks was an intimidating line of sharp spikes. These were most prominent along the neck, and some individual spikes may have been longer than the neck itself! The entire row projected outwards and upwards – perfect for spearing a leaping *Deinonychus*.

Sauropelta belongs to a subgroup of the ankylosaurian dinosaurs called the Nodosauridae. It is the third major ankylosaur subgroup, along with Ankylosauridae and Polacanthidae. Nodosaurids were characterized by several unique features, such as a rounded protuberance on the top end of the back of the head and fine ornamentation on the front of the snout. They generally had narrower snouts than the ankylosaurids, and also lacked the bulbous tail club of this other subgroup. *Sauropelta* is one of the oldest nodosaurids ever found, and is also one of the best-studied members of the group.

FOSSIL LOCATIONS

STATISTICS

Habitat:	North America (USA)
Period:	Early Cretaceous
Length:	16–26 ft (5–8 m)
Height:	2–5 ft (0.67–1.5 m)
Weight:	2.6–2.8 tons
Predators:	Theropod dinosaurs
Food:	Plants

CLASSIFICATION

Animalia
  Chordata
    Sauropsida
      Archosauria
        Dinosauria
          Ornithischia
            Ankylosauria
              Nodosauridae

SIZE COMPARISON

HYLAEOSAURUS

Meaning: 'forest lizard' **Pronunciation:** hy-lay-e-oh-SORE-uss

When Richard Owen first named the Dinosauria in 1842 he included three fossil saurians in his new group: *Megalosaurus*, *Iguanodon* and *Hylaeosaurus*. The first two animals are instantly recognizable. *Megalosaurus*, a giant carnivorous theropod, was the first dinosaur ever named. *Iguanodon*, a large ornithopod, was one of the first dinosaurs ever found and had been the subject of heated debate for nearly 200 years. *Hylaeosaurus* is the forgotten sibling of the trio, a poorly understood species doomed to obscurity because it is known from so few fossil remains. Only two decent specimens of *Hylaeosaurus* have been discovered, neither of which is very impressive. However, these are enough to show that *Hylaeosaurus* was an ankylosaur, a heavily armoured, quadrupedal herbivore. As such, it was the first armoured dinosaur ever discovered.

The first fossil of *Hylaeosaurus* was found in 1832 in the Tilgate Forest of West Sussex, deep in the southeastern corner of England. This scrappy specimen, which is mostly comprised of armour plates, was studied by pioneering palaeontologist

Gideon Mantell and named one year later. The 'forest lizard' had an interesting array of armour. Spikes lined the side of the neck and hips and rows of bony plates coated the back. It was clearly different from any large reptile that had ever been found. Two decades later, in 1853, a life-sized model of *Hylaeosaurus* was included in the famous Crystal Palace exhibit in London. It was the first armoured dinosaur ever exhibited, and helped to form the public perception of dinosaurs as strange, reptilian monsters.

SIZE COMPARISON

FOSSIL LOCATIONS

STATISTICS

Habitat:	Europe (England)
Period:	Early Cretaceous
Length:	10–20 ft (3–6 m)
Height:	2–3 ft (0.67–1 m)
Weight:	1985–2425 lb (900–1100 kg)
Predators:	Theropod dinosaurs
Food:	Plants

CLASSIFICATION

Animalia
  Chordata
    Sauropsida
      Archosauria
        Dinosauria
          Ornithischia
            Ankylosauria

MINMI

Meaning: named for a crossing near its discovery site in Australia **Pronunciation:** min-ME

Dinosaur fossils are rare in Australia, and most species are known only from a few scrappy specimens. However, the ankylosaur *Minmi* is amazingly common. At least five nearly complete skeletons are known, along with a truckload of more fragmentary fossils. This bounty of material makes *Minmi* the best-known Australian dinosaur, and also the most complete and well-studied ankylosaur from anywhere in the southern hemisphere.

Minmi is one of the smallest ankylosaurs that ever lived, measuring approximately 10 ft (3 m) in length and weighing only a few hundred kilograms. The skull was less than 10 in (25 cm) long, and held rows of leaf-shaped teeth perfect for shearing plants. The legs were long for an ankylosaur, but *Minmi* nevertheless moved at a sluggish pace. It didn't matter if predators could catch this herbivore, because the thick body armour provided a theropod-proof protective shell.

The armour of *Minmi* was different from that of other ankylosaurs. In most species the skull is heavily fused and roofed with a coat of bony plates, but *Minmi* had little cranial armour. On the main body, most of the armour consisted of small, oval plates that formed several long rows along the animal's back. This gave *Minmi* the appearance of a giant, reptilian hedgehog! The plates are broad and flat around the neck but get progressively smaller before turning into sharp spikes over the hind legs and tail.

SIZE COMPARISON

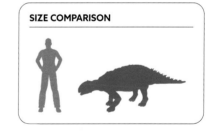

FOSSIL LOCATIONS

STATISTICS

Habitat:	Australia
Period:	Early Cretaceous
Length:	10 ft (3 m)
Height:	2–3 ft (0.67–1 m)
Weight:	440–463 lb (200–210 kg)
Predators:	Theropod dinosaurs
Food:	Plants

CLASSIFICATION

Animalia
  Chordata
    Sauropsida
      Archosauria
        Dinosauria
          Ornithischia
            Ankylosauria

IGUANODON

Meaning: 'iguana tooth' **Pronunciation:** ig-WAN-oh-don

Iguanodon holds a cherished place in the history of palaeontology. This large herbivore was one of the first dinosaurs to be discovered, the second dinosaur ever named and one of the first Mesozoic giants known from complete skeletons. But most importantly, *Iguanodon* was the first dinosaur to be recognized for what it really was: a giant, extinct, reptilian creature unlike anything that is alive today.

Iguanodon was discovered two decades before the name 'dinosaur' was even invented. The story of its discovery has reached legendary status, an historical mystery that is little more than palaeontological gossip. The standard tale has Mary Ann Mantell, the wife of country doctor Gideon Mantell, uncovering a strange leaf-like tooth while killing time as her husband visited a patient in 1822. It is equally likely that Gideon Mantell bought the teeth, or that they were donated to him.

But no matter how they came to light, these mysterious teeth obsessed Mantell. He probed museums and zoos in a desperate search for something similar. After several years, at the Royal College of Surgeons in London, Mantell saw the skeleton of an iguana and noticed the uncanny resemblance. His tooth must have come from an ancient, iguana-like monster. He named this new beast *Iguanodon*, or 'iguana tooth', in 1825, shortly after Buckland named *Megalosaurus*. Both would turn out to be 'dinosaurs', members of a bizarre group of 'terrible lizards' that ruled the Mesozoic.

Today *Iguanodon* is not merely the answer to a trivia question, but also one of the best-known dinosaurs. Its fossils are common not only across England, but also Europe and even North America. Complete skeletons are normal discoveries. At one site, in Belgium, coal miners came across nearly 40 different skeletons some 1000 ft (300 m) below the earth's surface. Few other dinosaurs are known from this abundance of fossils.

Iguanodon clearly was the dominant mid- to large-sized herbivore in its Early Cretaceous ecosystems. Its horse-like skull was long and narrow, with a large beak at the front for cropping vegetation and rows of leaf-shaped teeth for chewing. Approaching sizes of 36 ft (11 m) and six tons, *Iguanodon* was larger than some sauropods, and must have been a plant-guzzling machine. It probably walked on two legs much of the time, but the forelimbs were long and strong, and capped with blunt hooves, so it occasionally stood and even galloped on all fours. The first finger ended in a robust spike that was useful for warding off predators. The thumb could oppose the other digits, giving the hand a grasping function. This multi-purposed hand – useful for walking, weight support, protection and food gathering – is unlike that of any other dinosaur.

FOSSIL LOCATIONS

STATISTICS

Habitat:	Europe (Belgium, England, France, Germany, Spain), North America (USA)
Period:	Early Cretaceous
Length:	20–36 ft (6–11 m)
Height:	6–11 ft (1.8–3.3 m)
Weight:	3–6 tons
Predators:	Theropod dinosaurs
Food:	Plants

CLASSIFICATION

Animalia
   Chordata
      Sauropsida
         Archosauria
            Dinosauria
               Ornithischia
                  Ornithopoda

SIZE COMPARISON

OURANOSAURUS

Meaning: 'brave lizard' **Pronunciation:** oo-ran-o-SORE-uss

Few places conjure up such awe and wonder as Africa's Sahara Desert – thousands of miles of sand, punctuated by rare oases and populated by colourful bands of nomads. The Sahara has earned its reputation as one of the most inhospitable regions on the planet, but it is also one of the most productive dinosaur graveyards known. Despite the dizzying temperatures, choking sandstorms and scarcity of water, scientists have flocked to this desert for nearly half a century in the hopes of prying prize dinosaur fossils from Early Cretaceous rocks.

One of the most bizarre Saharan dinosaurs is *Ouranosaurus*, a close cousin of *Iguanodon*. Like its more famous relative, *Ouranosaurus* had a long and narrow skull with a beak and leaf-shaped teeth for chewing plants. It could probably walk on all fours, and had a spike on its thumb for warding off predators. Unlike *Iguanodon*, however, there was a knob-like bump on top of the skull in front of the eye. This may have supported a small keratin horn as in modern giraffes.

The most remarkable features of *Ouranosaurus* were the dorsal vertebrae, which expand into long, thin spines, some of which approach 3 ft (1 m) in length! These are tallest over the middle of the back and shortest over the pelvis. They also continue on the tail vertebrae and gradually become shorter towards the end of the tail. Together they may have formed a sail, or perhaps even a hump like in modern bison. If it was a hump, perhaps it helped to store water or fat. This is useful in desert-living camels, which can tap into these stored resources during dry periods.

The first remains of *Ouranosaurus* were discovered in the early 1960s by geologists from the French Atomic Energy Commission, whose primary goal was to search for uranium in Niger. After realizing what they had found, the Commission recruited a young palaeontologist named Philippe Taquet to study their fossils. Taquet travelled to Niger, where he proceeded to discover several well-preserved specimens.

Over the next several years Taquet continued to lead expeditions to the Sahara, and today he is considered one of the most successful field palaeontologists in history.

HYPSILOPHODON

Meaning: 'high-crested tooth' **Pronunciation:** hip-SILL-oh-pho-don

In the years after Mantell's discovery of *Iguanodon*, fossils of similar Early Cretaceous herbivores began surfacing all across England. Most of these did indeed belong to *Iguanodon*, and helped to make this giant herbivore one of the best-known dinosaurs. However, some specimens belonged to a much smaller animal. Mantell noted many resemblances to *Iguanodon*, such as a similar beak and teeth, and so he regarded them as juveniles. But some features were harder to explain. The skull was deeper, and its solid construction seemed strange for a young animal.

William Fox saw only one possible explanation: these smaller herbivores were members of a different species. Fox was a clergyman on the Isle of Wight, off the southern coast of England, but he spent most of his time away from his parish collecting fossils. Fox was no scientist, however, and he had little interest in describing fossils. Instead he begged Richard

Owen to name the new species, but the eminent anatomist passed. It was only several years later, in 1870, that equally eminent scientist Thomas Henry Huxley resurrected Fox's idea.

Huxley named this new dinosaur *Hypsilophodon*. It was a very small animal, slightly larger than a man in size but weighing only as much as a small child. *Hypsilophodon* was clearly a herbivore, and early scientists suggested that it lived and fed in the trees. Later studies, however, showed that it was a two-legged animal that was strongly adapted for running. Speed was a necessity for a small, unarmoured herbivore on the Isle of Wight, as it was infested with large predators like *Neovenator* and *Eotyrannus*. It is even possible that *Hypsilophodon* travelled in herds for protection, although this has not been demonstrated by clear fossil evidence.

SIZE COMPARISON

FOSSIL LOCATIONS

STATISTICS

Habitat:	Europe (England, Spain)
Period:	Early Cretaceous
Length:	6.5–8 ft (2–2.5 m)
Height:	24–30 in (60–75 cm)
Weight:	55–61 lb (25–28 kg)
Predators:	Theropod dinosaurs
Food:	Plants

CLASSIFICATION

Animalia
  Chordata
    Sauropsida
      Archosauria
        Dinosauria
          Ornithischia
            Ornithopoda

TENONTOSAURUS

Meaning: 'sinew lizard' **Pronunciation:** ten-on-toe-SORE-uss

Tenontosaurus was the most common plant-eating species in the Early Cretaceous ecosystems of the western United States. A mid-to-large-sized herbivore, it was the equivalent of a Cretaceous cow, an animal so common that its fossils are found in bunches. And just as humans lick their lips over a nice steak, *Deinonychus* must have salivated over *Tenontosaurus*. The sheer number of these animals made them the perfect prey. Today, teeth of these raptors are commonly found near *Tenontosaurus* fossils – a Cretaceous crime scene preserved in stone for 125 million years.

The predator–prey struggle between *Deinonychus* and *Tenontosaurus* is one of the most familiar tales of dinosaur palaeontology, frequently retold in children's books. However, *Deinonychus* is always the celebrity, while *Tenontosaurus* appears in a supporting role.

But *Tenontosaurus* was a fascinating and successful creature in its own right. Despite being relentlessly pursued by *Deinonychus*, it managed to thrive and dominate ecosystems.

The first fossils of *Tenontosaurus* were found by legendary fossil hunter Barnum Brown in Montana. The genus was later named by the equally legendary John Ostrom. More recently, several excellent fossils were found by seven-year-old Thad Williams while he was taking a walk with his father in Texas. These were named a new species.

Scientists recognize *Tenontosaurus* as a close cousin to *Hypsilophodon* and *Thescelosaurus*, and a more distant relative of *Iguanodon*. *Tenontosaurus* was a keystone herbivore well adapted to feeding on huge quantities of plants, and immediately distinguished from other ornithopods by its elongated, snake-like tail.

SIZE COMPARISON

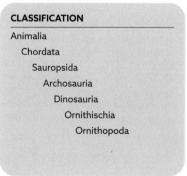

FOSSIL LOCATIONS

STATISTICS

Habitat:	North America (USA)
Period:	Early Cretaceous
Length:	23–26 ft (7–8 m)
Height:	5.5–6.5 ft (1.7–2 m)
Weight:	2200–2425 lb (1000–1100 kg)
Predators:	Theropod dinosaurs
Food:	Plants

CLASSIFICATION

Animalia
  Chordata
    Sauropsida
      Archosauria
        Dinosauria
          Ornithischia
            Ornithopoda

LEAELLYNASAURA

Meaning: named after Leaellyn Rich **Pronunciation:** lay-ell-in-uh-SORE-uh

Along the cold and misty coast of southeastern Australia is a set of secluded cliffs, which are constantly pounded by strong wind and waves. This is Dinosaur Cove, an area only accessible to scientists with helicopters and boats. Although it abounds with 100-million-year-old dinosaur fossils, excavating them isn't easy. Scientists have to use dynamite and heavy industrial machinery to pry fossils from the exceptionally hard rocks.

For years the husband-and-wife team, Tom Rich and Patricia Vickers-Rich, have painstakingly worked at Dinosaur Cove, and their Herculean efforts have paid off. Many of Australia's most important dinosaur discoveries come from this tiny speck of land, including a bizarre little herbivore that the Riches named after their daughter. This is *Leaellynasaura*, Leaellyn Rich's very own dinosaur species.

At first glance *Leaellynasaura* does not look very impressive. It was only a few feet long and weighed only slightly more than an infant human. It had no tank-like body armour, no spines and no large teeth. The most spectacular features of this dinosaur are much more subtle: the eyes of *Leaellynasaura* were enormous, and the brain had vastly enlarged optic lobes (the region that controlled sight). These combined to give *Leaellynasaura* a keen sense of sight – a very necessary adaptation to its environment. At the time this dinosaur lived, Australia was located far southwards, within the Antarctic Circle. Much of the year was cold and dark, so for any animal to thrive it needed good vision.

SIZE COMPARISON

FOSSIL LOCATIONS

STATISTICS

Habitat:	Australia
Period:	Early-middle Cretaceous
Length:	38–77 in (1–2 m)
Height:	1–3 ft (0.3–1 m)
Weight:	15–36 lb (7–16 kg)
Predators:	Theropod dinosaurs
Food:	Plants

CLASSIFICATION

Animalia
  Chordata
    Sauropsida
      Archosauria
        Dinosauria
          Ornithischia
            Ornithopoda

MUTTABURRASAURUS

Meaning: named after its discovery site in Australia
Pronunciation: mutt-a-burr-a-SORE-uss

Muttaburrasaurus is one of Australia's best-known dinosaurs. Only the ankylosaur *Minmi* is known from more complete fossils. *Muttaburrasaurus* closely resembled *Iguanodon* in nearly every aspect of its anatomy. Both were large herbivores with long, narrow skulls and leaf-shaped teeth that devoured foliage. Both walked upright but could switch to all fours if need be. And both possessed a hand that was useful for walking and grasping plants, but also had a heavy thumb spike for self-defence.

The most noticeable differences between these two mega herbivores have to do with size and skull shape. *Muttaburrasaurus* was slightly smaller than its better-known cousin, and it had a distinctive skull with a hollow, arched skull roof above the snout and a bony bump between the nostrils. These odd features, especially the hollow vaulted skull, may have been used to make sound for communication with other members of the species.

The first remains of *Muttaburrasaurus* were found in 1963 in the state of Queensland. These were named in honour of a local town in 1981.

In 1987, 14-year-old fossil hunter Robert Walker helped to discover a well-preserved skull.

SIZE COMPARISON

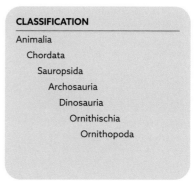

FOSSIL LOCATIONS

STATISTICS

Habitat:	Australia
Period:	Early–middle Cretaceous
Length:	23–25 ft (7–7.5 m)
Height:	7–7.5 ft (2.2 m)
Weight:	1.7–1.9 tons
Predators:	Theropod dinosaurs
Food:	Plants

CLASSIFICATION

Animalia
  Chordata
    Sauropsida
      Archosauria
        Dinosauria
          Ornithischia
            Ornithopoda

			Hettangian 199.6 – 196.5 MYA	Aalenian 175.6 – 171.6 MYA	
		Carnian 228.7 – 216.5 MYA	Sinemurian 196.5 – 189.6 MYA	Bajocian 171.6 – 167.7 MYA	Oxfordian 161.2 – 155.6 MYA
Induan 251.0 – 249.5 MYA	Anisian 245.9 – 237.0 MYA	Norian 216.5 – 203.6 MYA	Pliensbachian 189.6 – 183.0 MYA	Bathonian 167.7 – 164.7 MYA	Kimmeridgian 155.6 – 150.8 MYA
Olenekian 249.5 – 245.9 MYA	Ladinian 237.0 – 228.7 MYA	Rhaetian 203.6 – 199.6 MYA	Toarcian 183.0 – 175.6 MYA	Callovian 164.7 – 161.2 MYA	Tithonian 150.8 – 145.5 MYA

| EARLY TRIASSIC
251.0 – 245.9 MYA | MIDDLE TRIASSIC
245.9 – 228.7 MYA | LATE TRIASSIC 228.7
– 199.6 MYA | EARLY JURASSIC
199.6 – 175.6 MYA | MIDDLE JURASSIC
175.6 – 161.2 MYA | LATE JURASSIC
161.2 – 145.5 MYA |

TRIASSIC 251.0 – 199.6 MYA   **JURASSIC 199.6 – 145.5 MYA**

Dinosaurs of the Late Cretaceous

Berriasian 145.5 – 140.2 MYA

Valanginian 140.2 – 133.9 MYA

Hauterivian 133.9 – 130.0 MYA

Barremian 130.0 – 125.0 MYA

Aptian 125.0 – 112.0 MYA

Albian 112.0 – 99.6 MYA

Cenomanian 99.6 – 93.6 MYA

Turonian 93.6 – 88.6 MYA

Coniacian 88.6 – 85.8 MYA

Santonian 85.8 – 83.5 MYA

Campanian 83.5 – 70.6 MYA

Maastrichtian 70.6 – 65.5 MYA

EARLY-MIDDLE CRETACEOUS
145.5 – 99.6 MYA

LATE CRETACEOUS
99.6 – 65.5 MYA

The Final Act of the Dinosaurs

The Late Cretaceous was the heyday of the dinosaurs, the peak of their evolutionary success. At no other time were dinosaurs so diverse or in such complete control of ecosystems across the planet. The Cretaceous world – hot, wet and teeming with newly evolved flowering plants – was the perfect backdrop for the final act in a rich and complex drama that rivalled the best that Hollywood and Broadway have to offer.

By this time each separate continent had its own unique communities, the product of millions of years of isolation after the breakup of the supercontinent Pangaea. In many ways, the dinosaurs of the Late Cretaceous were similar to the mammals of today. They dominated all of the major ecological roles, were spread around the world, had evolved into a diverse array of body forms and made up complex, intricate communities that differed on each continent.

Many of the dinosaurs most familiar to us flourished during the Late Cretaceous. In the area that is now the Gobi Desert of Mongolia lived a stunning menagerie of species, ranging from sleek, ferocious hunters (*Velociraptor*) to bizarre bird-like theropods (*Oviraptor*) and vast herds of herbivorous ceratopsians (*Protoceratops*). Today's fossil hunters find all these species entombed in ancient sand dunes. Slightly later rocks from the same region show a somewhat different ecosystem, this one dominated by giant tyrannosaurid predators (*Tarbosaurus*), enormous hadrosaurid herbivores (*Saurolophus*), a supporting cast of aberrant theropods (*Gallimimus*) and rare sauropods similar to older Jurassic species (*Nemegtosaurus*).

In the ecosystems of the southern continents entirely different kinds of dinosaurs filled the same ecological niches. Instead of tyrannosaurids there were peculiar, short-armed abelisaurid theropods like *Carnotaurus* and *Majungasaurus*. Instead of small dromaeosaurs there were equally sleek noasaurids, such as *Masiakasaurus*. And, in the place of flocks of hadrosaurids and ceratopsians there was a diverse collection of sauropods that included the massive, armoured titanosaurs.

The best studied of all these ecosystems is the Hell Creek community of the western United States. Much of the great, sprawling prairie of Montana, South Dakota and North Dakota is underlain by a thick sequence of muddy and sandy rocks, which were deposited on vast floodplains during the waning days of the Cretaceous. These rocks, which date to about 67–65 million years ago, record the last great community of dinosaurs to exist on earth, an ecosystem dominated by such familiar faces as *Tyrannosaurus*, *Triceratops*, *Edmontosaurus*, *Ankylosaurus* and *Pachycephalosaurus*.

These Hell Creek species, among the most recognizable and popular dinosaurs of all, would have been witness to the great, fiery asteroid that pummelled the earth 65 million years ago. They would have choked in the cloud of dust thrown up by the impact, been scalded and incinerated by the global wildfires that followed, and swept out to sea by tsunamis as tall as ten-storey buildings. They were the last of their kind, wiped out by a sudden and catastrophic event with no forewarning. Up until this fateful moment, an explosive instant when earth's history changed forever, the dinosaurs had been continuing to evolve and diversify as if nothing would ever go wrong.

The 160-million-year reign of the dinosaurs was violently terminated by the impact of a large asteroid or comet 65 million years ago. This visitor from outer space hit the Yucatan Peninsula of Mexico, and immediately caused monstrous tsunamis, global wildfires and scalding acid rain.

CARNOTAURUS

Meaning: 'carnivorous bull' **Pronunciation:** car-no-TORE-uss

While *Tyrannosaurus* and its kin were terrorizing the northern hemisphere, a group of mega predators ruled supreme in the southern continents. These were the abelisaurids, a late-surviving offshoot of the primitive ceratosaurian lineage. The 'horned bull' *Carnotaurus* is the best known of these large theropods.

Carnotaurus lived during the Late Cretaceous in what is now Argentina. It was about the same size as *Allosaurus* and *Ceratosaurus*, but smaller than *Tyrannosaurus* and the carcharodontosaurids. The skull of *Carnotaurus* was truly strange: it was short and deep, covered with very rough bone texture and sported two large horns over the eyes. These horns were probably a display structure, but may have been used to headbutt prey. The rough bone texture is unique, and may indicate that much of the skull was covered in keratin, the same hard structure that comprises fingernails and hair.

The rest of the skeleton is equally strange. The hindlimbs are thin and elongated, and look particularly large in relation to the minuscule forelimbs. No other dinosaur has such pathetically short arms. They measure less than 2 ft (0.5 m) in length, a ridiculous size for an animal that was 30 ft (9 m) long and weighed over two tons. However, these short forelimbs are robust, covered with large scars, which indicates large muscles, and could move in nearly any direction. They must have been used for something – perhaps for holding food close to the body or to clutch a partner during mating – but what? Scientists are unsure of the answer.

Carnotaurus is only one of numerous abelisaurid theropods that have been found on the southern continents over the past few decades. Some species, such as *Aucasaurus*, have been discovered near *Carnotaurus* in South America. Others have come to light in Africa (*Rugops*), Madagascar (*Majungasaurus*) and India (*Rajasaurus*).

A few may have even migrated from the southern continents into Europe, a journey made possible by land bridges between the two landmasses. However, these predators are completely unknown in North America and Asia.

FOSSIL LOCATIONS

STATISTICS

Habitat:	South America (Argentina)
Period:	Late Cretaceous
Length:	23–30 ft (7–9 m)
Height:	9.5–12 ft (3–3.75 m)
Weight:	2.1–2.3 tons
Predators:	None
Food:	Sauropod and ornithischian dinosaurs

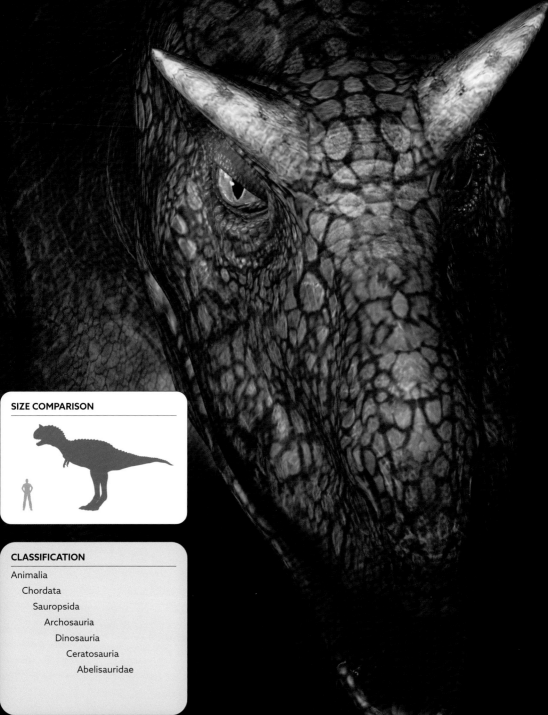

MAJUNGASAURUS

Meaning: named after a province in Madagascar **Pronunciation:** mah-jung-a-SORE-uss

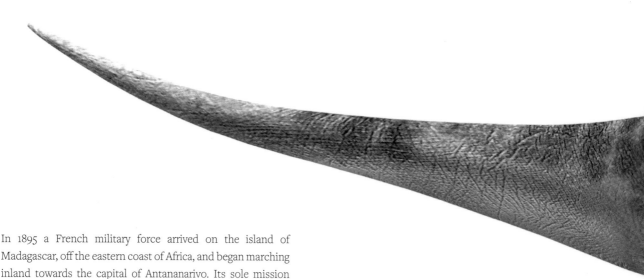

In 1895 a French military force arrived on the island of Madagascar, off the eastern coast of Africa, and began marching inland towards the capital of Antananarivo. Its sole mission was to take control of the island, which had long been caught in an imperialistic tug-of-war between Britain and France. But military physician Félix Salètes had other goals. He knew that their landing spot, the western coastal province of Majunga, was covered in Mesozoic rocks that had been little explored, so he dispatched an assistant to look for fossils, in the hope of finding Madagascar's first dinosaurs.

Salètes' hunch was correct; his assistant uncovered numerous fossils. They were sent to legendary French palaeontologist Charles Deperét. He described some of them – several teeth and vertebrae – as belonging to a new theropod, *Majungasaurus*. For years this predator was poorly known, but several recent American–Malagasy expeditions have uncovered a wealth of new fossils. These show *Majungasaurus* to be a large abelisaurid theropod, a close cousin to *Carnotaurus* and a member of a southern radiation of giant, primitive theropods.

Majungasaurus was very similar to other abelisaurids in many features of the skeleton: the skull was short and deep, with several small teeth and heavily textured bones, and the forelimbs were short. The neck was strong, due to robust and heavily fused vertebrae reinforced with ossified tendons for extra rigidity. However, *Majungasaurus* was unique in its possession of a dome-like horn on the top of its skull. For a long while isolated skull bones were thought to belong to the dome-headed pachycephalosaurs. One specimen was even given a new name – *Majungatholus* – but today this is recognized to be *Majungasaurus*.

Majungasaurus was clearly the apex predator in its ecosystem. The deep skull, strong neck and arsenal of small but sharp teeth would have been ideally suited to taking down large sauropods like *Rapetosaurus*. However, recent discoveries indicate a more disturbing predatory habit: cannibalism. Several isolated *Majungasaurus* bones have been found with bite marks that only match the teeth of the same species. This is the only clear evidence for cannibalism in dinosaurs that has ever been found.

FOSSIL LOCATIONS

STATISTICS

Habitat:	Madagascar
Period:	Late Cretaceous
Length:	23–30 ft (7–9 m)
Height:	9.5–12 ft (3–3.75 m)
Weight:	2.1–2.3 tons
Predators:	None
Food:	Sauropod and ornithischian dinosaurs

CLASSIFICATION

Animalia
  Chordata
    Sauropsida
      Archosauria
        Dinosauria
          Ceratosauria
            Abelisauridae

SIZE COMPARISON

New Research on the Tyrant Lizard King

Fossils of *Tyrannosaurus* have been known for over 100 years. More than 30 specimens have been discovered from across the western United States. These have been carefully studied by scientists, and today *Tyrannosaurus* is one of the best known of all the dinosaurs. But there is still much about this Cretaceous hypercarnivore that remains mysterious. How did it hunt? How fast did it grow and what sizes could it reach? Could it run or did it plod along? Sophisticated new techniques, which would have been unimaginable to the early discoverers of *Tyrannosaurus*, have suggested some answers.

Based on the depth and size of *Tyrannosaurus* bite marks on fossilized *Triceratops* bone, scientists have been able to estimate its bite forces. This research points to a remarkable conclusion: this beast had a bite that was powerful enough to crunch bone. Its bite was stronger than that of any other dinosaur and probably stronger than large living predators, such as crocodiles and lions. But why was the bite so strong? A careful look at *Tyrannosaurus* teeth provides the answer. The massive, banana-sized teeth are marked with deep, broad wear facets. These could only be produced in one way: tooth-on-bone contact. Instead of carefully stripping flesh and muscle from its prey, like any normal predator, *Tyrannosaurus* simply crunched right through the bone.

A more exact analysis of *Tyrannosaurus* feeding has been made possible by advances in computer software.

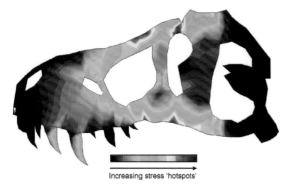

This diagram shows a computerised model of the skull of *Tyrannosaurus rex*. The red and yellow colours show which parts of the skull were thickened to help withstand the high forces of biting into the bones of prey. The model had 13,000 Newtons of force applied, roughly equivalent to 3,000 pounds per square inch. A modern hydraulic car crusher imparts 2,000 pounds per square inch.

Palaeontologists such as Emily Rayfield, of the University of Bristol, have utilized a sophisticated technique called Finite Element Analysis. Engineers use this complex program to test the strength of bridges and roads before they are built. Dr Rayfield has used it to look at how the skull of *Tyrannosaurus* would have reacted to the extreme stresses of bone crunching. It turns out that much of the skull, especially parts of the skull roof, are thickened, fused and strengthened to endure the forces produced by feeding. Numerous skull sutures – those areas where different bones contact – also acted to absorb stresses. The skull of *Tyrannosaurus* was a massive, robust killing machine that was well adapted to handle the heavy stresses of feeding on large prey.

There is no doubt that *Tyrannosaurus* fed on large herbivores like *Edmontosaurus* and *Triceratops*, but did this mega predator chase down its prey or ambush it? The answer depends on whether the 40-ft (12-m) long, seven-ton *Tyrannosaurus* could run, which has has been the subject of intense debate. New research by John Hutchinson and colleagues has reached an interesting conclusion. Based on comparisons with crocodiles and birds, the closest living relatives to dinosaurs, Hutchinson modelled the amount of leg muscle needed for running. It turns out that *Tyrannosaurus* would need more than 5.6 tons of leg muscle – some 80 per cent of its body mass – in order to run. Obviously, this is ludicrous. Hutchinson has followed up this study with computer-based analyses, which use animation software to accurately model how a *Tyrannosaurus* would have moved and how the individual muscles would have worked. These animations confirm his original conclusion: *Tyrannosaurus* was a slow animal that probably couldn't chase down its prey, which means it was more likely to be an ambush hunter.

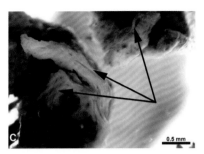

These insignificant looking blobs are actually examples of amazingly preserved soft tissue (blood vessels and red blood cells) found in a 67-million-year old *Tyrannosaurus rex* bone. The discovery of these tissues, which usually decay very rapidly after death, shocked scientists. The vessels, cells and proteins of *Tyrannosaurus* are very similar to those of modern birds.

The numerous fossil skeletons discovered include a wide range of sizes, from colossal 40-ft (12-m) long adults to much smaller juveniles. Gregory Erickson, of Florida State University, and his colleagues have used these fossils to examine how fast *Tyrannosaurus* grew. Erickson cuts dinosaur bones into very thin sections that can be examined under a microscope. This allows him to count growth lines – individual lines in the bone that represent a single year of growth, much like the rings of a tree trunk. These rings have helped Erickson determine that *Tyrannosaurus* grew astronomically fast, reaching adulthood in about 20 years. Juveniles grew at the jaw-dropping rate of nearly 5 lb (2.2 kg) per day, some four times faster than its closest relatives *Daspletosaurus* and *Albertosaurus*. In order to grow this fast *Tyrannosaurus* must have been warm-blooded.

Other palaeontologists have taken a more traditional approach to studying growth. Thomas Carr, of Carthage College, and Thomas Williamson, of the New Mexico Museum of Natural History, have examined nearly every *Tyrannosaurus* fossil ever found. They compare the anatomy of juveniles and adults in order to understand how the skeleton changed throughout life. One of their most important discoveries is that many animals long regarded as separate species, such as *Alioramus* and *Nanotyrannus*, are simply juvenile *Tyrannosaurus*. Juveniles had much longer legs and a more slender build than adults. They could probably run at fast speeds, and may have been pursuit predators instead of ambushers. In any case, they almost certainly fed in a different way than adults.

Some of the most remarkable work on *Tyrannosaurus* has focused on the cellular and molecular makeup of this giant predator. Mary Schweitzer, of North Carolina State University, and her colleagues have intensely studied the microscopic properties of *Tyrannosaurus* bone. They have identified blood vessels, individual blood cells and even minute proteins – all soft tissues that were thought to degrade as an animal fossilizes. The structure of the blood vessels and the chemical composition of the proteins are very similar to those of chickens, and add further support to the dinosaur–bird link. Perhaps most amazing of all, the discovery of proteins opens the door to finding dinosaur DNA. Actually re-creating dinosaurs will always be impossible because any DNA that scientists find is bound to be too fragmentary. However, dinosaur DNA can be used to study the evolution of this group, and perhaps to reveal how they were able to become so successful during the Mesozoic.

A tooth of *Tyrannosaurus rex* The smooth and serrated top of the tooth is the crown – the part that was actually exposed in the mouth. The more roughened bottom part is the root, which would have been implanted in the gums. The crown of a *Tyrannosaurus* tooth was thick and sharp for crushing bone, and the root was long and sturdy to brace the tooth against stresses during feeding.

TYRANNOSAURUS

Meaning: 'tyrant lizard' **Pronunciation:** ty-ran-o-SORE-uss

Tyrannosaurus is the undisputed king of the dinosaur world. This monstrosity of a predator is a true celebrity, the dinosaurian equivalent of a rock star. No other dinosaur is so popular or the subject of such intensive research. Indeed, the imaginations of both children and professional scientists flare at the thought of this seven-ton, 43-ft (13-m) long carnivore that ruled the North American plains during the final years of the Age of Dinosaurs.

Tyrannosaurus translates as 'tyrant lizard', a fitting description for a bone-crunching mega predator. Superlatives are often heaped upon *Tyrannosaurus*, but it is difficult to exaggerate the sheer strength and power of this ultimate dinosaur predator. The skull was enormous, measuring nearly 5 ft (1.5 m) in length. The jaws were chock-full of huge, banana-sized teeth – more than 50 in total. Some of these teeth were over 12 in (30 cm) long – some of the largest teeth ever seen in a predator! The forelimbs were tiny, measuring no more than 3 ft (1 m) long, but they were strong and robust, and were probably used to help subdue and hold prey.

But it wasn't only physical weapons that enabled *Tyrannosaurus* to become the most feared predator in history. The brain was large and well developed, and much bigger than in other large predators, such as carcharodontosaurids. It also had colossal olfactory lobes, the region of the brain that controls smell. In addition, the eyes of *Tyrannosaurus* faced partially forwards, resulting in binocular vision and greater depth perception. This all meant that *Tyrannosaurus* had very keen hunting senses, a further advantage for a carnivore already well endowed with crushing teeth and sharp claws.

Fossils of *Tyrannosaurus* are very common in the Hell Creek Formation, a Late Cretaceous rock unit in the western United States. More than 30 skeletons have been discovered, including many complete fossils. Some of these are found only a few feet below the Cretaceous–Tertiary extinction boundary, which proves that *Tyrannosaurus* was one of the last dinosaurs to live on earth.

Found alongside *Tyrannosaurus* are the fossils of large herbivores, such as the hadrosaurid *Edmontosaurus* and the ceratopsian *Triceratops*. It is certain that these were the favoured prey of the tyrant lizard. Some scientists have dismissed *Tyrannosaurus* as a mere scavenger, a seven-ton collector of dead carcasses that would have never hunted on its own. However, healed bite marks on *Edmontosaurus* and *Triceratops* bones, which prove the prey survived an attack, show that such an idea is nonsense. *Tyrannosaurus* was a hunter, a mega predator more ferocious than anything that has ever lived. But *Tyrannosaurus* was no normal mega predator: new research suggests that this beast may have been adorned with feathers, giving a bird-like appearance to the most terrifying hunter in our planet's history.

(overleaf) Tyrannosaurus rex – the apex predator of the Late Cretaceous period attempts to ambush a herd of hadrosaurs

FOSSIL LOCATIONS

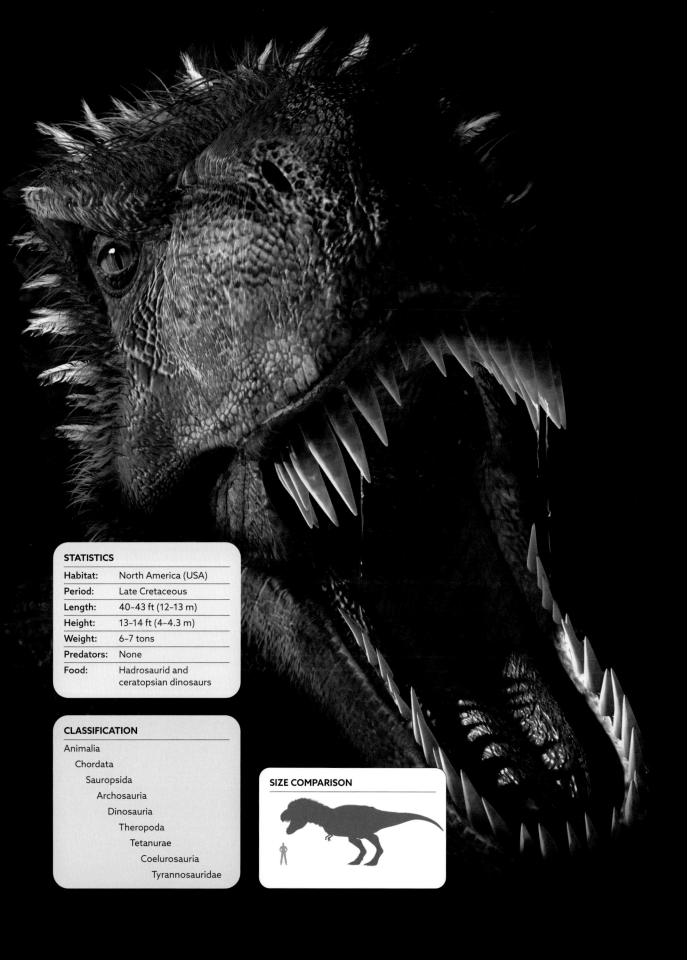

TARBOSAURUS

Meaning: 'alarming lizard' **Pronunciation:** tar-bo-SORE-uss

The Asian counterpart of *Tyrannosaurus* was *Tarbosaurus*: a giant, hypercarnivorous predator that terrorized ecosystems during the Late Cretaceous. *Tarbosaurus* and *Tyrannosaurus* were very close relatives, and some scientists even consider them the same animal. They were both enormous predators that reached lengths of more than 40 ft (12 m) and weights of seven tons, and both ripped apart prey with their strong skulls and foot-long, bone-crunching teeth.

Tarbosaurus is a very common discovery in the Late Cretaceous rocks of Mongolia and China. Only a few specimens have been described in detail, but at least 15 skulls and 30 skeletons have been discovered. In fact, there are more *Tarbosaurus* fossils than *Tyrannosaurus* specimens. Some of the best fossils come from the Nemegt Formation of Mongolia, a rock unit deposited during the final stage of the Cretaceous. Living alongside *Tarbosaurus* were large sauropods like *Nemegtosaurus*, which would have been an ideal prey species.

Tarbosaurus and *Tyrannosaurus* are the largest and most derived, or evolutionarily advanced, of the Late Cretaceous tyrannosauroid theropods. Slightly smaller and older cousins were common during earlier stages of the Cretaceous in North America. These genera included *Albertosaurus*, *Appalachiosaurus*, *Daspletosaurus* and *Gorgosaurus*, which reached lengths of about 25–30 ft (7.5–9 m) and weights of 2–3 tons. Several older, more primitive tyrannosauroids are also known. These animals, such as *Dilong* and *Eotyrannus*, are much smaller, more slender and similar in many ways to compsognathids and ornithomimosaurs.

Dilong, from the Early Cretaceous of China, was only 5 ft (1.5 m) long. It was covered in a dense array of simple, strand-like feathers, proving that some tyrannosauroids had these structures. Whether *Tarbosaurus* or *Tyrannosaurus* had feathers is unknown, but preserved skin impressions indicate that most of the body was covered by scales. Feathers, if present, were probably restricted to certain regions of the body and used solely for display.

SIZE COMPARISON

FOSSIL LOCATIONS

STATISTICS

Habitat:	Asia (China, Mongolia)
Period:	Late Cretaceous
Length:	40–43 ft (12–13 m)
Height:	13–14 ft (4–4.3 m)
Weight:	6–7 tons
Predators:	None
Food:	Hadrosaurid and sauropod dinosaurs

CLASSIFICATION

Animalia
  Chordata
    Sauropsida
      Archosauria
        Dinosauria
          Theropoda
            Tetanurae
              Coelurosauria
                Tyrannosauridae

ALXASAURUS

Meaning: named after tha Alaxa desert **Pronunciation:** al-ksa-SORE-uss

Alxasaurus, from the middle Cretaceous of China, belonged to the therizinosaur group. These tall, pot-bellied dinosaurs looked like a strange combination of a sloth and a turkey. The small, elongated skull seemed minuscule in comparison with the long neck and massive, rotund gut. The elongated hindlimbs supported the entire weight of the animal. The shortened forelimbs were capped with a set of long, wispy claws that reached up to 3ft (1 m) in length!

The therizinosaurs not only looked bizarre, but also possessed a truly peculiar combination of characteristics otherwise seen in very different dinosaur groups. The skull was very similar to that of a sauropod or prosauropod. Fronting the skull was a toothless beak, and filling the jaws were small, leaf-shaped teeth perfect for cropping plants. The foot was broad and contained four columnar digits, much like in sauropods. However, the pubis bone of the pelvis pointed backwards like in ornithischians and bird-like theropods.

It is no surprise that therizinosaurs long confused palaeontologists. The first therizinosaur was discovered in the 1950s and described as an enormous turtle! Later discoveries showed these animals to be dinosaurs, but nobody could agree what kind of dinosaur they represented. Some scientists thought they were prosauropods, others theropods and still others ornithischians. This confusion was finally put to rest in the early 1990s, when the discovery of *Alxasaurus* undoubtedly proved that these animals were theropods. Only theropods had a hand with three digits and a bird-like wrist. Later discoveries showed therizinosaurs to have a very theropod-like brain and even a body covering of feathers.

Alxasaurus was the turning point in this debate, the first therizinosaur known from reasonably complete fossils. Parts of five skeletons were discovered in 1988 in the Alxa Desert of Inner Mongolia, China, during a joint Chinese–Canadian expedition. When *Alxasaurus* was described in 1993, it was the oldest and most primitive therizinosaur. Since then, slightly older specimens have come to light in China and North America. These reinforce the theropod identity of these weird animals, and suggest that therizinosaurs were some of the closest cousins to birds.

FOSSIL LOCATIONS

DROMAEOSAURUS

Meaning: 'running lizard' **Pronunciation:** dro-me-oh-SORE-uss

Barnum Brown was one of the true legends of palaeontology, a swashbuckling man who made a living collecting fossils for the American Museum of Natural History in New York. He was notoriously eccentric, and often excavated fossils in some of the hottest parts of the world while wearing a full-length fur coat. He was apparently an intelligence officer during both World Wars, and picked up spare cash by spying on oil companies.

But fossil hunting is what Brown did best. Most of Brown's early efforts were focused on the Late Cretaceous rocks of Montana, where in 1902 he discovered the first fossils of *Tyrannosaurus*. But after a decade of work there he grew bored, and opened a new frontier of fossil exploration along the Red Deer River in Alberta. For several years he floated down the river on a large boat, stopping whenever his crew spotted fossils. One of his greatest discoveries was made in 1914, in a region that would later become Dinosaur Provincial Park. There he unearthed a skull and fragmentary foot bones that were later named *Dromaeosaurus*.

When *Dromaeosaurus* was discovered very little was known about small theropods. This fossil was the first sign of a major group of small-bodied Cretaceous carnivores, which were called dromaeosaurids in honour of this initial discovery. Today, these 'raptors' are among the best-known dinosaurs. Other members of this group include *Velociraptor*, *Deinonychus* and *Utahraptor*, which were clearly major predators in Cretaceous ecosystems across the globe.

Dromaeosaurus was also a fearsome predator, and would have gutted prey with its sickle-shaped foot claw and devoured flesh with its arsenal of sharp teeth. However, it lived alongside many larger carnivores, such as the tyrannosaurids *Albertosaurus*, *Daspletosaurus* and *Gorgosaurus*. This means that *Dromaeosaurus* must have occupied a different position in the ecosystem. It wasn't the giant apex predator, but rather a smaller, more cunning hunter that chased down prey in the shadow of the tyrannosaurids.

FOSSIL LOCATIONS

STATISTICS

Habitat:	North America (Canada, USA)
Period:	Late Cretaceous
Length:	5–6.5 ft (1.5–2 m)
Height:	18–28 in (46–70 cm)
Weight:	33–77 lb (15–35 kg)
Predators:	Giant theropod dinosaurs
Food:	Herbivorous dinosaurs

SIZE COMPARISON

CLASSIFICATION

Animalia
  Chordata
    Sauropsida
      Archosauria
        Dinosauria
          Theropoda
            Tetanurae
              Coelurosauria
                Dromaeosauridae

VELOCIRAPTOR

Meaning: 'speedy thief' **Pronunciation:** vel-oss-ih-rap-TOR

A decade after Barnum Brown's successful fossil-hunting trips in Montana and Alberta, the American Museum of Natural History began to expand its collecting efforts on a worldwide scale. Their next foray was into the Gobi Desert of Mongolia, one of the harshest and driest places on earth. Leading the expedition was explorer extraordinaire Roy Chapman Andrews, who is widely believed to be the inspiration for the fictional movie character, Indiana Jones.

In 1922 Andrews' team discovered a heavily crushed but remarkably complete skull of a small theropod. This skull was very similar to Brown's *Dromaeosaurus*, but found alongside was something palaeontologists had never seen before: a giant, curved and dangerously sharp toe claw. Two years later museum scientist Henry Fairfield Osborn named this new animal *Velociraptor*, the 'speedy thief'. It was a nightmarish creature, a human-sized carnivore that could rip prey apart with its lethal claws and array of knife-like teeth.

The American Museum expeditions had to leave Mongolia as Communist Russia's influence gradually engulfed the region.

But the fossil-rich badlands of the Gobi were not forgotten. Joint Russian–Polish expeditions picked up where the Americans left off, and amassed a vast collection of new dinosaur fossils. One of these is among the most remarkable fossils ever discovered: a *Velociraptor* locked in a deadly embrace with a *Protoceratops*, a primitive herbivorous ceratopsian. This specimen, the so-called 'Fighting Dinosaurs', is one of the few cases where a predatory act has been frozen in time in the fossil record.

Velociraptor was one of the keenest predators of the dinosaur world, a cunning hunter fully loaded with an arsenal of sharp claws and teeth, as well as a large brain and sharp eyesight. Many popular movies and books have portrayed this animal as a car-sized predator, but this reconstruction is actually based on the much larger *Utahraptor*. *Velociraptor* was no larger than a man and often merely the size of a dog. However, a pack of these violent, energetic carnivores would have been more than capable of taking down much larger animals.

FOSSIL LOCATIONS

STATISTICS

Habitat:	Asia (China, Mongolia)
Period:	Late Cretaceous
Length:	5–6.5 ft (1.5–2 m)
Height:	18–28 in (46–70 cm)
Weight:	33–39 lb (15–18 kg)
Predators:	Giant theropod dinosaurs
Food:	Herbivorous dinosaurs

CLASSIFICATION

Animalia
  Chordata
    Sauropsida
      Archosauria
        Dinosauria
          Theropoda
            Tetanurae
              Coelurosauria
                Dromaeosauridae

SIZE COMPARISON

TROODON

Meaning: 'wounded tooth' **Pronunciation:** TROO-o-don

The sleek, slender theropod *Troodon* is one of the best-known members of yet another group of small, bird-like theropods: the Troodontidae. Troodontids look like dromaeosaurs in many respects: both had long, narrow skulls with small, sharp teeth, both had an enlarged claw on the second toe and both were fast runners and keen hunters. In fact, scientists consider dromaeosaurs and troodontids to be each other's closest relatives.

The quintessential troodontid is *Troodon*, a dinosaur with a long, chequered and confusing history. This genus was first named in 1856 by Joseph Leidy, based on a single tooth. Apart from being one of the foremost anatomists of his day, Leidy was also a parasitologist and one of the pioneers of using scientific forensics to solve crimes. However, in the 1850s Leidy had few dinosaurs to compare his fossil to, so he regarded *Troodon* as a lizard. About 50 years later scientists recognized it as a dinosaur, but many argued that its strange, almost leaf-shaped tooth belonged to an ornithischian. Only with the discovery of more complete fossils in 1932 was *Troodon* revealed to be a theropod.

Troodon was well adapted for carnivory and speed. The skeleton was slender and light, with long legs suited for running. The skull was amazingly bird-like, with large, forward-facing eyes that may have given *Troodon* stronger vision than any other dinosaur. The brain was enormous, and one of the largest relative to body size of any dinosaur. Although these features all indicate that *Troodon* was a predator, it is also likely that this brainy theropod ate plants, seeds and insects. The teeth have large serrations and are somewhat leaf-shaped, a hallmark of herbivores. *Troodon* was probably a generalist feeder that ate a range of food, perhaps depending on the season.

Fossils of *Troodon* have been found in Late Cretaceous rocks across western North America, and have also turned up in Mexico and Russia. Several other troodontids are known from North America and Asia. They include small, primitive forms like *Sinovenator* and larger, stronger hunters like *Saurornithoides*. These dinosaurs were never particularly diverse, but formed an important component of northern ecosystems alongside dromaeosaurs and tyrannosaurids.

FOSSIL LOCATIONS

STATISTICS

Habitat:	North America (Canada, Mexico, USA)
Period:	Late Cretaceous
Length:	5–6.5 ft (1.5–2 m)
Height:	20–28 in (50–70 cm)
Weight:	110 lb (50 kg)
Predators:	Giant theropod dinosaurs
Food:	Small vertebrates, insects, plants

CLASSIFICATION

Animalia
   Chordata
      Sauropsida
         Archosauria
            Dinosauria
               Theropoda
                  Tetanurae
                     Coelurosauria
                        Troodontidae

SIZE COMPARISON

GALLIMIMUS

Meaning: 'chicken mimic' **Pronunciation:** gall-e-MIME-uss

Gallimimus was a Cretaceous ostrich, a theropod dinosaur that resembles the large flightless birds of today. Of course, ostriches are true birds and *Gallimimus* is an ornithomimosaurian theropod. However, ornithomimosaurs were close cousins to birds, and show just how astonishingly bird-like many theropod dinosaurs were.

Gallimimus is a typical ornithomimosaur, and one of the most famous members of the group. It really does look like an ostrich, albeit on a giant scale. *Gallimimus* measured about 20 ft (6 m) in length and weighed about 440 lb (200 kg), while ostriches are about half that size. However, like ostriches,

Gallimimus had elongated hindlimbs that carried the entire weight of the animal, shortened forelimbs with a weak hand and elongated, fragile skulls that lacked teeth. *Gallimimus* was probably covered in feathers, although the fossils are too poorly preserved to show this for certain.

Fossils of *Gallimimus* have been found in Late Cretaceous rocks in Mongolia, alongside the tyrannosaurid *Tarbosaurus* and the sauropod *Nemegtosaurus*. About ten other ornithomimosaurs are known, most from Asia or North America. Exactly how these colossal bird-like animals fit into Cretaceous ecosystems is a bit of a mystery, but recent fossils show evidence of a keratin-like beak sheathing much of the skull. It has been suggested that they filtered small aquatic invertebrates from lakes and ponds, but the beak may also have been used to crush seeds. What is certain is that *Gallimimus* and its kin were not sleek, keen, vicious hunters of large prey like most of their close theropod cousins.

SIZE COMPARISON

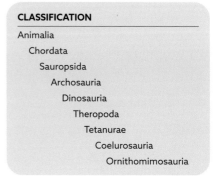

FOSSIL LOCATIONS

STATISTICS

Habitat:	Asia (Mongolia)
Period:	Late Cretaceous
Length:	16–20 ft (5–6 m)
Height:	8–10 ft (2.5–3 m)
Weight:	353–485 lb (160–220 kg)
Predators:	Giant theropod dinosaurs
Food:	Aquatic invertebrates, insects, seeds

CLASSIFICATION

Animalia
  Chordata
    Sauropsida
      Archosauria
        Dinosauria
          Theropoda
            Tetanurae
              Coelurosauria
                Ornithomimosauria

PELECANIMIMUS

Meaning: 'pelican mimic' **Pronunciation:** pell-eh-can-ih-MIME-uss

Pelecanimimus, a small theropod from the Early Cretaceous, is the most primitive member of the Ornithomimosauria, the group of 'ostrich mimics' that were especially common in the later Cretaceous. It is an important transitional form that links these abnormal theropods with their closest cousins, which were more traditional, sleek, predatory animals.

There are many differences between the primitive *Pelecanimimus* and later, more derived, or evolutionarily advanced, ornithomimosaurs. *Pelecanimimus* was much smaller than its advanced cousins, measuring only about 7 ft (2.1 m) in length and weighing no more than 88 lb (40 kg). In contrast, *Gallimimus* and later ornithomimosaurs were more than twice as long and perhaps six times as heavy. But it is really the skull of *Pelecanimimus* that was most distinctive. While *Gallimimus* and other ornithomimosaurs had a toothless beak for cracking seeds or straining microorganisms, *Pelecanimimus* had a jaw full of minuscule teeth. There were over 220 teeth in total, the highest number ever recorded for a theropod dinosaur!

Pelecanimimus is also unique in being the only ornithomimosaur found outside of North America and Asia. It is known from a single fossil, the skull and front half of the skeleton, found in the famous Las Hoyas fossil site near Cuenca, Spain. The site is renowned for its finely preserved fossils. Superb specimens of many primitive Mesozoic birds have been found there, often with feathers and soft tissues still visible. In fact, some soft tissue remains on the fossil of *Pelecanimimus*, and suggests that this primitive ostrich mimic had a gular pouch underneath its lower jaw. Many aquatic birds have a similar structure to store fish, so perhaps *Pelecanimimus* was also a fish eater.

SIZE COMPARISON

FOSSIL LOCATIONS

STATISTICS

Habitat:	Europe (Spain)
Period:	Early Cretaceous
Length:	6.5–8 ft (2–2.5 m)
Height:	3–4 ft (1–1.25 m)
Weight:	55–88 lb (25–40 kg)
Predators:	Giant theropod dinosaurs
Food:	Aquatic invertebrates, fish, seeds

CLASSIFICATION

Animalia
 Chordata
  Sauropsida
   Archosauria
    Dinosauria
     Theropoda
      Tetanurae
       Coelurosauria
        Ornithomimosauria

OVIRAPTOR

Meaning: 'egg thief' **Pronunciation:** oh-vih-rap-TOR

Oviraptor looks more like an alien life form than a cousin of *Tyrannosaurus* or *Allosaurus*. But overall appearances can be deceptive. *Oviraptor* is a member of a very specialized group of theropods called the Oviraptorosauria. These light, toothless animals were incredibly bird-like. Some scientists have even regarded them as true birds that lost the ability to fly, but most researchers consider them to be some of the closest cousins to birds.

Oviraptor measured about 7 ft (2.1 m) in length but weighed only 88 lb (40 kg), about the same as a young child. Its most characteristic feature was a highly modified skull, which was completely toothless but capped with a strong beak that may have been used to crack nuts or eat shellfish. Above this beak was a prominent but paper-thin crest, which was too weak to act as a defensive weapon but was well suited for display. Compared with other, more traditional theropods, the skull was short, deep and heavily fused.

The first fossil of *Oviraptor* was discovered by explorer Roy Chapman Andrews during his celebrated Central Asiatic Expeditions to Mongolia in the early 1920s. It was found atop a nest of eggs, which were presumed to belong to the ceratopsian *Protoceratops*. And so the new species was given the name *Oviraptor* – 'egg thief' – and was long considered to be an aberrant theropod adapted to eating the eggs of other dinosaurs. However, expeditions to Mongolia in the 1990s recovered startling evidence that demolished this idea. Small bones in the supposed *Protoceratops* eggs turned out to be the embryos of *Oviraptor*, and another fossil showed a large *Oviraptor* sitting on a nest in a protective fashion, covering and warming the eggs like a mother bird. *Oviraptor* was not an egg thief, after all, but a caring parent!

SIZE COMPARISON

FOSSIL LOCATIONS

STATISTICS

Habitat:	Asia (Mongolia)
Period:	Late Cretaceous
Length:	6.5–8 ft (2–2.5 m)
Height:	3–4 ft (1–1.2 m)
Weight:	77–88 lb (35–40 kg)
Predators:	Giant theropod dinosaurs
Food:	Aquatic invertebrates, seeds, nuts

CLASSIFICATION

Animalia
  Chordata
    Sauropsida
      Archosauria
        Dinosauria
          Theropoda
            Tetanurae
              Coelurosauria
                Oviraptorosauria

NEMEGTOSAURUS

Meaning: named after the rock formation it was discovered in
Pronunciation: neh-meg-toe-SORE-uss

Sauropods were very rare in the northern hemisphere during the Late Cretaceous, but a few of these large-bodied, long-necked giants inhabited Asia. The best known of these is *Nemegtosaurus*, a 70-ft (21-m) long herbivore that lived alongside the tyrannosaurid *Tarbosaurus* in Mongolia during the final years of the Age of Dinosaurs.

Nemegtosaurus is known only from a single skull, discovered during a joint Polish–Mongolian expedition to the arid badlands of southern Mongolia. But this skull is one of the most complete sauropod craniums ever found, and has been described in detail by scientists. It was tall and deep like the skulls of *Brachiosaurus* and *Camarasaurus*, but had a short row of pencil-like teeth at the front of the jaw as in diplodocoids. A strange combination of diplodocoid and *Brachiosaurus*-like features characterizes the rest of the skull, making this sauropod very difficult to place within the family tree.

Recent studies strongly conclude that *Nemegtosaurus* was a titanosaur, a member of a mostly Cretaceous radiation of enormous sauropods closely related to *Brachiosaurus*. Some titanosaurs, such as *Argentinosaurus*, were perhaps the largest animals ever to live on land. Most titanosaurs lived in the southern continents, but a handful of species dispersed into North America and Asia.

The Asian titanosaurs probably migrated from Europe in the Early Cretaceous, when the once isolated Asian continent collided with Europe. This was a major event in dinosaur history. Up to then Asia had been populated by primitive holdovers from earlier times, which had thrived on this isolated continent. New land connections helped to link Asia with Europe in the Early Cretaceous and North America in the Late Cretaceous. During the final years of the Cretaceous, European migrants like *Nemegtosaurus* shared ecosystems with animals like *Tarbosaurus* and *Gallimimus*, whose closest cousins were from North America.

SIZE COMPARISON

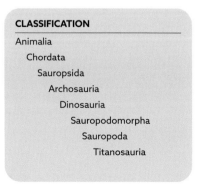

FOSSIL LOCATIONS

STATISTICS

Habitat:	Asia (Mongolia)
Period:	Late Cretaceous
Length:	70 ft (21 m)
Height:	20 ft (6 m)
Weight:	12–14 tons
Predators:	Giant theropod dinosaurs
Food:	Plants

CLASSIFICATION

Animalia
  Chordata
    Sauropsida
      Archosauria
        Dinosauria
          Sauropodomorpha
            Sauropoda
              Titanosauria

SALTASAURUS

Meaning: named after its discovery site in Argentina
Pronunciation: sal-tah-SORE-uss

Hadrosaurs and ceratopsians were the primary herbivores in the northern continents during the Cretaceous, but in the south the sauropods still ruled. The titanosaurian sauropods, a subgroup of large-bodied Cretaceous forms, were amazingly diverse. These sauropods are typified by *Saltasaurus*, a relatively small species from the Late Cretaceous of Argentina.

Saltasaurus was very small by sauropod standards, weighing only about seven tons and measuring about 40 ft (12 m). It was 'only' the size of *Tyrannosaurus*, and about half the length of its closest titanosaur cousins. At least five specimens have been discovered, in the same rock unit as large abelisaurid theropods. It appears that these two groups dominated South American ecosystems for much of the Cretaceous.

The most unique feature of *Saltasaurus* was its array of bony, plate-like body armour. This is commonly seen on ankylosaurs, but only very rarely in other dinosaur groups. In fact, when the large, oval plates of *Saltasaurus* were first found they were mistaken for the fossils of ankylosaurs. However, more complete skeletons proved that the plates belonged to *Saltasaurus*, and today a handful of other titanosaurs have also been found with armour. These were probably defensive structures, akin to the armour suit of medieval knights, used to protect *Saltasaurus* from abelisaurid attacks.

Saltasaurus is only one of several titanosaurs. At least 30 species have been described from the southern lands of South America, Africa, Australia, India and Madagascar. A handful of others are known from North America, Europe and Asia, many of which were probably immigrants. New titanosaurs are being uncovered at the astronomical rate of a few species a year, and are the subject of intensive research.

SIZE COMPARISON

FOSSIL LOCATIONS

STATISTICS

Habitat:	South America (Argentina)
Period:	Late Cretaceous
Length:	40 ft (12 m)
Height:	11 ft (3.3 m)
Weight:	6–7 tons
Predators:	Giant theropod dinosaurs
Food:	Plants

CLASSIFICATION

Animalia
  Chordata
    Sauropsida
      Archosauria
        Dinosauria
          Sauropodomorpha
            Sauropoda
              Titanosauria

ANKYLOSAURUS

Meaning: 'stiffened lizard' **Pronunciation:** ang-ki-lo-SORE-uss

Ankylosaurus was a military tank some 65 million years before its time, a big, plodding creature covered from head to toe in impenetrable armour and furnished with offensive weapons that could cripple even the most ferocious predator.

Ankylosaurus, the 'fused reptile', was the quintessential ankylosaur, the genus for which this large group of plated, armadillo-like herbivores was named. It had all of the characteristics of the group: a short, stocky body that walked on four legs, a fused and triangular skull perfect for slicing through plants and an array of body armour that would make a medieval knight proud.

But *Ankylosaurus* was no ordinary ankylosaur. It was the largest member of the group and the last to survive. Individuals reached lengths of 33 ft (10 m), about the same size as *Allosaurus*, and weights of up to eight tons. The body was astoundingly bulky, measuring up to 6.5 ft (2 m) in width – much greater than an average man's height! However, the skull

was tiny, less than 2 ft (0.5 m) in length. It was heavy and solidly fused, with two horns projecting from the back end on each side and a series of small, interlocking, oval-shaped plates engulfing the roof. Each jaw held over 60 minuscule teeth, each measuring less than ½ in (1cm) in length, that were ideal for cropping plants.

The most remarkable feature of *Ankylosaurus* was its globular tail club, which resembles a mace (a heavy club used to bludgeon and crush opponents in medieval times). It was an enormous structure, nearly the size of the skull, and comprised of a complicated mass of fused vertebrae, tendons and armour plates. Seven strongly fused tail vertebrae anchored the base of the club, which was sheathed by two major osteoderms and several smaller ossicles. This would have been a devastating and deadly weapon, and a deterrent that would have made tyrannosaurids and other predators think twice before attacking.

FOSSIL LOCATIONS

STATISTICS

Habitat:	North America (Canada, USA)
Period:	Late Cretaceous
Length:	26–33 ft (8–10 m)
Height:	7–9 ft (2–2.75 m)
Weight:	5.8–8 tons
Predators:	Giant theropod dinosaurs
Food:	Plants

CLASSIFICATION

Animalia
  Chordata
    Sauropsida
      Archosauria
        Dinosauria
          Ornithischia
            Thyreophora
              Ankylosauria
                Ankylosauridae

EUOPLOCEPHALUS

Meaning: 'well-armed head' **Pronunciation:** u-oh-plo-CEPH-uh-luss

Euoplocephalus is undoubtedly the best-known ankylosaur: over 40 specimens have been discovered from Late Cretaceous rocks in western North America, including more than 15 skulls. In contrast, the fossils of its closest, and more famous cousin, *Ankylosaurus*, can be counted on one hand. As a result, much of what is known about ankylosaur anatomy, biology, diet and habits is based on careful study of *Euoplocephalus*.

Euoplocephalus had all of the major ankylosaur features: a heavily armoured body, a small skull with tiny teeth, and a slow-moving, four-footed gait. But it also has two intriguing features. Firstly, the foot has only three toes, whereas all other ankylosaurs have four or five. Secondly, an extra bone is present over the eye socket. This bone, called the palpebral, would have formed a bony eyelid, the most extreme example of cranial armour among the fused and reinforced skulls of the ankylosaurs.

This bony-eyed species was a member of the Ankylosauridae, a subgroup of ankylosaurs that possessed a predator-smacking tail club. The club of *Euoplocephalus* was similar to that of

Ankylosaurus but had a different shape. Whereas the club of *Ankylosaurus* was spherical, that of *Euoplocephalus* was shaped like a frisbee. Viewed from above the club was a large, circular structure, but from the side it was slightly thicker than the vertebrae that supported it. Studies show that the club was held only a few inches off the ground and had little vertical flexibility. However, it could more easily move from side to side. The bony tendons helping to connect the club to the rest of the tail were perfect for transmitting muscle forces, which means that *Euoplocephalus* could swing its weapon with vigour. Any theropods looking for a meal would have to face the consequences.

SIZE COMPARISON

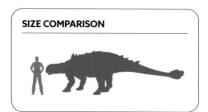

FOSSIL LOCATIONS

STATISTICS

Habitat:	North America (Canada, USA)
Period:	Late Cretaceous
Length:	16–20 ft (5–6 m)
Height:	4–6 ft (1.2–1.8 m)
Weight:	2–4 tons
Predators:	Giant theropod dinosaurs
Food:	Plants

CLASSIFICATION

Animalia
  Chordata
    Sauropsida
      Archosauria
        Dinosauria
          Ornithischia
            Thyreophora
              Ankylosauria
                Ankylosauridae

EDMONTONIA

Meaning: named in honour of Edmonton, Alberta **Pronunciation:** ed-mon-TONE-e-uh

Living alongside *Euoplocephalus* on the Late Cretaceous floodplains of the American west was a more distantly related ankylosaur, *Edmontonia*. Whereas *Euoplocephalus* belonged to the club-bearing ankylosaurids, *Edmontonia* was a nodosaurid, a member of the second major ankylosaurian subgroup. It lacked a tail club, and instead had to rely on its armour for protection from mega predators like *Albertosaurus*.

The skull of *Edmontonia*, and other nodosaurids, was longer and narrower than the stout, triangular head of ankylosaurids. The skull roof is covered by a less complex pattern of fewer, larger osteoderms. However, *Edmontonia* was unique in possessing an extra bony plate, located in the cheek region on the side of the mouth.

Its function is hard to understand. Perhaps it was a feeding adaptation, which helped to keep plant matter in the mouth as *Edmontonia* haphazardly devoured foliage by the ton. Or, possibly it protected the vulnerable soft tissues of the mouth from predatory attacks.

The body armour of *Edmontonia* is generally similar to that of other nodosaurids. A series of broad osteoderms covered the neck, and smaller, more circular plates sheathed the back. A series of spines projected sideways along the body. The largest of these were in the shoulder region, some of which angled backwards and others forwards, probably forming its major defensive weapon. Unlike the club-tailed ankylosaurids *Edmontonia* would have faced its predators head-on.

SIZE COMPARISON

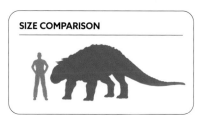

FOSSIL LOCATIONS

STATISTICS

Habitat:	North America (Canada, USA)
Period:	Late Cretaceous
Length:	20–23 ft (6–7 m)
Height:	6–7 ft (1.8–2.1 m)
Weight:	4–5 tons
Predators:	Giant theropod dinosaurs
Food:	Plants

CLASSIFICATION

Animalia
  Chordata
    Sauropsida
      Archosauria
        Dinosauria
          Ornithischia
            Thyreophora
              Ankylosauria
                Nodosauridae

MAIASAURA

Meaning: 'good mother lizard' **Pronunciation:** my-uh-SORE-uh

The discovery of *Maiasaura* was a watershed moment in palaeontology. Along with the discovery of the bird-like *Deinonychus*, Jack Horner's description of the herbivorous *Maiasaura* helped to change the general perception of dinosaurs. Instead of viewing the 'terrible lizards' as unintelligent, sluggish animals doomed to extinction, scientists began to see them as energetic, dynamic creatures that dominated the Mesozoic world.

Many early scientists thought that dinosaurs simply abandoned their eggs. *Maiasaura* was the first species to prove conclusively that some dinosaurs were keen parents that actively watched and fed their children. The evidence for this revolutionary conclusion was remarkable: a 75-million-year-

old nesting ground preserved in the Cretaceous rocks of Montana. Deep in the sparsely populated badlands, Horner and Bob Makela uncovered numerous nests, chock-full of 30 to 40 eggs the size of a rugby ball. Bones of small embryos, juveniles and adults were found alongside the nests, suggesting that *Maiasaura* nested in large groups. The bones of the hatchlings were very weak, which meant that these rabbit-sized dinosaurs must have moved very slowly and awkwardly, and

FOSSIL LOCATIONS

STATISTICS

Habitat:	North America (USA)
Period:	Late Cretaceous
Length:	30 ft (9 m)
Height:	10 ft (3 m)
Weight:	3 tons
Predators:	Giant theropod dinosaurs
Food:	Plants

CLASSIFICATION

Animalia
  Chordata
    Sauropsida
      Archosauria
        Dinosauria
          Ornithischia
            Ornithopoda
              Hadrosauridae
                Hadrosaurinae

SIZE COMPARISON

could not possibly have fed on their own. However, their teeth showed clear signs of wear caused by plants. Only one possibility existed: the parents gathered food for their young and weaned them through their early life.

The range of juvenile and adult specimens helped Horner to demonstrate that *Maiasaura* grew exceptionally fast, much like modern birds. Hatchlings weighed only about 2.2 lb (1 kg), and measured less than 2 ft (0.5 m). Adults, on the other hand, were 30-ft (9-m) giants that weighed three tons. Studies of growth lines in the bones showed that hatchlings reached full adult size in less than ten years – a remarkable rate that must have been powered by a warm-blooded metabolism.

Maiasaura was a generalized hadrosaurid. It had a long skull fronted with a downturned beak and jaws packed with a dense battery of teeth, perfect instruments for processing vast quantities of plants. *Maiasaura* not only nested in colonies, but also travelled in herds. One fossil site contains the remains of at least 10,000 individuals, ranging in size from juveniles to adults. This is the largest dinosaur bonebed ever found. Perhaps this herbivore, which had no heavy armour or tail spikes, needed to travel in large herds to protect itself from tyrannosaurids and other mega predators

PARASAUROLOPHUS

Meaning: 'near crested lizard' **Pronunciation:** par-ah-SORE-oh-loph-us

The hadrosaurid *Parasaurolophus* boasted one of the most unusual features ever seen in a dinosaur: a long, curved cranial crest that looked like a snorkel. Many hadrosaurids sported some kind of skull ornamentation, ranging from thin, arched crests similar to those of modern cassowaries to spike-like protuberances jutting off the top of the skull. But none of these were as large or bizarre as the long, hollow tube of *Parasaurolophus*.

The crest of *Parasaurolophus* was colossal. It extended for approximately 4 ft (1.25 m) – about the height of a human child! The crest began at the front of the skull, right above the narrow beak used to crop plants. Here two large, tapering nostrils led into separate hollow tubes, which extended all the way to the back of the crest. The end of the crest was thick, solid bone, and the tubes did not pierce through in an opening. Instead, they turned around and headed back down the centre of the crest. The inside of the crest, therefore, was not solid bone, but a complicated maze of nasal sinuses.

No modern animals possess anything remotely similar, and scientists were long confused over why a plant-eating dinosaur would have needed a 4-ft (1.25-m) long hollow tube extending from its head. Many fanciful suggestions were thrown around: perhaps it was a snorkel for underwater feeding, the bony support for an elephantine trunk or even a capsule for large glands. These ideas may appear comical, but show just how difficult it was to interpret this strange structure. Today, most scientists believe that the crest was probably a display device used to attract mates. It may have also helped to cool the animal, and was capable of producing sound to communicate with other members of the species. The unique crest of *Parasaurolophus* was probably a multi-purpose tool.

Parasaurolophus is one of the rarest of the hadrosaurids. Only a handful of fossils have been found in the Late Cretaceous rocks of western North America, whereas animals like *Edmonotosaurus* and *Maiasaura* are known from thousands of specimens. Perhaps *Parasaurolophus* was a more solitary animal that did not travel in the large herds characteristic of these other species.

FOSSIL LOCATIONS

STATISTICS

Habitat:	North America (Canada, USA)
Period:	Late Cretaceous
Length:	26–33 ft (7.8–10 m)
Height:	7.5–10 ft (2.3–3 m)
Weight:	4–6 tons
Predators:	Giant theropod dinosaurs
Food:	Plants

CLASSIFICATION

Animalia
  Chordata
    Sauropsida
      Archosauria
        Dinosauria
          Ornithischia
            Ornithopoda
              Hadrosauridae
                Lambeosaurinae

SIZE COMPARISON

GRYPOSAURUS

Meaning: 'hooked-nose lizard' **Pronunciation:** gry-po-SORE-us

The most diverse, the longest-lived and the most widely spread hadrosaurid genus was *Gryposaurus*, a large animal distinguished by an awkward-looking bump on its nose. Four species of *Gryposaurus* have been named. They ranged across the entire western region of North America for over five million years during the Late Cretaceous. Today, *Gryposaurus* fossils are common discoveries from Alberta to Utah, a distance of some 1200 miles (1900 km).

Gryposaurus measured up to 30 ft (9 m) in length and weighed three tons. Apart from the skull, its skeleton was typical for hadrosaurids, and like most species it could walk on either two or four legs.

The skull, however, is unlike that of any other member of the group. It bears a distinctive bony bump on its nose, above the nostril. Akin to the distinguished 'Roman nose' of some

humans, this bump gives *Gryposaurus* its name of 'hooked nose'. The bump was probably a display feature, but its thickened, roughened texture suggests that it may also have been used as an aggressive weapon, perhaps for gentle headbutting between males competing for mates.

Gryposaurus is a member of a subgroup of hadrosaurids called the hadrosaurines. These were the non-crested hadrosaurids, and include animals like *Maiasaura*, *Edmontosaurus* and *Brachylophosaurus*, many of which are found in vast bonebeds. The other major subgroup, the lambeosaurines, comprises those species with ornate cranial crests. The most familiar member of this group is *Parasaurolophus*, and others include *Lambeosaurus* and *Corythosaurus*.

SIZE COMPARISON

FOSSIL LOCATIONS

STATISTICS

Habitat:	North America (Canada, USA)
Period:	Late Cretaceous
Length:	23–30 ft (7–9 m)
Height:	8–11 ft (2.5–3 m)
Weight:	2–3 tons
Predators:	Giant theropod dinosaurs
Food:	Plants

CLASSIFICATION

Animalia
  Chordata
    Sauropsida
      Archosauria
        Dinosauria
          Ornithischia
            Ornithopoda
              Hadrosauridae
                Hadrosaurinae

ANATOTITAN

Meaning: 'duck titan' **Pronunciation:** AN-at-oh-tit-an

Deposited on a lush floodplain during the waning days of the Cretaceous, the Hell Creek Formation of the western United States has yielded an incredibly diverse assemblage of dinosaurs. Many of these species, such as *Tyrannosaurus* and *Triceratops*, are some of the most familiar in the dinosaur world. But the most common members of the Hell Creek community were hadrosaurids, 'duck-billed' giants like *Edmontosaurus* and *Anatotitan* that filled the main herbivore role.

Edmontosaurus is known from more fossils than nearly any other dinosaur, and some bonebeds preserve remains of thousands of individuals. Much rarer is a close cousin, *Anatotitan*, which grew to massive sizes almost unheard of among hadrosaurids. Some individuals reached lengths of 40 ft (12 m) – the same size as the contemporaneous *Tyrannosaurus* – and weights of five tons. No armour plates or spikes adorned the skeleton, and it is likely that large body size was protection enough against tyrannosaurid predators.

Anatotitan is immediately distinguished by a very long skull, the longest and lowest cranium of any dinosaur. The head was about 4 ft (1.25 m) long but only about 12 in (30 cm) deep, giving it an elongated, tubular appearance like the stretched skull of a modern horse. At the front of the head was a humongous, spoon-shaped beak, the quintessential 'duck bill' of hadrosaurids. No other species had such a large beak, which was as wide as the rest of the skull in *Anatotitan*. Behind the beak was a long toothless gap, which would have given the tongue ample room for moving plant matter around the mouth to be chewed. Behind this gap was the tooth row, which was very short but included a stunning battery of teeth that would have chomped through plants with gusto. *Anatotitan* was a plant-guzzling machine, perfectly adapted for feeding on the flowering plants that spread like wildfire across the Cretaceous landscape.

SIZE COMPARISON

FOSSIL LOCATIONS

STATISTICS

Habitat:	North America (USA)
Period:	Late Cretaceous
Length:	33–40 ft (10–12 m)
Height:	10–12 ft (3–3.7 m)
Weight:	3–5 tons
Predators:	Giant theropod dinosaurs
Food:	Plants

CLASSIFICATION

Animalia
  Chordata
    Sauropsida
      Archosauria
        Dinosauria
          Ornithischia
            Ornithopoda
              Hadrosauridae
                Lambeosaurinae

LAMBEOSAURUS

Meaning: named in honour of palaeontologist Lawrence Lambe
Pronunciation: lam-bee-oh-SORE-uss

The lambeosaurine hadrosaurids, the subgroup with ornate cranial crests, are named after *Lambeosaurus*, one of the most fantastic dinosaurs of the Late Cretaceous. This large herbivore was one of the most common animals on the warm floodplains of western Canada 75 million years ago. It is immediately distinguished from other crested species by the unique shape of its headgear.

Unlike the elongated tubular crest of *Parasaurolophus*, the crest of *Lambeosaurus* was shorter, taller and did not extend far behind the rest of the skull. For a long while scientists named numerous species of *Lambeosaurus*, based on minor differences in crest shape, but today these are recognized as different growth stages and sexes of two species.

One species, *L. lambei*, is characterized by a hatchet-shaped crest. The blade of the hatchet is a tall, arched hump above the eye, while the handle is a thin prong that extends backwards behind the eye to slightly overhang the rest of the skull. The other species, *L. magnicristatus*, has a single large, rounded crest that curves slightly forwards. It looks like the crest of the modern cassowary bird, and vaguely resembles the quiffed hairstyle of Elvis Presley!

Both of these species were standard-sized hadrosaurids, measuring about 30 ft (9 m) long and weighing a few tons. However, a third species from Mexico appears to have been a giant, and may have reached lengths of 50 ft (15 m) and weights of over 10 tons. However, these estimates are based on very fragmentary fossils, which scientists are unsure even belong to *Lambeosaurus*.

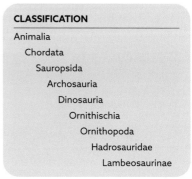

SIZE COMPARISON

FOSSIL LOCATIONS

STATISTICS

Habitat:	North America (Canada, Mexico)
Period:	Late Cretaceous
Length:	30–50 ft (9–15 m)
Height:	10–15 ft (3–4.5 m)
Weight:	3–8.5 tons
Predators:	Giant theropod dinosaurs
Food:	Plants

CLASSIFICATION

Animalia
  Chordata
    Sauropsida
      Archosauria
        Dinosauria
          Ornithischia
            Ornithopoda
              Hadrosauridae
                Lambeosaurinae

CORYTHOSAURUS

Meaning: 'helmet lizard'
Pronunciation: co-rith-oh-SORE-uss

The 'helmet-crested' herbivore *Corythosaurus* is one of the most characteristic lambeosaurines. It is probably the closest relative of *Lambeosaurus*, and the two genera looked nearly identical. Both were about the same size, had astonishing adaptations for herbivory in the skull and possessed short, tall and rounded cranial crests.

However, minor details of the crest distinguish *Corythosaurus* and *Lambeosaurus*. While *Lambeosaurus* had two crest forms – a two-pronged hatchet and a single rounded dome – *Corythosaurus* only had a single dome. And, while the dome in *Lambeosaurus* arched forwards like Elvis Presley's quiff of hair, the crest of *Corythosaurus* stood straight upwards, like the orderly haircut of a soldier.

The arched, semi-circular crest of *Corythosaurus* was gigantic, making the skull deeper than it was long. The crest was rounded and hollow inside, much like a pith helmet. Hence the name: 'helmet lizard'.

More than 20 fossils of *Corythosaurus* have been found in 80-million-year-old rocks in Alberta, in the same area where *Lambeosaurus* is common. However, a closer look at the rocks suggests that *Corythosaurus* is slightly older than *Lambeosaurus*, and that the two genera probably did not live together. This makes sense, as the two very similar animals would have been competing for the same food and other resources. Perhaps *Corythosaurus* evolved into *Lambeosaurus* as environmental conditions shifted.

SIZE COMPARISON

FOSSIL LOCATIONS

STATISTICS

Habitat:	North America (Canada)
Period:	Late Cretaceous
Length:	30–33 ft (9–10 m)
Height:	10–11 ft (3–3.5 m)
Weight:	5–5.2 tons
Predators:	Giant theropod dinosaurs
Food:	Plants

CLASSIFICATION

Animalia
  Chordata
    Sauropsida
      Archosauria
        Dinosauria
          Ornithischia
            Ornithopoda
              Hadrosauridae
                Lambeosaurinae

PSITTACOSAURUS

Meaning: 'parrot lizard' **Pronunciation:** sit-ack-o-SORE-uss

The small, Early Cretaceous *Psittacosaurus* may look unremarkable, but it is one of the oldest and most primitive ceratopsians. It was an early progenitor of the horned-and-frilled, rhino-like behemoths such as *Triceratops* and *Chasmosaurus* that were common in North America during the Late Cretaceous. The genus is divided into at least ten species that ranged across Asia during the Early Cretaceous, making it the most species-rich dinosaur genus. It was also one of the most widespread and long-lived dinosaurs that ever existed.

Looking at *Psittacosaurus*, it is hard to believe that this tiny, fragile animal is closely related to the massive, thundering ceratopsids of the Late Cretaceous. Most species of *Psittacosaurus* measured only a few feet in length and weighed no more than a toddler. *Psittacosaurus* walked on two legs and was probably a fast runner. In contrast, *Triceratops* reached 30 ft (9 m) in length and 8 tons in weight (some other ceratopsians must have been ever larger) and plodded slowly around on all fours.

However, there is no doubt that *Psittacosaurus* was an early ceratopsian. It possessed numerous features only seen in these dinosaurs, most importantly an extra bone at the front of the upper jaw called the rostral and cheekbones that flared off to the side. The rostral bone comprised part of the sharp, toothless beak that cropped plants, and the expanded cheeks, which were capped with a small horn, may have been used to attract mates or ward off predators. In later ceratopsians these horns would become enormous structures to complement additional horns on the top of the skull.

Psittacosaurus is one of the best-known dinosaurs. Over 400 specimens have been found across Asia, and thousands more remain entombed in rock. One finely preserved specimen from China was found with hollow, quill-like structures along its back. Another amazing discovery in China shows an adult *Psittacosaurus* fossilized alongside over 30 juveniles, demonstrating clear evidence for parental care.

SIZE COMPARISON

FOSSIL LOCATIONS

STATISTICS

Habitat:	Asia (China, Mongolia, Russia, Thailand)
Period:	Early Cretaceous
Length:	39–79 in (1–2 m)
Height:	14–28 in (35–70 cm)
Weight:	55 lb (25 kg)
Predators:	Theropod dinosaurs
Food:	Plants

CLASSIFICATION

Animalia
  Chordata
    Sauropsida
      Archosauria
        Dinosauria
          Ornithischia
            Ceratopsia
              Psittacosauridae

PROTOCERATOPS

Meaning: 'early horned face' **Pronunciation:** pro-toe-SER-a-tops

Another well-known primitive ceratopsian is *Protoceratops*, first discovered during Roy Chapman Andrews' legendary Central Asiatic expeditions (see page 182) and today represented by over a hundred skeletons from the Gobi Desert. It was among the favourite prey of *Velociraptor*, but the sheer number of fossil specimens proves that *Protoceratops* was a remarkably successful dinosaur.

Protoceratops is also important for understanding the evolution of the giant, thundering ceratopsids of the Late Cretaceous. It is a critical bridge in the evolutionary sequence linking small, sleek early species like *Psittacosaurus* and later, larger ones like *Triceratops*.

Protoceratops is clearly more advanced than *Psittacosaurus*, since it possessed several characteristic features of later ceratopsians not present in its more primitive cousin. For instance, *Psittacosaurus* walked on two legs and lacked any sort of cranial frill, while *Protoceratops* walked on four legs and had an elaborate, plate-like frill projecting from the back of its skull. However, *Protoceratops* did not have the enlarged nostrils, nasal horns and additional vertebrae supporting the pelvis of *Triceratops* and its kin.

Protoceratops was a small herbivore, about the size of a sheep. It probably filled a similar role in its ecosystem: that of a small, generalized grazer of low plants. The beak was large and sharp, the teeth formed a scissor-like array and the frill anchored strong jaw muscles – all features that helped *Protoceratops* mow through shrubs and bushes. The frill was probably also useful in attracting mates; males seemed to possess larger and more prominent frills than the females.

SIZE COMPARISON

FOSSIL LOCATIONS

STATISTICS

Habitat:	Asia (China, Mongolia)
Period:	Late Cretaceous
Length:	5–6.5 ft (1.5–2 m)
Height:	20–26 in (50–67 cm)
Weight:	529 lb (240 kg)
Predators:	Theropod dinosaurs
Food:	Plants

CLASSIFICATION

Animalia
  Chordata
    Sauropsida
      Archosauria
        Dinosauria
          Ornithischia
            Ceratopsia
              Protoceratopsidae

TRICERATOPS

Meaning: 'three-horned face' **Pronunciation:** try-SER-a-tops

Triceratops, together with *Tyrannosaurus*, *Brachiosaurus* and *Stegosaurus*, is one of the most widely known and popular dinosaurs. There is no mistaking *Triceratops* with its characteristic three-horned face, shield-like cranial frill and sturdy four-legged stance. This was the rhino of the Late Cretaceous, a large, ferocious-looking creature that was actually just a plant eater. But it could get angry if provoked. *Triceratops* is seen as a hero for underdogs everywhere, a simple herbivorous species that stood up to the neighbourhood bully, *Tyrannosaurus*.

In many ways *Triceratops* was the culmination of 85 million years of ceratopsian evolution. It was the last surviving species, enduring right up to the mass extinction at the end of the Cretaceous 65 million years ago. In fact, it was one of the latest surviving dinosaurs anywhere in the world. It was also one of the largest ceratopsians, weighing up to eight tons and measuring nearly 30 ft (9 m) in length. The skull was absolutely enormous, comprising one-third of the entire length of the animal – some 10 ft (3 m)! This was one of the largest skulls ever seen in a land-living animal; only a few close cousins had bigger heads.

The most notable feature of *Triceratops*, and the basis for its name, was the sharp trio of horns emanating from the top of the skull. The number and type of horns varied incredibly among ceratopsids, making them an important feature for distinguishing species. *Triceratops* had a single short horn on top of the snout and a larger, stronger and longer horn projecting from above each eye. These were up to 3 ft (1 m) long, and covered with a dense network of blood vessels that probably supported a keratin shell, like that in modern horned mammals.

The function of these horns has been the subject of intense debate. They may have been used mostly for display purposes, or perhaps in shoving matches between males competing for mates. However, some horns show damage caused by *Tyrannosaurus* bites, and one mutilated *Triceratops* skull records the unfortunate result of a face-to-face death match with this mega theropod. There is no doubt then that the horns were also powerful defensive weapons.

All *Triceratops* fossils come from the Hell Creek Formation and other end Cretaceous rock units of western North America. The first fossil, a pair of brow horns found in 1887, was mistaken for a prehistoric bison. Since that time scientists have found hundreds of specimens, which have been described as 18 different species! Recently palaeontologists have determined that these are nothing more than different growth stages of one or two species. In fact, the horns and frills of *Triceratops* dramatically changed shape throughout growth, meaning that adults and juveniles looked completely different.

FOSSIL LOCATIONS

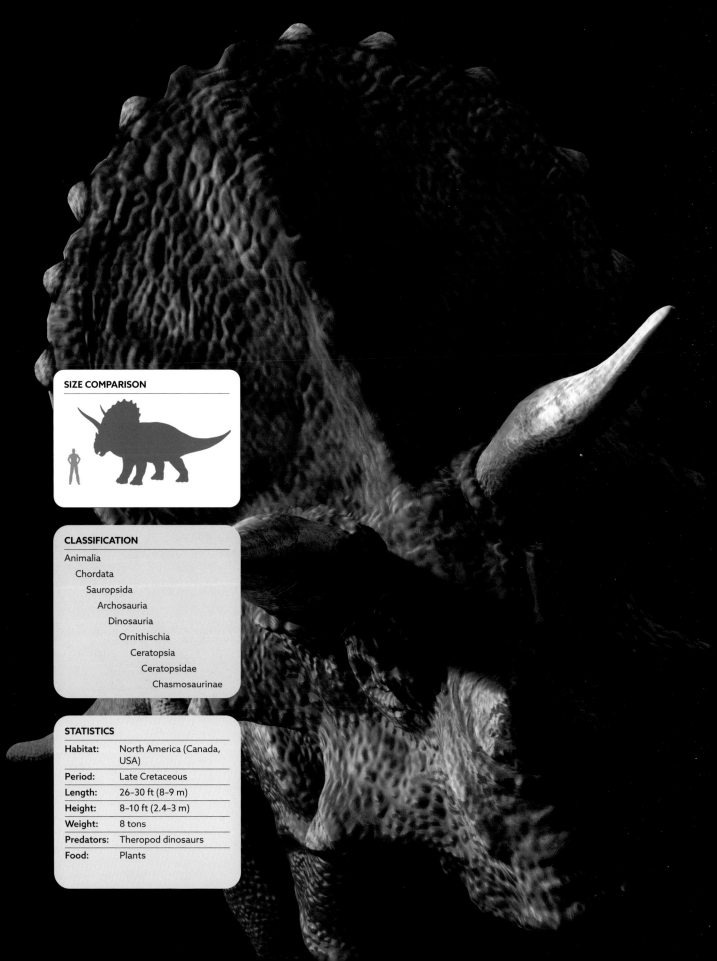

SIZE COMPARISON

CLASSIFICATION

Animalia
  Chordata
    Sauropsida
      Archosauria
        Dinosauria
          Ornithischia
            Ceratopsia
              Ceratopsidae
                Chasmosaurinae

STATISTICS

Habitat:	North America (Canada, USA)
Period:	Late Cretaceous
Length:	26–30 ft (8–9 m)
Height:	8–10 ft (2.4–3 m)
Weight:	8 tons
Predators:	Theropod dinosaurs
Food:	Plants

TOROSAURUS

Meaning: 'bull lizard' or 'perforated lizard' **Pronunciation:** tore-oh-SORE-us

Torosaurus was a close cousin of *Triceratops*, and the two genera are found alongside each other in Late Cretaceous rocks across the American west. *Torosaurus*, however, has a much longer, larger and more massive skull than its more famous relative.

In absolute size the head of *Torosaurus* was slightly smaller than that of *Triceratops* – about 9 ft (2.75 m) compared to its cousin's 10 ft (3 m) length. However, *Torosaurus* was a much smaller animal, measuring a good 5 to 10 ft (1.5–3 m) less than *Triceratops*. This makes the skull of *Triceratops* about a third of the length of the body, while that of *Torosaurus* comprised 40 per cent of the entire skeleton. This is truly mind-boggling.

Among the whole panoply of land-dwelling vertebrates that has ever lived, only another close cousin, *Pentaceratops*, had a similarly gargantuan head.

Triceratops, *Torosaurus*, *Pentaceratops* and a handful of other species comprise one of the two main subgroups of ceratopsid dinosaurs, the chasmosaurines. These ceratopsians are united by many features, such as an enlarged rostral bone at the front of the snout and triangular-shaped epoccipitals, novel nubbins of bone that surround the frill. The other main group, the centrosaurines, includes genera such as *Centrosaurus*, *Einiosaurus* and *Styracosaurus*, which have much smaller horns above the eyes and a shorter frill. Both groups were widespread in North America during the final few million years of the Cretaceous.

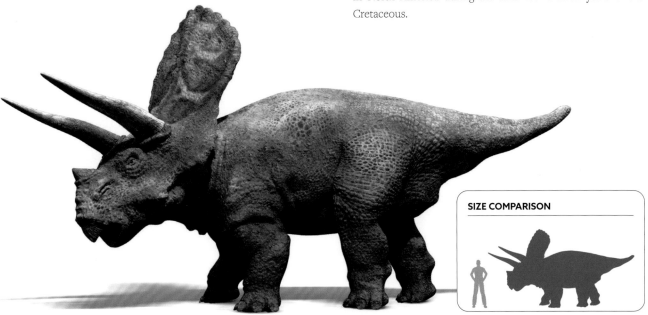

SIZE COMPARISON

FOSSIL LOCATIONS

STATISTICS

Habitat:	North America (Canada, USA)
Period:	Late Cretaceous
Length:	23–26 ft (7–8 m)
Height:	7.5–8 ft (2.3–2.4 m)
Weight:	5–7 tons
Predators:	Theropod dinosaurs
Food:	Plants

CLASSIFICATION

Animalia
  Chordata
    Sauropsida
      Archosauria
        Dinosauria
          Ornithischia
            Ceratopsia
              Ceratopsidae
                Chasmosaurinae

PENTACERATOPS

Meaning: 'five-horned face' **Pronunciation:** PEN-tah-ser-a-tops

Pentaceratops, like its slightly younger cousin *Torosaurus*, had a massive skull, measuring some 9 ft (2.75 m) in length. On average *Pentaceratops* was probably about the same size as *Torosaurus*, meaning that it also had a skull that comprised about 40 per cent of the body. These measurements are truly astounding, and give *Pentaceratops* a slightly awkward appearance. The skeleton looks as if it is about to tip over forwards, literally head over heels.

Pentaceratops lived about five million years before *Torosaurus* and 10 million years before the Cretaceous–Tertiary extinction. Its name refers to its unique skull. Whereas close relatives such as *Triceratops* had three horns, *Pentaceratops* had an additional

two horns projecting from the side of the skull, in the region of the cheeks. All ceratopsians have some sort of bony protuberance in this region, but in most species it is nothing more than a low, rounded bump. However, the bumps of *Pentaceratops* are elaborated into massive, sharp horns that would have been well positioned for delivering a powerful blow to predators such as the tyrannosaurid *Daspletosaurus*.

Several skulls of *Pentaceratops* have been discovered, mostly in the states of New Mexico and Colorado. The first fossils were unearthed in 1921 by Charles H. Sternberg, one of the giants of 20th-century dinosaur palaeontology. Sternberg cut his teeth collecting fossils in Kansas for E.D. Cope during the infamous 'Bone Wars' of the late 1800s. He later became his own boss, and collected dinosaur fossils across the American and Canadian West, which he sold to museums around the world. His three sons continued the family's fossil-hunting tradition well into the 1970s.

SIZE COMPARISON

FOSSIL LOCATIONS

STATISTICS

Habitat:	North America (USA)
Period:	Late Cretaceous
Length:	20–26 ft (6–8 m)
Height:	6–8 ft (1.8–2.4 m)
Weight:	5–7 tons
Predators:	Theropod dinosaurs
Food:	Plants

CLASSIFICATION

Animalia
  Chordata
    Sauropsida
      Archosauria
        Dinosauria
          Ornithischia
            Ceratopsia
              Ceratopsidae
                Chasmosaurinae

CHASMOSAURUS

Meaning: 'opening lizard'   **Pronunciation:** kas-mo-SORE-us

Chasmosaurus was one of the most common dinosaurs in the Late Cretaceous landscape of western North America. It was a close cousin to *Triceratops* and the namesake genus of the subgroup Chasmosaurinae.

Chasmosaurus was a mid-sized ceratopsian, measuring less than 20 ft (6 m) in length and a few tons in weight. *Triceratops* was much larger overall, and other close cousins such as *Torosaurus* and *Pentaceratops* had much more gigantic heads. But *Chasmosaurus* was more widespread and diverse than its relatives. Scientists have found over 40 skulls and other specimens of *Chasmosaurus* from across western North

America, ranging from the badlands of Alberta to the southernmost tip of Texas. These constitute at least four distinct species.

As with most ceratopsians, the head of *Chasmosaurus* was its most distinctive feature. The skull was long and low, and the frill was flat and faced upwards, much like a tabletop. In contrast, many other close cousins had a more upright frill that faced strongly forwards. No other ceratopsian had such a wide frill, which gave the skull of *Chasmosaurus* a strongly triangular appearance when viewed from above. In the middle of the frill were two enormous holes, which give the animal its name. These openings, the parietal fenestrae, were covered by skin and muscles externally and would have lightened the frill and made it easier to carry.

SIZE COMPARISON

FOSSIL LOCATIONS

STATISTICS

Habitat:	North America (Canada, USA)
Period:	Late Cretaceous
Length:	16–18 ft (5–5.5 m)
Height:	5–5.5 ft (1.5–1.65 m)
Weight:	2–3 tons
Predators:	Theropod dinosaurs
Food:	Plants

CLASSIFICATION

Animalia
  Chordata
    Sauropsida
      Archosauria
        Dinosauria
          Ornithischia
            Ceratopsia
              Ceratopsidae
                Chasmosaurinae

STYRACOSAURUS

Meaning: 'spiked lizard' **Pronunciation:** sty-rack-o-SORE-us

The ceratopsians are renowned for the weird array of spikes and horns projecting from their skulls. Most species had three spikes: one over the nose and one above each eye. Others, such as *Pentaceratops*, added a horn on each cheek. But one ceratopsian took its skull ornamentation to the extreme. The centrosaurine *Styracosaurus* had more spikes and horns emanating from its head than any other ceratopsian. Instead of three or five spikes, most individuals had nine horns!

Styracosaurus had one of the most fantastic skulls of any dinosaur, an alien cranium that defies logic. Like most centrosaurines the frill was short, and excavated by two large openings to lighten its weight. Also, like most other ceratopsians, there was a single large horn over the nose, a long and pointed structure that measured up to 2 ft (0.5 m) in length.

But this is where the similarities end. *Styracosaurus* had horns spreading sideways from each cheek, and another six horns arranged in a semi-circular array on the back of the frill. The largest of these, a pair located at the midline of the frill, were as long or longer than the nasal horn. With nine horns in total, *Styracosaurus* would have been well prepared for predators like *Daspletosaurus*. However, some of the horns were so small and fragile that they must have been used for display only.

Styracosaurus is known from 75-million-year-old rocks in Dinosaur Provincial Park, Alberta. Discovered in slightly older rocks is *Centrosaurus*, the quintessential centrosaurine and closest cousin to *Styracosaurus*. These two genera do not widely overlap, and it appears that *Styracosaurus* supplanted its older cousin as the primary centrosaurine in the Dinosaur Park ecosystem. Perhaps *Styracosaurus* even evolved directly from *Centrosaurus*.

SIZE COMPARISON

FOSSIL LOCATIONS

STATISTICS	
Habitat:	North America (Canada)
Period:	Late Cretaceous
Length:	16–18 ft (5–5.5 m)
Height:	5–5.5 ft (1.5–1.65 m)
Weight:	2–3 tons
Predators:	Theropod dinosaurs
Food:	Plants

CLASSIFICATION

Animalia
  Chordata
    Sauropsida
      Archosauria
        Dinosauria
          Ornithischia
            Ceratopsia
              Ceratopsidae
                Chasmosaurinae

EINIOSAURUS

Meaning: 'buffalo lizard' **Pronunciation:** ie-nee-oh-SORE-uss

Seventy-five million years before the bison, large ceratopsian dinosaurs thundered across the plains of western North America. One of these, *Einiosaurus*, is named after the Blackfoot Indian word for bison. But this 'bison lizard' really didn't look like the large, shaggy mammals

that were so prized by Native Americans. True, both *Einiosaurus* and the bison had horns projecting from their skulls. However, the horns of this Late Cretaceous ceratopsian were much more fantastic, forming some of the most bizarre cranial ornaments ever seen in an animal.

Einiosaurus is a centrosaurine, a member of the ceratopsid subgroup characterized by short frills and reduced brow horns. It is a close relative of *Styracosaurus*, and was thought to be a

new species of this genus when first discovered in Montana in the mid-1980s. However, more careful study revealed amazing differences in cranial ornamentation. *Einiosaurus* had two horns radiating from the back of the frill, while *Styracosaurus* had six. And, while *Styracosaurus* had a long, thin horn on its nose, *Einiosaurus* had a fat, short spike that curved forwards, much like a can-opener!

Fossils of *Einiosaurus* have been found only in Montana, in an approximately 75-million-year-old rock unit called the Two Medicine Formation. At least 15 individuals are known from two bonebeds. Although not as large as some hadrosaurid bonebeds, which contain bones of more than 10,000 individuals, these fossil assemblages suggest that *Einiosaurus* travelled in herds. Many other centrosaurines, as well as some chasmosaurines, are also known from bonebeds, indicating that herding behaviour was widespread among ceratopsians. Perhaps it was an effective way to deter predators, find food or survive long periods of drought.

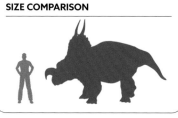

SIZE COMPARISON

FOSSIL LOCATIONS

STATISTICS

Habitat:	North America (USA)
Period:	Late Cretaceous
Length:	24–25 ft (7.2–7.6 m)
Height:	7–7.5 ft (2.1–2.3 m)
Weight:	4.5–5 tons
Predators:	Theropod dinosaurs
Food:	Plants

CLASSIFICATION

Animalia
  Chordata
    Sauropsida
      Archosauria
        Dinosauria
          Ornithischia
            Ceratopsia
              Ceratopsidae
                Centrosaurinae

PACHYRHINOSAURUS

Meaning: 'thick-nosed lizard' **Pronunciation:** pack-ee-rhy-no-SORE-uss

Pachyrhinosaurus was an average-sized ceratopsian, smaller than giants like *Triceratops* and *Einiosaurus* and about the same size as *Chasmosaurus*. The skull followed the generalized centrosaurine pattern: deep facial region, short frill and reduced ornamentation over the eyes.

The cranial decoration, on the other hand, was truly bizarre. As in other centrosaurines, two thin horns projected from the back of the frill, but there the similarities end. Two short, unique horns protruded upwards from the centre of the frill between the large oval-shaped fenestrae (openings). And the entire region above the eyes and nose was engulfed in a mass of thick, rough bone. This is called a cranial boss.

A similar pattern is seen in a close cousin, *Achelousaurus*, but in this animal there were separate bosses over the eyes and the nose.

The function of this strange headgear is a matter of speculation. However, it is difficult to imagine that the dense, swollen head of *Pachyrhinosaurus* was an effective anti-predator device. Instead, like most bizarre ornamentation in dinosaurs, the primary purpose of the cranial bosses and smaller horns was probably for display and attracting mates. This idea is supported by the fact that many of these structures did not develop until the animal was an adult, and ready to mate. If they were primarily defensive weapons they would probably be present on juveniles, which would have been weaker, smaller and more prone to attack.

SIZE COMPARISON

FOSSIL LOCATIONS

STATISTICS

Habitat:	North America (USA)
Period:	Late Cretaceous
Length:	18–20 ft (5.5–6 m)
Height:	5.5–6 ft (1.6–1.8 m)
Weight:	2–2.4 tons
Predators:	Theropod dinosaurs
Food:	Plants

CLASSIFICATION

Animalia
  Chordata
    Sauropsida
      Archosauria
        Dinosauria
          Ornithischia
            Ceratopsia
              Ceratopsidae
                Centrosaurinae

PACHYCEPHALOSAURUS

Meaning: 'thick-headed lizard'   **Pronunciation:** pack-ee-seph-uh-LOH-sore-uss

One of the last-surviving groups of dinosaurs, the pachycephalosaurs were perhaps the most mind-boggling and bizarre creatures of the Mesozoic. At least 10 genera have been discovered, most from the Late Cretaceous of North America and Europe. The prototypical pachycephalosaur is the namesake of the group, *Pachycephalosaurus*. This Late Cretaceous herbivore lived alongside *Tyrannosaurus* and endured up until the very end of the reign of dinosaurs. At 16 ft (5 m) long and about 660 lb (300 kg), the two-legged *Pachycephalosaurus* was the largest known genus. Other species were tiny, with heads the size of a golf ball.

Pachycephalosaurs seem straight out of a fantasy novel or a science fiction movie. Their most unique feature was undoubtedly the swollen, bony head, which was studded with a fabulous array of spikes, bumps and bony blisters. No other dinosaurs had such peculiar features. The skull was heavily fused and incredibly robust, and individual bones are hard to distinguish. The skull roof is amazingly thickened, and in *Pachycephalosaurus* is comprised of 10 in (25 cm) of solid bone! In most species the top of the skull is rounded into a dome, which is surrounded by numerous small, odd-shaped nubbins of bone that project in all directions. Similar pustules erupt from the top surface of the snout. The front of the skull was capped with a short beak, which was used to crop plants. Small, leaf-shaped teeth filled the jaws, but pachycephalosaurs probably could not extensively chew their food like many other ornithischians.

The heavy, fused skulls of pachycephalosaurs are common fossils because they are so easily preserved. Other skeletal remains are poorly known, but a few nearly complete fossils show that the neck was short and strong, the gut was broad and the tail was long and stiffened by ossified tendons. These features suggest that pachycephalosaurs processed most of their food in the gut like in sauropods and therizinosaurs, and were dynamic, active animals that used their tail for balance.

The dome-shaped skull has prompted much speculation. Some of the first scientists to study pachycephalosaurs suggested that they butted heads in competition for mates, much like modern bighorn sheep. However, this idea seems unlikely. Firstly, the spherical dome was poorly shaped for headbutting, as two colliding skulls would have slid past each other like impacting billiard balls. Secondly, no breaks, bone lesions or other injuries have ever been found on a dome, which would be expected if they were commonly used as battering rams. Thirdly, the internal structure of the dome was solid but probably not rigid enough to protect the brain from impact-related trauma. It seems more likely that the skulls were used to attract mates or to differentiate species.

FOSSIL LOCATIONS

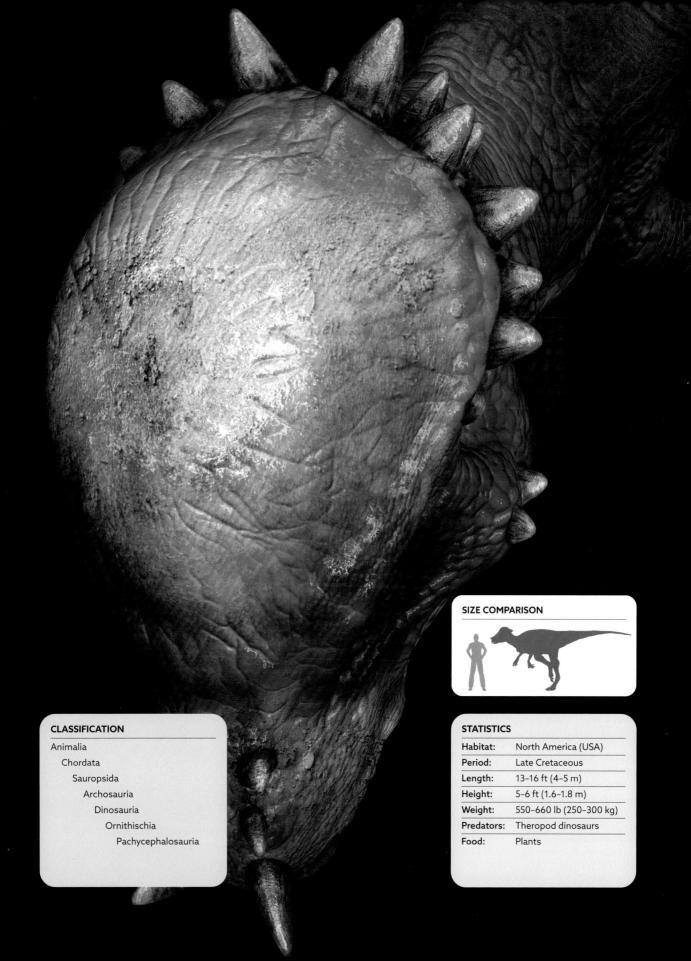

CLASSIFICATION

Animalia
   Chordata
      Sauropsida
         Archosauria
            Dinosauria
               Ornithischia
                  Pachycephalosauria

SIZE COMPARISON

STATISTICS

Habitat:	North America (USA)
Period:	Late Cretaceous
Length:	13–16 ft (4–5 m)
Height:	5–6 ft (1.6–1.8 m)
Weight:	550–660 lb (250–300 kg)
Predators:	Theropod dinosaurs
Food:	Plants

The End
of the
Dinosaurs

The most important lesson we can learn from the study of geology and palaeontology is that everything changes. Continents move around, mountain ranges ascend to the sky and then erode to dust and seas expand and contract. Organisms originate, evolve and spread. Some groups become amazingly diverse, flourish around the world and dominate ecosystems. But nothing is permanent. Even the most successful groups ultimately go extinct, resetting the evolutionary clock and paving the way for other groups to rise in their place. This is what happened to the dinosaurs 65 million years ago.

The extinction of the dinosaurs, which happened at the boundary between the Cretaceous and Tertiary periods of the geologic time scale (known as the 'K–T Boundary'), is the most famous example of a mass extinction. It is tangible proof of an ever-changing world that is at worst cruel, at best indifferent. Like the rise and fall of human civilizations, the fate of the dinosaurs is a cautionary tale whose lessons should be heeded.

This book has focused on the rise of the dinosaurs: the evolutionary journey of an insignificant group of small, fragile animals that slowly supplanted other land-dwelling vertebrates in the Triassic, dominated every corner of terrestrial ecosystems in the Jurassic, and continued to change and diversify in the Cretaceous. Their story ends 65 million years ago, with one of the most devastating moments in earth history.

What caused the extinction of the dinosaurs? This question has haunted palaeontologists ever since the first remains of giant, primeval 'saurians' turned up in England. Many early scientists simply dismissed dinosaurs as evolutionary failures – slow, stupid, sluggish animals that were ultimately doomed to extinction. It was their fate to die out and allow the more advanced mammals to take over the world. But this explanation is unsatisfactory. We now know that dinosaurs were not failed experiments destined for extinction, but dynamic animals that dominated the world for 160 million years. So what could cause such a successful group to simply disappear from the fossil record so suddenly at the end of the Cretaceous?

As with many keystone moments in geological history the answer seems to lie in a singular, cataclysmic event. It was an asteroid or comet impact that ended the Cretaceous and abruptly terminated the reign of the dinosaurs. The evidence for this idea is conclusive. In the late 1970s University of California geologist Walter Alvarez noticed something unusual while studying the thin layer of clay that marked the Cretaceous–Tertiary boundary in central Italy. This clay was enriched in iridium, an element that was exceptionally rare on earth but very common in outer space. Further research identified 'iridium spikes' at K–T boundary rocks across the globe. About a decade later scientists discovered the smoking gun: a 65-million-year-old crater hidden underneath the sandy beaches of Mexico.

There was no mistaking the evidence: an extraterrestrial object, probably several kilometres wide, smashed into the Yucatan Peninsula of Mexico at the end of the Cretaceous. Up until this point the dinosaurs were doing quite well. Their diversity was slightly lower than it had been earlier in the Cretaceous, but such peaks and valleys in diversity were common throughout the Mesozoic. There was no reason to believe that they were gradually going extinct. The sudden and explosive visitor from outer space changed everything. It hit earth with a force of several thousand nuclear bombs, and poisoned the planet nearly to the point of no return.

Within a few thousand years all of the dinosaurs were gone, save for their avian descendants – the victims of impact-induced climate change and ecosystem devastation. Dust from the explosion swept into the atmosphere and blocked out the sun, killing off plants and drenching the earth in scalding, acid rain. Wildfires blazed across the globe, and colossal tsunamis pummelled the coasts of North and South America. Along with the dinosaurs went all of the pterosaurs and most, but not all, species of mammals and birds. The oceans were also devastated. A few fortunate animals survived, but the dinosaurs were probably too large, unable to protect themselves underwater or in burrows. Or perhaps it was just bad luck on a massive scale.

The course of earth history changed forever on that day. Gone was the group that had dominated the planet for 160 million years. Hypercarnivores like *Tyrannosaurus* and plant-munching vacuum cleaners like *Triceratops* and *Edmonotosaurus* were no more. All of a sudden ecosystems were empty. Although devastated, the earth was not demolished. It took time, but life rebounded. The playing field was open, the clock was reset, and a new competition for dominance began. Ultimately the mammals and birds won out, and today fill most of the niches once occupied by dinosaurs. But mammals have gone one step further than the dinosaurs ever did. We humans are only here because the dinosaurs went extinct, and must remember that most important lesson of earth history: change is inevitable.

Glossary

Abelisaurids
A subgroup of theropods (meat-eating dinosaurs) that lived primarily in the southern continents (Gondwana) during the Cretaceous; well-known examples include *Abelisaurus*, *Carnotaurus* and *Majungasaurus*.

Advanced
A feature or characteristic of an animal that is new and inherited from more recent evolutionary ancestors.

Aetosaurs
A subgroup of archosaurs and close cousins to crocodiles that lived during the Triassic, ate plants and were covered with a tank-like shield of armour plates and spikes.

Angiosperms
The flowering plants, which evolved during the Cretaceous period and include most major groups of modern plants such as grasses.

Ankylosaurids
A subgroup of ankylosaurs (armoured, tank-like dinosaurs) characterized by a bony tail club; examples include *Ankylosaurus* and *Euoplocephalus*.

Ankylosaurs
A group of ornithischian (bird-hipped) dinosaurs, characterized by a plant-eating diet and a tank-like body covered in armour shields, plates and spikes. Ankylosaurs are divided into two subgroups: ankylosaurids and nodosaurids.

Antorbital fenestra
An opening in the skull in front of the eye that housed an extensive sinus (internal spaces) and is the distinguishing feature of archosaurs (the 'ruling reptiles').

Archosaurs
The so-called 'ruling reptiles', a major group of reptiles that first evolved in the Triassic period. It includes crocodiles, birds, dinosaurs, pterosaurs and several other extinct groups.

Bipedal
Walking on two legs.

Carcharodontosaurids
A subgroup of tetanuran theropods, closely related to *Allosaurus*, that includes some of the largest predators ever to live on earth (*Carcharodontosaurus* and *Giganotosaurus*).

Centrosaurines
A subgroup of ceratopsian (horned and frilled) dinosaurs characterized by a short frill and short horns above the eyes; examples include *Centrosaurus*, *Einiosaurus* and *Styracosaurus*.

Ceratopsians
The 'horned dinosaurs', a subgroup of ornithischian (bird-hipped) dinosaurs, characterized by a plant-eating diet and a skull bearing horns and a frill (shield).

Ceratosaurs
A subgroup of theropods (meat-eating dinosaurs) with primitive features that includes *Ceratosaurus* and the abelisaurids.

Chasmosaurines
A subgroup of ceratopsian (horned and frilled) dinosaurs characterized by a long frill and a deep beak; examples include *Chasmosaurus*, *Torosaurus* and *Triceratops*.

Coelophysoids
A subgroup of theropods (meat-eating dinosaurs) with primitive features that lived during the Triassic and Early Jurassic; examples include *Coelophysis* and *Liliensternus*.

Coelurosaurs
A subgroup of theropods (meat-eating dinosaurs) with advanced features, including many birdlike characteristics; examples include tyrannosauroids, troodontids, dromaeosaurs and birds, which evolved from coelurosaurs.

Cretaceous
The third and final period of the Mesozoic Era (the Age of Dinosaurs), during which coelurosaurian predators, ornithischian herbivores (ornithopods, ceratopsians) and titanosaurid sauropod herbivores dominated ecosystems.

Derived
See advanced.

Dinosaurs
The 'fearfully great reptiles', a subgroup of reptiles that dominated the Mesozoic world and evolved into modern birds.

Dinosauromorphs
A subgroup of archosaurs that includes true dinosaurs and the closest cousins of dinosaurs, such as *Lagerpeton*, *Marasuchus* and *Silesaurus*.

Diplodocids
A subgroup of sauropod (long-necked) dinosaurs, which includes *Apatosaurus* and *Diplodocus*, that were common in the Jurassic period.

Dromaeosaurs
A subgroup of coelurosaurs (birdlike theropods), most of which were small or medium-sized predators with enlarged claws on their feet; examples include *Deinonychus*, *Dromaeosaurus*, *Microraptor* and *Velociraptor*.

Era (geological time)
See periods.

Genus (plural, genera)
A formal term in the classification system of living organisms that refers to a group of closely related species. For example, *Tyrannosaurus* is the genus name of the dinosaur species *Tyrannosaurus rex*.

Gondwana
A large landmass comprised of modern-day Africa, South America, India, Australia and Madagascar that split apart from the northern continents (Laurasia) during the breakup of the supercontinent Pangaea.

Hadrosaurs
The 'duck-billed dinosaurs', a subgroup of ornithopod (large plant-eating) dinosaurs characterized by hoof-like feet and a large beak at the front of the snout.

Jurassic
The second period of the Mesozoic Era (the Age of Dinosaurs), during which large ceratosaur and tetanuran predators and sauropod herbivores dominated ecosystems.

Lambeosaurines
A subgroup of hadrosaurs (duck-billed dinosaurs) characterized by an elaborate crest on top of the head; examples include *Corythosaurus*, *Lambeosaurus* and *Parasaurolophus*.

Laurasia
A large landmass comprised of modern-day North America, Europe and Asia that split apart from the southern continents (Gondwana) during the breakup of the supercontinent Pangaea.

Mesozoic Era
The Age of Dinosaurs, an era of geological time that is subdivided into the Triassic, Jurassic and Cretaceous periods and ended with the extinction of all dinosaurs except for birds.

Nodosaurids
A subgroup of ankylosaurs (armoured, tank-like dinosaurs) characterized by narrow snouts and the lack of a club on the tail; examples include *Edmontonia*, *Nodosaurus* and *Sauropelta*.

Ornithischians
The 'bird-hipped dinosaurs', one of the three major subgroups of the dinosaurs (along with theropods and sauropodomorphs), so named because the pubis bone of the pelvis is oriented backwards as in birds. This subgroup includes many plant-eating dinosaurs such as the stegosaurs, ankylosaurs, ceratopsians, pachycephalosaurs and ornithopods.

Ornithomimosaurs
The 'ostrich mimic dinosaurs', a subgroup of coelurosaurs (birdlike theropods), most of which resembled large birds such as ostriches; examples include *Gallimimus* and *Pelecanimimus*.

Ornithopods
A subgroup of ornithischian (bird-hipped) dinosaurs that ate plants and is divided into its own subgroups, such as *Iguanodon* and hadrosaurs.

Osteoderms
Plates and shields of bone, often thickened and covered with a rough texture, which help protect an animal.

Oviraptorosaurs
A subgroup of coelurosaurs (birdlike theropods), most of which are characterized by a bizarre and lightweight skeleton and a crested skull that lacks teeth; examples include *Caudipteryx* and *Oviraptor*.

Pachycephalosaurs
The 'domed dinosaurs', a subgroup of ornithischian (bird-hipped) dinosaurs characterized by an incredibly thick skull that is shaped like a rounded dome.

Palaeontology
The scientific study of fossils and ancient life, including dinosaurs.

Pangaea
A supercontinent, or landmass, comprised of all of the world's conjoined continents, that existed before the Age of Dinosaurs and began to break apart during the Triassic period.

Periods (geological time)
A span of time in the history of the earth that is formally recognized by geologists (scientists who study the earth and rocks). Examples are the Triassic, Jurassic and Cretaceous: the three periods of the Age of Dinosaurs. Periods are subdivisions of eras and can be further subdivided into epochs.

Permo-Triassic Extinction
The largest mass extinction in the history of the planet, in which up to 95 per cent of all species on earth died out approximately 250 million years ago at the boundary between the Permian and Triassic periods.

Phytosaurs
A subgroup of archosaurs and close cousins to crocodiles that lived during the Triassic and were ambush predators that fed on fish and other reptiles.

Predators
Animals that hunt and eat other animals (meat eaters).

Primitive
A feature or characteristic of an animal that is 'old fashioned' and inherited from distant evolutionary ancestors.

Prosauropods
A subgroup of sauropodomorphs that lived during the Triassic and Early Jurassic, ate plants and are characterized by a mid-sized body with a long neck and small head with a beak; they may have walked on two or four legs.

Pterosaurs
A subgroup of archosaurs, commonly known as pterodactyls, that was a major group of flying reptiles during the Age of Dinosaurs. Pterosaurs are close cousins of dinosaurs but are not included within Dinosauria.

Quadrupedal
Walking on four legs.

Rauisuchians
A subgroup of archosaurs, closely related to crocodiles, which were large predators during the Triassic period. Some resembled large meat-eating dinosaurs but are only distant cousins.

Reptiles
A general name for those vertebrate animals with scaly skin that lay eggs. They include crocodiles, snakes, lizards and dinosaurs. Since birds evolved from dinosaurs, modern classification systems include birds within the group Reptilia even though they look very different.

Saurischians
The 'lizard-hipped dinosaurs', a major subgroup of dinosaurs that includes the sauropodmorphs and theropods, so named because the pubis bone of the pelvis is oriented forwards as in reptiles.

Sauropodomorphs
One of the three major subgroups of the dinosaurs (along with theropods and ornithischians), which includes the prosauropods and sauropods (long-necked dinosaurs).

Sauropods
The 'long-necked dinosaurs', a subgroup of sauropodomorphs that arose during the Triassic and were the primary plant-eating dinosaurs during the Late Jurassic. They are characterized by a massive body with an extremely long neck, a small head and quadrupedal posture.

Species
A formal term in the classification system of living organisms that refers to a group of living organisms that can breed together and reproduce offspring, but cannot breed with members of another species. For example, *rex* is the species name of the dinosaur species *Tyrannosaurus rex*.

Sphenosuchians
A subgroup of primitive crocodiles that lived during the Late Triassic and Early Jurassic; they were small, lightweight and fast runners.

Spinosaurids
A subgroup of tetanuran theropods characterized by a large sail on the back and possibly a fish-eating diet; examples include *Baryonyx*, *Irritator* and *Spinosaurus*.

Stegosaurs
The 'plated dinosaurs', a subgroup of ornithischian (bird-hipped) dinosaurs characterized by large plates that covered the back and massive spikes on the tail; examples include *Huayangosaurus*, *Kentrosaurus* and *Stegosaurus*.

Tetanurans
A subgroup of theropods (meat-eating dinosaurs) with advanced features such as a stiff tail and a hand reduced to three fingers; examples include *Allosaurus*, coelurosaurs and birds.

Therizinosaurs
A subgroup of coelurosaurs (birdlike theropods), characterized by a skull with a beak and teeth for eating plants, a large gut, enormous hand claws and sturdy legs; examples include *Alxasaurus* and *Beipiaosaurus*.

Theropods
One of the three major subgroups of the dinosaurs (along with sauropodomorphs and ornithischians), which includes all of the meat-eating dinosaurs. Subgroups of theropods include coelophysoids, ceratosaurs, tetanurans, coelurosaurs and birds.

Thyreophorans
The 'shield-bearing dinosaurs', a subgroup of ornithischian (bird-hipped) dinosaurs that includes the plated and armoured stegosaurs and ankylosaurs.

Titanosaurs
A subgroup of sauropod (long-necked) dinosaurs, which includes *Argentinosaurus* and *Saltasaurus*, that were common in the Cretaceous period and especially prevalent on the southern continents (Gondwana).

Triassic
The first period of the Mesozoic Era (the Age of Dinosaurs), during which dinosaurs originated, diversified and spread across the globe.

Tyrannosauroids
A subgroup of coelurosaurs (birdlike theropods) that lived during the Jurassic and Cretaceous. It includes small-bodied predators such as *Guanlong* and monstrous carnivores such as *Tyrannosaurus* and *Tarbosaurus*.

Index

Page references in **bold** are for illustrations
Species names in *italics*

A

abelisaurids 78, 164, 166–169
Abrictosaurus 70
Acrocanthosaurus **126–127**
Aetosauria 13
aetosaurs 17
Agassiz, Louis 17
Age of the Sauropds 76
Albertosaurus 195
allosaurids 52, 119, 126–130
Allosauroidea 53, 83
allosaurs 82–85
Allosaurus 52, 53, 76, **82–83**, 106
Alvarez, Walter 218
alvarezsaurids 86
Alxasaurus 87, **178–179**
Amargasaurus 61, **144–145**
Anatotitan **201**
Andrews, Roy Chapman 182, 188, 205
Angaturama 124
Ankylosauria 9, 68
Ankylosauridae 110, 148, 150, 194
ankylosaurs 68, 72, 110, 148–153,
    192–195
Ankylosaurus 9, 68, **192–193**
Antarctica 51
antorbital fenestra 12
Apatosaurus 61, 76, **102**
Appalachiosaurus 176
Archaeopteryx 9, 53, 87, 90, 91,
    92–93, 94–95, 132
'Archaeoraptor' 136
Archosauria 12–13, 18
archosaurs 12, 14, 18, 22, 28
Argentinosaurus 8, 60, **146–147**
Arizonasaurus 18
armour *see* body armour
asteroid impact 164, 218
Aucasaurus 166
Avemetatarsalia 13

B

Baldwin, David 30
Barapasaurus 61, **64–65**
Baryonyx **122–123**
Batrachotomus 18
Beipiaosaurus 133
birds 8, 12, 53, 87, 91, 187
    evolution 86, 90–91, 132
    origin 90–01
    wings 20
body armour 72, 104–111, 148–153,
    191–195
Bonaparte, Jose 43
Bone Wars 30, 76, 78
bonebeds 130, 196, 212
bony head 214
bony plates *see* body armour
Brachiosaurus 61, **98–99**
Brachytracelopan 144

Brontosaurus 102
Brown, Barnum 159, 180
Buckland, William 56

C

Camarasaurus 61, 76, 77, **103**
Camptosaurus **112–113**
carcharodontosaurids 83, 126–131
Carcharodontosaurus 126, **128–129**
Carnegie, Andrew 100, 101
Carnotaurus **166–167**
Caudipteryx 133, **138**
Cedarosaurus 142
centrosaurines 208, 211–213
Ceratopsia 9
ceratopsians 68, 69, 119, 164, 204–213
ceratosaurs 8, 78–
Ceratosaurus 8, 53, 69, **78–79**
Cetiosaurus 65
Chasmosaurinae 210
chasmosaurines 208–211
Chasmosaurus **210**
Chinshakiangosaurus 60
cladograms 7, 8
Archosauria 13
Avemetatarsalia 13
Coelurosauria 53, 87
Crurotarsi 13
Deinonychosauria 91
Dinosauria 8–9, 29
Diplodocoidea 61
Dromaeosauridae 91
Macronaria 61
Maniraptora 87
Marginocephalia 9, 69
Neosauropoda 61
Ornithischia 9, 68–69
Ornithopoda 69
Paraues 87, 91
Saurischia 8, 29
Sauropoda 61
Sauropodomorpha 8, 29
Tetanurae 8, 53
Theropoda 29
Theropoda 8
Thyreophora 9, 68
    classification 8
club *see* tail club
Coelophysoidea 32
Coelophysis 8, 29, **30–31**, 32, 53l
coelophysoids 8, 28, 32, 34, 78, 86
Coelurosauria 53, 86–87
coelurosaurs 52, 86, 88, 89
Coelurus 86
common ancestor 24
communication 98, 161, 198
Compsognathidae 88
compsognathids 86, 90
Compsognathus 53, 87, **88**, 90, 132
Confuciusornis 90, 133
convergent evolution 16

Cope, E.D. 30, 76
Corythosaurus **203**
cranial boss 213
crests 48, 54, 188, 198–203
Cretaceous 118–119, 146
    Early–Middle 116–161
    Late 162–215
crocodiles 12, 16
crocodilians 16, 19
Crocodylomorphia 13
crocodylomorphs 19
Crurotarsi 13
Cryolophosaurus 48, **50–51**

D

Dacentrurus 108
Daspletosaurus 176
Deinonychosauria 91
Deinonychus 90, 91, 132, **140–141**, 159
Desmatosuchus 17
Dicraeosaurus 144
Dilong 133, 176
Dilophosauridae 48, 51
Dilophosaurus 32, **48–49**
dinosaur evolution 32, 34, 47
see also cladograms, extinction, fossils
dinosaur–bird link 90, 92
dinosaur wings 136
Dinosauria 7, 8–9, 13, 56, 68
dinosauromorphs 13, 22
Diplodocoidea 61, 102
Diplodocus 29, 61, 76, **100–101**
Dong Zhiming 59
Dracovenator 51
Dromaeosauridae 53, 87, 91
dromaeosaurids 86, 90, 133, 136, 140,
    142, 180–183
Dromaeosaurus 29, **180–181**
Dryosaurus **114–115**
duck-bill 201

E

Edmontonia **195**
Edmontosaurus 201
Effigia 18
Efraasia 29, **42**
eggs 188, 196
Einiosaurus **212**
Elaphrosaurus 78, **80–81**
Enatiornithes 90
Eocursor 68
Eoraptor **24**
Eotyrannus 158
Eudimorphodon 13, **20–21**
Euoplocephalus **194**
Euparkeria 13
Euparkeria 13, **14–15**, 28
Eustreptospondylus **58**
exhibitions 100
Crystal Palace 58, 152
extinctions 28, 164

Cretaceous–Tertiary 218
Triassic–Jurassic 46–47
eyes 160, 172, 184

F

feathered dinosaurs of China 90,
    132–133, 134–139
feathers 90, 92, 132, 133, 136–139, 172,
    176, 178
'Fighting Dinosaurs' 182
fish eaters 122, 124, 187
flight 20, 132
flowering plants 118, 119
fossils 6–7
    first definite 28
    transitional 60
Fox, William 158
frills 205, 206, 208–213

G

Gallimimus 87, **186**
Gargoyleosaurus **110–111**
Gasosaurus **59**
Gastonia 142, **148–149**
Giganotosaurus 126, **130–131**, 146
Gojirasaurus 32
Gondwana 47, 118
Gorgosaurus 176
growth 38, 40, 196
growth series 40
Gryposaurus **200**

H

Hadrosauridae 69
hadrosaurids 118, 119, 164, 196–203
hadrosaurs 68, 69
Hammer, William 51
herds 148, 196, 212
Herrera, Victorino 25
Herrerasaurus 13, **25**
heterodontosaurids 68, 70
Heterodontosaurus 29, 69, **70–71**
Horner, Jack 196
horns 78, 166, 206, 208, 209, 211–213
Huayangosaurus **104–105**
hunting in packs 140, 142
Huxley, Thomas Henry 17, 90, 158
Hylaeosaurus 68, **152**
Hypsilophodon 69, **158**

I

Iguanodon 68, 69, 122, **154–155**
Incisivosaurus **139**
iridium 218
Irritator **124–125**

J

Jurassic
    Early–Middle 44–73
    Late 74–115

Juravenator 88
juveniles 40, 171, 196

K
Kentrosaurus **108**
keystone species 76, 130, 159
Kotasaurus 60
K–T Boundary 218

L
Lagerpeton 22
Lagosuchus 22
lambeosaurines 198, 200, 201–203
Lambeosaurus **202**
L. lambei 202
L. magnicristatus 202
largest dinosaurs 98, 146
Laurasia 47
Leaellynasaura **160**
Lessemsaurus 60
Lewisuchus 22
Liaoning, China 132, 136–139
Ligabueino 144
Liliensternus 29, **32–33**
long-necked dinosaurs
    see sauropods
Lycorhinus 70

M
Macronaria 61
Maiasaura **196–197**
Majungasaurus 166, **168–169**
Majungatholus 168
Mamenchisaurus **96–97**
Maniraptora 87
Mantell, Gideon, 152, 154, 158
Mantell, Mary Ann 154
Mapusaurus 130
Marasuchus 13, **22–23**
Marginocephalia 9
Marsh, O.C. 30, 87, 78, 89, 102
mass extinctions see extinctions
Megalosaurus **56–57**, 58
Megapnosaurus 30
metriorhynchids 19
Microraptor 91, 132, 133, **134–135**,
    136–137, 142
Minmi **153**
Monolophosaurus 53, **54–55**
Morrison Formation 76–77
Mussaurus 29, **40–41**
Muttaburrasaurus **161**

N
naming of dinosaurs 42, 56, 59, 154,
    158
Nemegtosaurus 186, **190**
Neosauropoda 61, 96
neosauropods 96
Neovenator 158
nest of eggs 188, 196
noasaurids 164
Nodosauridae 150
nodosaurids 118, 150, 195

O
Omosaurus 108
opposite birds 90

Ornithischia 9, 68–69
ornithischians 7, 28, 34, 47, 68–69,
    76
Ornitholestes 86, **89**
Ornithomimosauria 87, 187
ornithomimosaurs 86, 186–187
Ornithopoda 9, 69
ornithopods 69, 76, 112–115, 154–161
Ornithurae 90
ostriches 186, 187
Ostrom, John 90, 132, 159
Ouranosaurus **156–157**
Oviraptor 87, 91, **188–189**
Oviraptorosauria 87, 91, 188
oviraptorosaurs 86, 138, 139
Owen, Richard 56, 68, 72, 108, 158

P
Pachycephalosauria 9
pachycephalosaurs 68, 69, 119, 214
Pachycephalosaurus 9, 69, **214–215**
Pachyrhinosaurus **213**
Pangaea 28, 46–47
Parasaurolophus 9, 69, **198–199**
Parasuchus 13, **16**
Paraues 87, 91
parenting 188, 196, 204
Patagosaurus 65
Pelecanimimus **187**
pelvis, bird-like 68
Pentaceratops **209**
Phytosauria 13
phytosaurs 16
Pisanosaurus 68
Planicoxa 142
Plateosaurus 8, 29, 34, **38–39**
plates 14, 78
    see also body armour
Plot, Robert 56
Polacanthidae 148, 150
Polacanthus 148
Postosuchus 13, **18**
pristichampsines 19
Proceratosaurus 86
Procompsognathus 32
prosauropods 8, 28, 34–35, 36, 38, 42,
    60, 62
Protoarchaeopteryx 133
Protoceratops 182, 188, **205**
Pseudolagosuchus 22
Psittacosaurus **204**
Pterosauria 13
pterosaurs 20
pubis bone 68, 127, 178

Q, R
Quetzalcoatlus 21
Rajasaurus 166
Rapetosaurus 146
raptors 8, 136, 140, 142
rauisuchians 13, 18, 28
Rich, Tom, Patricia Vickers- and
    Leaellyn 160
Riojasaurus 29, **43**
Romer, Alfred 22
rostral bone 204, 208
Rugops 166
ruling reptiles 12

S
sails 120, 122, 158
Saltasaurus 61, 146, **191**
Saltoposuchus 13, **19**
Saurischia 8, 29
Sauropelta **150–151**
Sauropoda 61
Sauropodomorpha 8, 28, 29
sauropodomorphs 7, 34
sauropods 8, 29, 47, 60–61, 76,
    96–113, 119
transitional 62, 65
Sauroposeidon 98
Saurornithoides 184
Scelidosaurus 68, **72–73**
science of dinosaurs 6–7
scutes see body armour
Seeley, Harry Govier 68
Segisaurus 32
Seismosaurus 60
Sellosaurus 42
Sereno, Paul 24, 25, 128
Shunosaurus 61, **66–67**
Silesaurus 22
Sinornithosaurus 133
Sinosauropteryx 88, 132, 133
Sinovenator 184
Sinraptor 83, 84
Sinraptoridae 84
Solnhofen Limestone deposits 88, 92
sphenosuchians 19
spikes see body armour, frills
spines 144, 156, 195
spinosaurids 52, 58, 120–125
Spinosauroidea 53
Spinosaurus 53, **120–121**
Spinostropheus 78
Stagonolepis 13, **17**
Stegosauria 9, 68, 104
stegosaurs 68, 72, 104–109
Stegosaurus 9, 68, 76, **106–107**
Sternberg, Charles H. 209
Stromer, Ernst 120, 128
Styracosaurus 211
supercontinent see Pangaea
Syntarsus 30

T
tail club 66, 192, 194
Tarbosaurus **176–177**, 186
Tendaguru expeditions 80, 98, 109,
    114
Tenontosaurus 140, **159**
Terrestrisuchus 19
Tetanurae 8, 52, 53, 54
tetanurans 52–53, 54–59, 78, 86
Thecodontosaurus **36–37**
therapsids 14
therizinosaurids 86, 178
Therizinosauroidea 87
Theropoda 8, 29
theropods 7, 24, 28, 29, 30, 3247, 48,
    52, 86, 164
Thyreophora 9, 68, 72, 104
thyreophorans 68, 72
Titanosauria 61, 146
titanosaurs 60, 164, 190–191

Torosaurus **208**
Torvosaurus 78
tree-living creatures 136
Triassic 14, 5
Late 26–35
Triassic–Jurassic extinction 46–47
Triceratops 9, 170, **206–207**
Troodon 87, 91, **184–185**
Troodontidae 87, 91, 184
troodontids 86, 184
Typothorax 17
Tyrannosauroidea 53, 87
tyrannosaurids 86, 119, 164, 172–177
tyrannosaurs 8
Tyrannosaurus rex 8, 53, 87, **172–173**,
    174–175
recent research 170–171
tyrant lizard king see *Tyrannosaurus
    rex*

U, V
Utahraptor 91, **142–143**
Velociraptor 8, 53, 87, 91, **182–183**
Vulcanodon 61, **62–63**

W
Walker, Robert 161
Walker, William 122
walking 22, 34, 36
Williams, Thad 159

Y, Z
Yangchuanosaurus 83, **84–85**
Young, C.C. 86
Yucatan Peninsula 218
Zhao Xijin 54
Zupaysaurus 32, 51

Acknowledgements

Steve Brusatte would like to thank the following individuals: my two academic advisors, Paul Sereno and Mike Benton, for constant support and encouragement; Lynne Clos, the editor of Fossil News magazine, for publishing my monthly series of dinosaur profiles from which this book stemmed; Allen Debus, Mike Fredericks and the community of avocational dinosaur writers who were very supportive when I began writing about dinosaurs as a teenager; my research collaborators: Roger Benson, Thomas Carr, Josh Mathews, Scott Williams, Thomas Williamson, and many others for teaching me so much about dinosaurs; and my fellow graduate students, Graeme Lloyd, Manabu Sakamoto, Mark Young, and many others; and finally, the Marshall Scholarship for study in the United Kingdom

and all of the funding agencies and museum curators who have made my research travels possible. Last but most important, I thank my family, Anne my fiancee, my parents Jim and Roxanne and my brothers Mike and Chris for their unwavering support.

ARTWORK CREDITS

All artwork in this book has been supplied by Jon Hughes and Russell Gooday of Pixel-shack.com, except P28 Late Triassic Earth, P46 Pangaea, P47 Late Jurassic Earth © Quercus Publishing Plc.

PHOTOGRAPHIC CREDITS

P6 Palaeontology students excavating Late Jurassic dinosaur fossils in Wyoming, USA © Steve Brusatte, P7 Two pages from Steve Brusatte's field notebook, detailing a July 2005 excavation of Triceratops fossils in Montana, USA © Steve Brusatte, P12 Euparkeria skull © Iziko South African Museum, P35 Plateosaurus skeleton next to a man © Louie Psihoyos/Corbis, P52 (top) The skull of the tetanuran theropod Allosaurus © Getty Images/Jason Edwards, P52 (bottom) The hand of the tetanuran theropod, Allosaurus © Michael S. Yamashita/CORBIS, P77 (top left) Morrisson Formation rocks in Wyoming, USA © Steve Brusatte, P77 (bottom left, top right, bottom right) Palaeontology students excavating the skeleton of Diplodocus in Wyoming, USA © Steve Brusatte, P93 Archaeopteryx Fossil © Louie Psihoyos/CORBIS, P118 Butterfly bushes and desert oaks on red sand, Northern Territory, Australia © Theo Allofs/zefa/Corbis, P132 Fossil of Microraptor gui © Xinhua/Xinhua Photo/Corbis, P133 (top) Detail of the fossilized skull of Sinosauropteryx prima, 120 million years old. © O. Louis Mazzatenta/National Geographic/Getty Images, P133 (bottom): Fossil of Confuciusornis sanctus © Layne Kennedy/CORBIS, P165 Meteorite disaster© Sanford/Agliolo/CORBIS, P170 Finite element analysis of Tyrannosaurus rex skull © Emily Rayfield/University of Bristol, P171 (top left) Fragments of tissue lining the marrow cavity of a Tyrannosaurus rex thigh bone © epa/Corbis, P171 (right) Tyrannosaurus rex tooth © Thomas E. Williamson/New Mexico Museum of Natural History & Science

First published in Great Britain in 2008 by
Quercus Editions Ltd
Carmelite House
50 Victoria Embankment
London EC4Y 0DZ
An Hachette UK company

This new edition published in 2024

Copyright © 2008 Quercus Editions Ltd

The moral right of Steve Brusatte to be identified as the author of this work has been asserted in accordance with the Copyright, Designs and Patents Act, 1988.

A CIP catalogue record for this book is available from the British Library

HB ISBN 978 1 52943 839 0

10 9 8 7 6 5 4 3 2 1

Picture research by Alex Spears
Edited by Sally MacEachern
Index by Lynn Bresler
Designed by Neal Cobourne

Printed in China